"Y50, SHOW US THE LAST DEMONSTRATION."

"Now?" Y50 put the tray of drinks down on the hall table.

It was my turn to be astonished. Aide robots do not ask questions like that. "Yes, now."

Y50 started ticking.

"Why is it doing that?" asked Zak.

"I don't know." I tried to turn the robot off again, but discovered that an illegal protecto plate had slid over the switch. I tried to get access to Y50's brain, but the case was locked beyond my ability to open it.

"Y50, release the locks on your brain case."

The case remained locked; the ticking went on.

Zak laughed. "Sounds like an old-fashioned bomb."

I thought of the threat that someone at the GWS banquet would become fatally ill. Y50 would have been there if I hadn't ordered it to give the last demonstration now.

"I can't tell if it's a bomb or not, Zak, but I strongly suggest that you leave the apartment while I deal with this situation."

"I was only joking, Arda. Who would put a bomb in a household robot?"

"Y50—I order you to stop the demonstration!"

Y50 said and did nothing—except continue to tick.

"Zak, please leave."

"You think it is a bomb, don't you?"

"I don't know. We can't take chances. Leave. . . ."

MURDER AT THE GALACTIC WRITERS' SOCIETY

ISAAC'S UNIVERSE 2

by

Janet Asimov

DAW BOOKS, INC.
DONALD A. WOLLHEIM, FOUNDER
375 Hudson Street, New York, NY 10014

ELIZABETH R. WOLLHEIM
SHEILA E. GILBERT
PUBLISHERS

First Printing, January 1995
1 2 3 4 5 6 7 8 9

DAW TRADEMARK REGISTERED
U.S. PAT. OFF. AND FOREIGN COUNTRIES
—MARCA REGISTRADA
HECHO EN U.S.A.

PRINTED IN THE U.S.A.

ACKNOWLEDGMENTS

Many thanks to Martin H. Greenberg for persuading Isaac to invent a universe for other writers to use, and for suggesting that I write one of the books.

Thanks to Robert Silverberg, who thought up "Erthumoi" and added a seventh to Isaac's six intelligent species.

And thanks to my niece, Patti Lynn Jeppson, because her passion for archaeology gave me inspiration.

Most of all, I am deeply grateful for the memory of Isaac and thirty-three years of love.

PART ONE

Chapter 1

"How can I infiltrate the Galactic Writers' Society when I have not yet published anything?"

In the Director's office of Smith's Employment Agency, nobody seemed to notice my slight emphasis on the word "yet."

My employer ignored the implication that I could be interested in anything other than Agency work. She patted her gray curls and said, "Arda, your new job is as housekeeper to Fortizak, president of the Galactic Writers' Society. Their annual banquet is to be held tonight, under the roof dome of Fortizak's apartment building. As Fortizak's servant, you will be in a good position to observe the situation and help these operatives, who work as a team."

Neither operative was Erthumoi, as aliens call anyone born or made on Earth or its colonies. I assumed that the team was Locrian and Naxian for intelligence and muscle, in that order.

I might as well kill the suspense at once by revealing that although the Agency had a legitimate business supplying household and office help of all kinds, it was primarily one of the cover organizations of the Terran Federal Bureau of Investigation. Nobody loves the TFBI, but they pay well and they always believe there's something worth investigating.

I was a recent employee of the TFBI, assigned to the Agency, but so far I had done no investigating. I had only worked in ordinary per diem jobs like receptionist or secretary, never as an agent, and certainly not as anyone's housekeeper.

"But if I'm going to help these agents, how can I do it as a lowly domestic—programming and monitoring kitchen electronics?"

"Are you questioning the assignment?" Director Smith was a sloppily preserved middle-aged human, but there was nothing sloppy about the way she ran the Agency. She was known for firing uncooperative employees.

I thought about the high cost of living on Earth, especially in Manhattan, that most expensive of all the far-flung Terran Federation's real estate. "I will be happy to accept the assignment, Director."

"You're not supposed to be happy or sad," said Smith, "but perhaps you are practicing."

The Locrian emitted a creaky laugh, slightly muffled inside the transparent breather that filters out what Locrians consider to be the excessive oxygen content of Earth's atmosphere.

"At any rate," Smith said, "you will not be in the kitchen, because the GWS has hired two human cooks to prepare the food. During the banquet you will wait on the writers with the assistance of a work robot."

"What kind?" Some of them are incredibly stupid.

"Since Fortizak's housekeeper left, he had to rent one of the Y series from the Robotics Division. It can do the menial chores so that you will be able to keep watch when Naxo and Dee-four have to sit down at tables after the banquet starts."

"Your Arda is very new," said the Naxian, staring at me with his reptilian eyes. "Blonde, pretty, young, and innocent. That has its advantages. Don't you agree, Dee-four?"

"Yes." The Locrian tilted her head for a second. They don't have facial expressions, but the degree and angle of head movements can be very expressive.

Smith said, "Arda, only members of the GWS are invited to the banquet, but as Fortizak's housekeeper you'll be allowed to function as a waitress. You must help Naxo and Dee-four guard against any untoward event that could embarrass the Terran Federation. We of the TFBI are particularly concerned about preventing a robbery of those present at the banquet in person."

I was disappointed. It was just a simple protection job, nothing to do with high-level espionage.

Dee-four said, "Protecting the GWS members should not be difficult because there won't be a large crowd. At the regular monthly GWS meetings, most members attend by hycom, so they're present only as holov images. At the banquet some will be there in person, particularly those who like to eat. It's traditional that the food served is that of the species whose planet hosts the banquet that year. Most of the Six Species like human food."

"If I'm to be there as Fortizak Human's housekeeper, how will you two get in?"

Dee-four said, "I work for the TFBI because writing, unless you are Fortizak, doesn't pay well, but I am a regular member of the GWS. I write articles on interspecies scientific research."

"A real *writer,*" I said in awe. I am always impressed by published writers, and you must be published in order to belong to the Galactic Writers' Society.

I turned to the Naxian. "And you, sir—um—mizz . . ."

"I'm male and you Erthumoi call me Naxo, although my real name is much more impressive."

Dee-four sighed into her breather. "In loose translation, Naxo's name means 'Coiled Brawn With Fantastic Reproductive Apparatus' though I wouldn't know."

I wouldn't, either. I hadn't seen many Naxians, but I had certainly never seen them extrude anything but fringelike "hands" from those seemingly seamless snake bodies.

Director Smith tapped impatiently on her desk. "We're wasting time. Arda must get over to Fortizak's soon. We must make some tests. Naxo, will Arda pass?"

Naxo's human height, snaky body stretched taller as he peered at me, rather like a cobra contemplating a kill. I was suddenly bothered by the fact that the Naxian Major Talent is the capacity for sensing emotions, even in organics alien to themselves.

"She looks right, but I can't sense a thing," Naxo said. Terrans usually expect a Naxian to hiss when speaking, but that happens only when a Naxian is very angry. "It's just as well I'll be the only Naxian at the banquet to sense emotions, so Arda will pass anyone else's inspection, except yours, Dee."

Dee-four proceeded to demonstrate the Locrian Major Talent. Above the breather, her face was dominated by an enormous, delicate eye protected by a transparent cover. Suddenly Dee-four retracted her eyecover.

Director Smith's jowls tightened and a visible quiver rippled down Naxo's body. Locrians can be unnerving when the eye is fully exposed, for then a Locrian sees three-dimensionally into anything.

Dee-four shrugged. "However correct Arda looks, she'll never pass a Locrian inspection, but it won't matter at the GWS banquet. The only other Locrian who will be there in person is so old his eyecover is no longer removable. Others will be there holographically, but we must be in person to deeplook."

More than six intelligent species inhabit the Galaxy, but only six of these use hyperdrive and travel away from their home solar systems. Since those six prefer different kinds of planets, they get along with each other in spite of problems and the fact that one of the Six Species is the Crotonites.

"Surely no Crotonites will attend in person," I said, hoping this was true.

"They'll be there, loaded with jewels," said Dee-four.

Smith said, "Criminals might kill a Crotonite in the course of a jewel robbery—with Galactic repercussions."

Naxo's tail twitched. "It hardly seems like a crime to kill Crotonites. I can't stand them. I can't tell what they think, but their emotions are positively polluting—waves of greed that are not necessarily restricted to sex. I don't object to sex, you understand, but the Crotonites are so incredibly crude about it."

Smith said, "I have been informed that two Crotonites will be at the banquet in person. The male, named Kolix, is already here in Manhattan, where he has business connections. He is also a member of the Galactic Writers' Society."

"Unfortunately," Dee-four said. "Kolix's articles try to prove that Crotonite wings are better than all other methods of flight found in the Galaxy, and the Crotonite heroes of his fiction always demonstrate that Crotonites are smarter than the rest of the Six Species."

"Will he eat at the banquet?" I asked, envisioning the preparation of Crotonite food which, I'd read, is eaten alive, on the wing.

"I doubt it," said Smith. "Fortizak informed me,

when he rented the work robot, that Crotonite food capsules have been delivered to his apartment so the royal couple can try them at the banquet."

"Try them?" asked Dee-four. "Are they experimental?"

"I made inquiries. They are new, but Crotonite scientists assure me that the capsules are harmless, if utterly devoid of taste. They serve only to provide nutrition when everyone else is eating food Crotonites won't touch because it's already dead. I was told, however, that no other species should try the capsules because their chemical components may be rather stimulating."

"Stimulating?" Naxo asked eagerly.

"In certain ways of arousal that might be embarrassing for other species." Director Smith was reputed to be prudish.

Naxo grinned, an unsettling phenomenon because it revealed his fangs. "I can think of some interesting experiments, like dropping a capsule into a Cephallonian's tank."

"A capsule might improve Pleltun's turgid deep-sea novels," said Dee-four, "and it's too bad our Samian member doesn't eat food or capsules. Hjeg's squashed-box of a body might disassemble in front of everybody. At least it would spare us a recitation of one of her narrative poems."

"Long narrative poems?" I asked enviously. When I'd tried writing one myself, it had petered out after two cantos.

"Very long, and they translate badly into Galactic Basic."

Naxo's lower body coiled tighter and he said, "This banquet promises to be fun and games."

"Are you a writer, too?" I asked.

"No, Arda. I'll be masquerading as a Naxian writer

of romances who happens to be a distant cousin and doesn't like to travel any more than Fortizak does."

"Naxians have no romance," said Dee-four. "Just sex."

"My cousin says his novels sell well to Erthumoi."

"Who, no doubt, search for what seems to be pornographic but is only a manifestation of the peculiar Naxian sense of humor."

Director Smith tapped her desk harder this time. "You have not yet told Arda that the jewels she must help protect are the property of Kolix's wife. He is getting married this afternoon in the Naxian embassy here, and will bring his wife with him, although she is not a GWS member."

"Special dispensation," said Naxo. "According to the TFBI, Kolix insisted. The wife is Crotonite royalty—Crown Princess Vush, no less—and nobody can afford to irritate Crotonites these days, what with the way they have a stranglehold on Seventh Species artifacts and charge the rest of us supergalactic prices. Such an obnoxious species."

Dee-four's head swayed to and fro and she said dreamily, "I can hardly wait to remove my eyecover for a look into Vush's ruulogem. It's said to be the biggest ever found in the Galaxy."

"We'd better get going," said Naxo. "I want a long soak in my bath to freshen my scales and improve my appetite."

Dee-four and Naxo went to the door together—Dee-four's feet clicking, Naxo's coils slithering.

As the door closed, I heard Naxo ask, "How much would you say that big ruulogem is worth?"

Chapter 2

"I've never seen a ruulogem," I said. "Have you, Director Smith? Are they so beautiful?"

"I've never been fond of jewelry. It is typical of Crotonites that Princess Vush would insist on wearing a priceless gem not only to her wedding this afternoon but when she accompanies her new husband to the GWS banquet afterward. She should keep the ruulogem in her palace safe."

"I can understand why there'd have to be three of us to guard the jewel, but aren't Locrians physically frail?"

"Dee-four is one of the most intelligent agents we have, and her eye can find guns hidden by others. Naxo is not as bright as she is, but once he coils around a suspect, he never lets go. They make a good team, but the problem is that they are supposed to be GWS members, so they will have to be sociable, and sit down with the others at the banquet tables. You, Arda, will be able to stay near the Crotonites during dinner."

"I see."

"You don't, yet. Naxo can joke about killing Crotonites, but it could happen. There is reason to believe that it might. I did not tell Naxo and Dee-four because Naxo is not the most discreet agent in the Galaxy, and I don't want to alarm the GWS unnecessarily."

Behind her, another door opened, evidently to a

bathroom, and from it walked—well, he was so magnificent that I could not speak. His features were aristocratic, his wavy hair much blonder than mine. He was taller than I and possessed a slim but muscular shape enticingly outlined by a black bodysuit. . . .

Those were my thoughts. Some of them. And whenever I write paragraphs like the last one, I no longer wonder why I am as yet an unpublished writer.

He spoke. "I am Dr. Elson, Arda." His voice was so mellifluous it made my name sound like a poem. He lowered his firm buttocks to the edge of Smith's desk and smiled seductively at me. I instantly wished I needed a doctor's attention.

"Arda," Director Smith said coldly, "you needn't stare at Dr. Elson. We need his help. Because the Galactic Writers' Society banquet is being held on Earth this year, it is a potential threat to the Terran Federation. We will be blamed if an alien gets sick. There might even be war if one dies."

Dr. Elson smiled again. This smile was the sort doctors use to raise your confidence in the powers of medical science as embodied by them.

"My specialty is the medical care of sick aliens."

"Dr. Elson must be at the banquet, in case anyone gets sick. But because he is not a writer . . ."

I had always been of the firm opinion that writers represented the evolutionary peak in any species, but doctors now supplanted them in my mind. I smiled back at Dr. Elson.

". . . and because it must not be known that we anticipate any medical problems, Dr. Elson must go to the banquet disguised."

"Arda, I'll be at the banquet as your boyfriend, called in to help you with the proceedings."

"But—Dr. Elson . . ."

"Just call me Elson. If you develop the habit, you won't forget and call me doctor in public."

"Yes, Arda," said Director Smith. "As Fortizak's housekeeper, you will inform him that you need your boyfriend to help serve at the banquet, and that he is well-trained as a butler. Elson will then be on hand to take over if anyone—human or alien—becomes ill. What have you learned about alien anatomy and physiology, Arda?"

"Accessing . . ." The words slipped out, to my shame.

"Smith, you old devil, you've been testing me. Arda is an android, isn't she?"

"Yes. One of the most recent lifelike models, with extra intelligence and strength. You needn't access your knowledge of the Six Species, Arda. Elson has studied them all."

Elson walked over to me, fingered my long straight hair, caressed my cheek, and even touched my resilient breasts. I could not help it; my eyelids fluttered once.

"Well, well," said Elson. "I'll bet you have the latest in emotive circuits, young Arda."

"Yes," I said, cursing them.

"And are you programmed for pleasure?"

"No, Doctor. I'm a detective, not a plaything." I wanted to tell him that I was willing to learn anything he wanted to teach me about pleasure, but he smiled again.

"Then tell me, fair Arda, what is the Major Talent of each of the Six Species?"

I didn't mind Elson testing me. "To begin with the worst, Crotonites are said to be the Galaxy's biggest con artists."

"Excellent," said Elson. "Most convincingly human. She's been programmed with the colloquial usage of Galactic Basic."

My positronic brain seethed with despair at being talked about as if I were the latest model of refrigerator. I hadn't been activated for long, but it was long enough to be fully aware of the unfairness of organic chauvinism. As the immortal Charlotte Bronte might have put it if she'd been in similar circumstances—Reader, I suffered.

I said, "I was *not* programmed. I have learned."

"Nevertheless, you are an android," Smith said angrily.

Humans, the organic Erthumoi, seem to have a Major Talent for suppressing the progress of their most intelligent robots. But I restrained myself and continued.

"The aquatic Cephallonians are supposed to have a Major Talent for intuitive thinking. Samians ingest minerals and energy, can stick to anything, and go anywhere because they can tolerate every environment from high gravity to outer space. Naxians can detect emotions, but only from organic brains. Locrians can see into the inner structure of anything. Humans are the most recent of the Six, with a talent for technology."

"A good summary," Elson said. "Since only agents Dee-four and Naxo can detect that Arda is an android, I'm sure she will pass nicely as my girlfriend. She's been programmed to be most convincingly human."

My emotive circuits couldn't take it any longer. "Doctor—I mean, Elson—perhaps you don't realize that more advanced androids not only have high intelligence and emotive circuits, but we acquire information best by learning it, the way humans do, only faster. We are not electronically stuffed with exactly what we need to know, the way stupid aide robots are."

"And," said Elson, "you have a delightfully human body."

My emotive circuits quivered. "Furthermore, we androids differ from robots, although bound by the laws of robotics, because we are intelligent, have emotive circuits, and are self-aware. We are legally recognized as independent sentient beings with full citizenship in the Terran Federation—although many organics retain prejudice against nonorganics . . ."

"Stop lecturing us," said Smith. "The point is that since the writer and banquet host, Fortizak, hires only housekeepers who are female and organic, you must pass as one in order to arrange for Elson to be at the banquet. A doctor's presence must be concealed to avoid alarming anyone. We at the TFBI are doing everything we can to avoid a Galactic Incident."

"You seem to think someone may indeed become ill," I said. "Are some of the members sickly?"

"No."

"Then why . . . ?"

"A message appeared on my office computer three days ago. It was electronically cued to erase evidence of its origin after its transmission was accomplished. The exact words were, 'Gems can be fatal at banquets.' The TFBI chiefs and I agreed to keep quiet about this but to have three operatives at the banquet and a doctor as well. I sent to Luna City for Dr. Elson, known as a specialist in alien medicine—including that for Crotonites."

"The threat may be a joke," I said. "Or, if not a joke, then someone may have informed on the would-be thief because he knows the thief will take the ruulogem even if it means disabling or killing the crown princess."

"Good thinking, young Arda." Elson beamed at me.

Smith said, "I'm sure there are also members of the GWS who would think such a thing was amusing. One of the writers might have sent the threat in order to set up one of those mystery evenings so popular here on Earth."

"Do any of the GWS members write mysteries?"

"Fortizak writes mysteries, as well as everything else. The only other mystery writer who will be physically present at the banquet is Kolix, whose fictional Crotonite detective is made to seem smarter than Sherlock Holmes and Hercule Poirot combined."

"Then maybe it really is just a nasty joke by a mystery writer, trying to take revenge on Kolix," I said.

Smith scowled. "We cannot take the risk. You will see to it that Elson is present in case the Crotonites are in danger."

"But shouldn't we tell the GWS about the threats?"

"No, Arda. Not if one them has sent the messages. I'm sure Dee-four and Naxo can stop any robbery."

I smiled at Elson. "And you'll be able to stop anybody from making anyone else sick."

"Unless it's from listening to long poems."

Elson and I laughed together—oh, joy—and I said, "It must be a joke. Why else would the perpetrator give advance notice of what he, she, or it intends to do?"

Smith pursed her lips. "It is not uncommon for sentient beings to take irrational pleasure in playing games they think they can win."

"Especially if the game is to embarrass the Federation," said Elson, smiling—alas—at her.

"You may go now, Arda," she said. "Let Elson into the banquet, and don't get in the way if anything does happen."

I felt denigrated to the status of a robotic tool that was needed only to open a banquet door for a doctor.

Chapter 3

I like to walk. It makes me feel more human and seems to assist my thought processes.

When I left Smith's Employment Agency, I walked up Fifth Avenue and then through the park to Fortizak Human's building on Central Park West. By the time I entered the vestibule and cued in the lobby computer, I should have thought myself well into my role of housekeeper-spy.

Instead, I was wondering how a real writer would describe Central Park, so full of delicate shades of pink and cream among the different greens of early spring. I tried out sentences in my positronic brain and found myself saying one aloud.

"Central Park is an oasis for Erthumoi and from Erthumoi."

The baritone voice that issued from the computer plate was unaccompanied by any visual representation of its owner.

"If that's supposed to be the latest open sesame code, it isn't. Besides, I don't have one. And yours is a terrible cliché."

"Sir, I am here . . ."

"Young woman, I see in my visicreen that you are good-looking and no doubt eager, but I'm in the middle of five books and I'm too busy for an interview, or anything else. Go away and write a letter to me explaining what you want."

"No one writes letters any more."

"That will save both of us a lot of time and trouble."

"I am your new housekeeper!"

"Oh? You're much too young, but you might as well come up. The blasted banquet of the Galactic Writers' Society has been dumped on me this year and I need immediate *help*."

With the anguish in that "help" reverberating through my circuits, I took the antigrav lift to the top floor.

Fortizak Human was waiting in the open doorway of his apartment, shoving one hand through his disheveled, curly dark hair. He was not dressed in one of the conservative gray bodysuits he seemed to wear on all the holov talk shows or for the portraits of himself on jackets of the old-fashioned books he insisted be printed in spite of the fact that most people read, if they read at all, from holoscreens.

The famous writer was wearing worn baggy pants, shoes with genuine laces, rumpled socks, and a real undershirt. He bore no resemblance to the handsome Elson, but he did have dark blue eyes, high cheekbones in his broad face, and shoulder muscles enlarged from his insistence on actually using a keyboard to write his books. I'd read up on him, and knew that he'd had two wives, each of whom had left him because he wrote too much.

"If you're through marveling at my godlike appearance, new housekeeper, you might as well enter my sanctum. What's your name and why do you look more intelligent, and certainly prettier than most housekeepers?"

"My name is Arda, Mr. Fortizak." I was careful to

leave out the "Human" that all robots and androids affix to the proper name of organics. "I can't help how I look or my intelligence."

"Arda, eh? You can call me Zak." He ushered me into the spacious, book-lined hall of his apartment and pointed to a small, metallic robot standing in a corner. It was one of the unintelligent work models found in almost every household these days. This one was labeled Y50.

"Fix that robot or send it back to Smith's. I rented it from them to cope with the chores until they could find me a real live human housekeeper, but this robot's a dud."

"It has malfunctioned?"

"Uh-huh. I don't know how to make it function. While I understand the theory of robotics, in hands-on applications I have no talent . . ." His gaze traversed my form. "Well, that depends on the applications."

I felt I understood why his previous housekeeper had left. "I gather you don't have housekeepers for long?"

"You gather nothing of the sort. Hilda was with me for fifteen years and left to join her sister in a retirement colony. I always hire housekeepers who are quiet, more than middle-aged, and devoid of curiosity." He glared at me.

"What is wrong with Y50?"

"Nothing, at first. Hilda programmed it to inquire into the state of my health five times a day and to serve me low-calorie meals, so after she left I sent it back to Smith's for reprogramming. It returned this morning, stood here in the hall, and wouldn't respond to commands. I turned it off."

I used my wrist communicator to speak to the adjustments department of Smith's Robot Division, which will repair any of our robots that malfunction.

As I spoke to the head of the department, I noted that Zak's former housekeeper had the right idea. Zak had no discernible waistline, so low calorie meals were still advisable.

"Did any malfunction occur in Y50 when the programming was changed yesterday?" I asked the human manager.

"Robot Y50 never arrived for reprogramming."

"Are you certain?"

"Positive. We check 'em in at the repair entrance. You want a repair truck to pick this one up?"

"Not until I see if I can repair Y50."

As I clicked off, Zak said, "Maybe Y50 couldn't follow orders because it was even then out of whack, the way it is now. Maybe it just wandered around and came back because this was the last destination its muddled brain could remember."

"That's possible."

"The GWS expected me to use Y50 as butler for the banquet tonight, but I suppose we can do without it now that you're here, Arda. As for my own needs, I prefer managing with only a household computer and a live housekeeper."

I wondered if a human like Fortizak would, if he knew my actual identity, believe that I am truly alive. A fifty-year-old T. Federation Supreme Court ruling states that androids are to be considered alive, but many humans still don't agree.

"Mr. Forti—I mean, Zak—my boyfriend Elson will be able to function as a butler tonight."

Zak sighed. "Naturally you'd have a boyfriend. Competent, attractive?"

"Very."

He sighed again. "Butler, then—for tonight only. Tell your Elson to wear appropriate garb. The banquet's formal. Are you mentally, psychologically, and manually skilled enough to help an informal writer into formal clothes?"

"Well, I . . ."

"And tell Elson to arrive early. The cooks will be at work by five p.m., and you'd both better be up there to oversee things."

"Yes, sir."

"I assume that your eagerness to get your boyfriend a temporary job means that you can't or won't repair that robot?"

"I will endeavor to initiate self-repair in Y50," I said, walking over to it. "But even if I can get Y50 functioning again, it's best to have Elson on hand. Y50 may not be reliable, and Elson is a much better looking butler, in addition to being organic and highly intelligent."

I opened Y50's command plate. Nothing seemed out of order. I turned the robot on. In Y50's metallic head, the sensor devices made to resemble eyes began to glow softly.

"Hey, Y50," Zak called out. "Are you in there? What happened to you after I ordered you to return to Smith's?"

Y50 continue to stare straight ahead. It did not answer.

I held my work ID card in front of Y50's eyes, careful not to let Zak see it. "Y50, I am an accredited employee of Smith's. You will obey me. Do you understand?"

Y50 emitted a brief, faint hum as it scanned my card and then said, "Yes."

"Excellent. You are to help me at the Galactic Writers' Society banquet tonight. Scan yourself for malfunctions and perform needed self-repair. If self-repair is not possible, go back to Smith's."

Y50 hummed again, longer. "No malfunction."

"It's lying through its metallic teeth," said Zak.

"Simple robots have no teeth, and they are unable to lie. Y50, we must test the adequacy of your functioning. Demonstrate your functions as butler for the banquet."

"Demonstrate? Do you wish to see the last demonstration?"

I had no idea what Y50 meant. "Right now demonstrate how you will serve drinks."

Y50 walked to a closed door in the hall, opened it, and went out of sight.

"That's the door to the kitchen," Zak said. "Should we follow it to make sure it doesn't break anything?"

"It seems to be functioning adequately," I said. "We asked it to demonstrate being a butler, so we'd better wait."

Y50 soon returned bearing several small glasses of assorted drinks on a tray. It offered them to Zak, not to me. Y50 was undoubtedly functioning well enough to read the fine print on my ID card, stating that I am an android.

Zak downed what seemed to be orange juice, smiled and said, "Good. Y50 is on the ball again."

Since I had studied colloquialisms, I was not perturbed by Zak's irrational last statement. "Y50, what did you mean by the last demonstration?"

"I do not mean. I am programmed to demonstrate."

Robots like Y50 do not understand language nuances. "Y50, you asked if we wished to see the last demonstration. We do."

"That doesn't make sense," said Zak. "Maybe we'd better just let it do its thing as a butler."

"As an accredited member of Smith's staff, I must disagree. Y50 should not have asked such a question.

We must find out what it means. With your permission, sir."

"Oh, go ahead, Arda. I suppose it's just as well you take your job so seriously."

"Y50, show us the last demonstration."

"Now?" Y50 put the tray of drinks down on the hall table.

It was my turn to be astonished. Aide robots do not ask questions like that. "Yes, now."

Y50 started ticking.

"Why is it doing that?" asked Zak.

"I don't know." I tried to turn the robot off again, but discovered that an illegal protecto plate had slid over the switch. I tried to get access to Y50's brain, but the case was locked beyond my ability to open it.

"Y50, release the locks on your brain case."

The case remained locked; the ticking went on.

Zak laughed. "Sounds like an old-fashioned bomb."

I thought of the threat that someone at the GWS banquet would become fatally ill. Y50 would have been there, if I hadn't ordered it to give the last demonstration now.

"I can't tell if it's a bomb or not, Zak, but I strongly suggest that you leave the apartment while I deal with this situation."

"I was only joking, Arda. Who would put a bomb in a household robot?"

"Y50—I order you to stop the demonstration!"

Y50 said and did nothing—except continue to tick.

"Zak, please leave."

"You think it is a bomb, don't you?"

"I don't know. We can't take chances. Leave."

Zak tapped his prominent chin. "Fascinating. Whatever this robot is presently doing, the probability is that someone must have abducted it on its way back to

Smith's. The someone must have reprogrammed it to start a countdown sequence at the end of the banquet, and when you asked to see the last demonstration that activated . . ."

"Zak! Leave—now!"

"I can't leave a pretty girl to be blown to proverbial smithereens—interesting word, smithereens, but I can't remember its origin. . . ."

"Mr. Fortizak! You must not take chances. I will again attempt to take this robot apart, but you must leave."

I turned back to the robot and heard the outer door open and close. I still couldn't open the brain case, much less the protecto plate. Suddenly the ticking stopped and Y50 began to burp, slowly and loudly, every two seconds.

I was lifted up, carried into the kitchen, and shoved behind a large metal cabinet. Zak squirmed in beside me, puffing slightly.

"You're heavier than you look."

"You would be safer out of the building," I said. But there wasn't time. My superior ears heard Y50, out in the hall, give a burp that rose to a crescendo. I covered Zak's body with mine.

The sound of the ensuing explosion was not as loud as that of Zak laughing.

"Arda, much as I'm enjoying your protectiveness, I think we should get up and find out what's happened. Y50 isn't ticking or burping or exploding at the moment."

I insisted on leading the way back into the hall, but the danger was indeed over.

Y50's body storage compartment was open, the contents spread over the hall floor. Zak picked up one of them.

"Listen to this, Arda," he said, chuckling as he read the front of the leaflet in his hand. " 'Greetings, fellow members of the Galactic Writers' Society. You are here to celebrate the marriage of your most famous member, the renowned Kolix. Enjoy these souvenirs of the occasion.' "

"The Crotonite."

"Who has outdone himself." Zak turned the pages of the leaflet. "There's more. The marriage announcement is followed by the entire family trees of Kolix and his bride. And on the next page . . ." Zak stopped and snorted.

"What's the matter?"

"That egotistical hack! He's reprinted favorable reviews of his latest so-called masterpieces—they're actually of low literary quality but such is the prevailing stupidity of most members of the Six Species that they do, unfortunately, sell rather well—not as well as mine, of course, but . . ."

"Is there something worse, Zak?" His jaw had tightened and he looked like a Plarrtian marsh-beast about to dismember a tourist.

"Crotonites! That miserable little bat-winged demon called Kolix! He has added samples of unfavorable reviews of what other GWS members have written. Even some of mine!"

"Hardly a major tragedy," I said, touching Y50.

"And you call yourself a fit housekeeper for a *writer?*"

I ignored him. "Y50, how did Kolix reprogram you?" There was no answer.

"Where did you receive the programming for this last demonstration, Y50?"

Then I saw that Y50's eyes were dull, and this time when I tried to unlock the brain case, I was successful.

Zak came over and peered at Y50 with me. "I don't think I've ever actually seen a positronic brain."

"This is a very simple one, like those in all robots—except . . ."

"Except what?"

"This brain is dead."

Zak's square-tipped fingers touched the brain, and he grunted. "But why? There wasn't a real bomb in Y50's body, only a lot of suspicious noise to scare everyone before the body opened to shower the party with these scurrilous leaflets."

I felt strangely sad, a sensation with which my emotive circuits had, so far in my short life, little experience. "Zak, there was a bomb, a tiny one placed in Y50's brain. Presumably the bomb was set to go off as soon as Y50 had fulfilled its last demonstration—the leaflets."

"You mean that whoever did this made sure that Y50 couldn't reveal who the programmer was?"

"Yes, but that doesn't make sense either. Everyone would suspect Kolix, because of the leaflets."

Zak shook his head. "Not necessarily. Kolix could argue that because the robot was instantly deactivated before anyone could ask it questions, someone else must have been the perpetrator of this stupid joke, designed to embarrass the Crotonites and increase hostility toward them. That would let Kolix off the hook, but he'd still have had his little joke, putting down his fellow writers."

"Very odd behavior," I said.

"I've always thought that Crotonites had all the integrity and social skills of piranha," said Zak. "But we've found Kolix out this time. Thanks to you, Arda. I'd never have been able to get Y50 to give that end demonstration prematurely. It would have gone to the banquet and at the last minute everyone would have received those leaflets if you hadn't tested it."

"But Kolix deliberately killed a robot to make it look as if he's innocent!" I was trying not to show Zak my outrage.

"The robot is just deactivated," Zak said. "Can't Smith's send someone to take it back for refitting with a new brain?"

"Yes, but it won't be the same Y50."

"Arda, it doesn't pay to be sentimental about inanimate objects. Y50 was not a person."

"It had a brain, and some slight intelligence. Perhaps even some self-awareness."

"Nonsense. Not a simple aide robot. Now, Arda, you'd better get to work. After you've cleaned up here, there's a package of Crotonite food capsules in the kitchen that has to go up to the caterers. Too bad I can't doctor those capsules to make Kolix extremely sick to his stomach, or whatever the Crotonites use for digestion."

"But . . ."

"Now in the kitchen you'll find a door to your own bedroom and bathroom suite. When not working, you may also relax in the living room—that's over there— but you are not allowed to enter my library and office unless I send for you on the intercom. If you need me, the main computer will hear you speak my name and then I'll hear you. The main computer has been programmed by my previous housekeeper with complete instructions on how to take care of the household, and me. Ignore the instructions on diet."

"Sir, I . . ."

"I must go to work now, Arda. I work every day, and I always have deadlines. My most pressing one is a magazine article to instruct the lay public in up-to-date scientific matters. I must explain the new modifications of hyperdrive to people who have never understood hyperdrive in the first place. You do your work, and I will do mine."

He opened another door, onto a corridor leading to the other side of the apartment. "And, Arda, get rid of that robotic hulk."

"Yes, sir."

As he left, my emotive circuits signaled anger. Humans didn't care about robots. Fortizak Human was not upset about the death of a lowly robot like Y50.

Death? Could I call it that?

If I am legally alive, won't I be legally "dead" when my brain no longer functions? When does the word "death" stop applying to inorganic beings?

Y50's death had been caused deliberately.

Was that not murder?

Chapter 4

Smith's pickup service removed poor dead Y50. I took the Crotonite food capsules up to the roof dome and began helping the caterers, a married human couple who were busy in the kitchen just off the large space to be used as the banquet hall. They welcomed my assistance because there were no servorobots, thanks to the GWS's assumption that Zak's Y50 would be available. I assured the caterers that my boyfriend and I would pass around hors d'oeuvres, serve drinks, and dish out the buffet food.

The dome and its surrounding terrace were spacious and pleasant with trees and flower-bearing plants from all over the Galaxy. On one of the unwindowed walls was hung a large banner saying "The Galactic Writers' Society" in white letters on a purple background, so the floral table decorations were white and purple tulips.

I had not had a chance to see the view from Zak's building because in his apartment the blinds were down and tightly closed. Here in the roof dome I could gaze out over all of Central Park, still acclaimed as one of the urban wonders of the Galaxy. The towers of the city glistened in the golden light of the setting sun as I tried to decide which adjectives to use in case I ever wrote this up.

Inside the dome there was an assortment of chairs

and cushions that could be used by most of the Six Species except Samians. One always hopes that Samians will refrain from sticking to whatever surface they are on, or to whomever is nearby. Samians are generally good-natured, but being stuck to a Samian doesn't bring out the good nature of other beings.

I put platters of unsynthesized Terran food on a long table at one end of the room. The banquet had to be buffet style because it would be undiplomatic to judge the correct amount and kind of food for each of the Six Species.

I added a dish containing the food capsules I'd labeled "For the Crotonites only." They were still in their sealed package, which I intended to open only after the Crotonites arrived. Doctoring the Crotonite food capsules would be a good way of insuring that the most obnoxious of the Six Species would get sick, perhaps as fatally as the warning had said.

The regular food was simple, hearty, and exactly what Fortizak had ordered. Fortunately, at least some Terran food can be eaten by each of the Six Species except the fussy Crotonites.

The primarily vegetarian Cephallonians relish Terran salads and breads, but are not averse to sampling smoked salmon and pickled herring. Locrians, who eat only synthesized food at home, like the same Erthumoi food plus deviled eggs, ham wrapped around cheese, chili, and marinated pieces of chicken.

Samians are said to enjoy absorbing Terran drinks put into a depression that appears on the top of their blocklike form. Their highly mobile component parts may possibly eat minerals, but disassembling is something they try to do only in private.

Naxians will eat anything.

The dome computer announced that Zak wanted me

to come down to his apartment. Since Elson was supposed to arrive soon, coming directly to the roof, I was perturbed, but Zak was ostensibly my employer. I had to go.

In my short lifetime I had already absorbed more information about human culture than most organic Erthumoi ever do. Therefore, I was prepared for the fact that most human males still wear the formal garb that has always been prevalent in their particular petty cultural group.

In Zak's case, that of the typical North American male, formal garb continues to mean a tuxedo. His was only slightly shiny in the seat and at the elbows, but it was distinctly loose, and not in style.

"I've lost weight since I bought this."

"In your early youth, no doubt." I was struggling to insert the studs in his white shirt front. "Considering the ease of hypervelcro, this antiquated means of closing up a garment must be symptomatic of the innate conservatism of the human male who prefers to look as if he belonged in some other century."

"On the contrary, I hate tuxedos. I wanted to wear my best tunic and least repulsive pair of pants, but, unfortunately, the rest of the GWS voted for formal clothes."

I finished the shirt front and deftly fastened Zak's steel cufflinks, noting that each was ornamented by a tiny blue-enameled representation of Earth.

"Given to me by a fan," he said.

"Won't the nonErthumoi members resent Terran chauvinism?"

"Not at all. I'm famous for it. The foreign GWSers derive great pleasure from making fun of my refusal to leave Earth."

"You never leave Earth?"

"I never have, and won't if I can help it."

"But think of what's out in the rest of the Galaxy! Such beauty, such adventures . . ."

"You've been there?"

I paused. I could not tell him I'd been alive only a short time. "I hope to go."

"Then you better find an employer who travels." The gaze of his dark blue eyes suddenly softened as he looked at me, perhaps surmising that my emotive circuits—I mean my feelings—were hurt. "But not yet. I like you, Arda. You're efficient, and you didn't bother me while I was writing."

The fact that he had bothered me while I was trying to help the caterers did not occur to him, but then an employer tends to assume that a servant can perform all ordered tasks regardless of interruptions.

He shoved up one bejeweled cuff and glanced at his wrist chronometer. "In fact, you've fastened me into my tuxedo so quickly that I have time to do a little more writing before I must go up and play host. When does your boyfriend arrive?"

Coincidences do happen, for at that moment the lobby computer announced, "Elson requests entry."

I was about to tell Elson to go directly to the roof, but Zak touched the response panel and said, "Come up to my apartment, Elson. Then you can take Arda back up to the roof."

"Why should he come here first?" I asked Zak.

"I think I should inspect the boyfriends of my hired help. Especially when I'm developing a deep appreciation for said help. You very fond of this Elson?"

"I have developed an emotion of sincere passion for him." At least it felt sincere, and distinctly resembled what humans refer to as passion. But as soon as I said the words, they did not sound at all right.

"Sincere passion, eh? That's a good one. You interest me, Arda. You certainly do. I hope Elson appreciates you."

Elson's entry into Zak's apartment was magnificent. He was dressed in faultless evening apparel, a phrase I may have picked up somewhere, and looked like a perfect gentleman—or butler, in this case. I have read that perfect butlers always look more gentlemanly than their employers. Comparing Zak and Elson, this was certainly true.

"I have read many of your books, Mr. Fortizak," Elson said, using the right approach. "I believe it is true that you are the genius everyone says."

"I say it, too," said Zak. "What do you do, Elson, when you're not romancing my new housekeeper?"

"I am an actor," said Elson. "Currently unemployed except for this unpaid venture as a butler."

That was clever of Elson, I thought. Everyone knows that most actors are unemployed much of the time.

Zak said, "Elson, are you a good bouncer?"

"A what?"

"A person, usually working in a bar, who notices unruly patrons and throws them out of the establishment."

Elson expanded his magnificent smile. "I can do that."

"You may have to. Before Arda arrived today, I received word that there will be two Crotonites at the banquet, and that can mean trouble."

I said, "It's so sweet of Kolix to want his bride with him at the banquet. He must love her very much." It is not true that I am obsessed with the idea of romance, but if one is to become a writer, one must know about such things. Besides, I wanted Elson to know that I could appreciate the value of true love.

"Bah," said Zak. "It's an arranged marriage. No doubt Kolix has seen her only a few times before, on formal occasions."

I wanted to show Elson—and Zak—how much general information I possessed. "Are not Crotonite arranged marriages made years before, so the couple can experiment with sex to see if they are compatible?"

I had given considerable thoughts to experiments with sex, which I had never been given the opportunity to make into reality. I had studied the claims of scientific literature, and some not so scientific, that first-class androids not only can perform sexually but can also enjoy the activity. I couldn't help resenting the ease with which so many nonErthumoi species learn about and incorporate sex into their daily lives, while we androids are usually deprived.

Elson answered my question. "Ordinarily, Crotonite marriages are arranged with premarital contact to insure that both are sexually proficient before getting legal about it. In the case of the Crotonite crown princess, she needs no introduction to sex, for Kolix will be her second husband. The first is said to have died from overexertion due to extraordinary sexual demands made by Vush."

"Well, well," Zak said happily. "How pleasant to think of Kolix caving in under his marital exertions. The Galactic Writers' Society was founded on the premise that the Six Species get to know each other better through their written words, but after reading Crotonite books I wonder if it's worth it."

"Arda, you and I must still protect the Crotonites from any would-be thief or assassin," Elson said.

"We will, Elson. I am strong and observant. And I have kept the package of food capsules sealed."

"The very words food capsules almost makes me

sympathize with Kolix," Zak said. "Elson, are you sure you know how to be a butler—which side to serve from, and all that sort of crap?"

"Oh, yes, Mr. Fortizak. Arda, I think we should go to the roof now, to be ready for the guests." Elson took my arm, demonstrating his masterfulness and his attachment to me.

"Then run along," said Zak, as if we were children. "Call me when the first guests arrive. I have work to do."

I looked back as I opened the apartment's front door, and saw Zak standing motionless in the middle of the hall, his full lower lip pushing in and out, his eyes unfocused.

"Mr. Fortizak! Are you ill?"

"I'm thinking!" he snarled. "Go away!"

We went. As Elson and I entered the roof dome, he said, "Have you told Fortizak about the anonymous messages?"

"Certainly not! I work for Smith's. This job is merely a cover. Fortizak Human only thinks he's my employer."

"Good. We'll work well together, Arda."

I was in seventh heaven. I read that phrase in a novel, but I have not yet found out what it means. Whatever, I was in it.

Chapter 5

An hour later, heaven seemed more like chaos because the guests were arriving. Writers, once loosed from their solitary occupations, have a pressing need to talk.

Dee-four came up to me for a Locrian fizz, one of the nonalcoholic drinks I was dispensing from behind a long table. Locrian fizz is a pale yellow-green with large brown bubbles in it, and appeals only to Locrians.

"Where's Zak?" she asked, sipping the fizz through a straw.

"I notified Mr. Fortizak that the guests were arriving, but he said he was in the middle of an important chapter."

"That's Zak. Have you seen Naxo?"

"Not yet."

"Smithy called him in for a last-minute briefing which must have gone overtime. I suppose he's on his way. Frankly, I suspect that Smithy doesn't think either of us agents is competent, but I've known Naxo for years, and aside from his various Naxian peculiarities, he's reliable, and so am I."

It was then that I noticed the low rectangular block beside me. It was not an additional side table, for a pulsating wave was passing slowly across its surface.

It spoke. "Are you still in the agent business, Dee-four? Don't your books sell at all?"

The Locrian did not pull back her eyecover—they hate doing that in what they consider our oxygen-polluted atmosphere—but she peered over the main table to inspect the block.

"Hello, Hjeg. Of course my books sell. I'm still an agent because it pays and it's fun. You meet so many nice people, like sneaky Samians who listen in to other people's conversations."

"I wasn't being sneaky. I was just here, absorbing the sense impressions of the party for my next poem. Why did the TFBI assign agents to this affair, Dee-four?"

The Locrian clicked in annoyance. "Protecting the jewels, Hjeg. When the Crotonite crown princess shows up, she'll be wearing several."

"And the TFBI expects one of us from the GWS to steal it!"

"I don't know. The help has been vouched for, in case you were wondering. That's the caterers and Arda, here."

"And my boyfriend, Elson. He's the butler taking hors d'oeuvres around over there."

"Indeed?" asked Dee-four, gazing at him with that covered huge eye.

"Director Smith has okay'd him," I said.

"I suppose she's checked him out with the TFBI files, too," said Dee-four. "And that's probably what Smithy was telling Naxo."

"Who is Naxo?" asked Hjeg.

"A Naxian TFBI agent. The GWS promised the princess that she would have two bodyguards."

Hjeg's voice—I was never able to tell where it emerged from her strange body—rose higher. "Don't tell me the idiot Crotonites have brought the ruulogem?"

"What do you know about ruulogems, Hjeg?"

"Only that the Crotonites have the biggest and best. They call it their royal gem. Do you know who's supposed to steal it, or are you and the Naxian just here to keep Vush from accidentally flushing it down an Erthumoi toilet?"

"Not funny, Hjeg. Perhaps you're here to steal the ruulogem. You've never come to a meeting in person before."

Another ripple dimpled Hjeg's surface. "What would I do with a gem, Dee-four? I don't even need the money you'd get from selling it, if you could. I don't need anything—except possibly a little champagne."

I dutifully poured a glass into the depression that formed in Hjeg's surface.

"Everyone needs money," said Dee-four, taking some more Locrian fizz. "Even you. If you stole the ruulogem, nobody would know you had it hidden inside your body. Then you'd sell it later."

"Why would I do that?"

"If somebody paid you enough for it and said it was in a good cause. You Samians tend to believe anyone's sob story."

"I don't, Dee-four, but I'm thinking of writing them because poetry sells badly. In the meantime, I shall look forward to seeing that ruulogem. It's said that gazing into the larger stones promotes higher thought."

Dee-four laughed. "Naxo told me ruulogems promote distinctly lower thoughts."

"How typically Naxian," said Hjeg, unsticking herself from the floor and slowly moving (I'm not sure how) over to a group of human writers sipping drinks in a corner of the room. One of the humans poured another glass of champagne into a depression that formed in Hjeg's top, and the liquid quickly disappeared.

Dee-four waggled her head. "Now everyone will know Naxo and I are here to guard the jewels, but perhaps it's just as well. It might deter the thief, if there is one, from trying to steal the gem."

"What's it like when you use your eye to look into the depths of a ruulogem?" I asked.

Dee-four's mandible clicked. "An exquisite sensation of delving into a cascade of color. With a ruulogem as big as the Crotonite royal gem, I might even enter an altered state of consciousness. Thanks for the drinks, Arda. Wasn't the fizz a bit fizzier than usual?"

"I don't know. I confess that I've never seen any of these special beverages for nonErthumoi. The drinks were all here when I came up to help the cooks."

Elson came over to offer hors d'oeuvres to Dee-four and she made another clicking noise. Locrians do that in almost any emotional situation. She also moved her head up and down, scanning his perfectly fit shape.

Wheezing into her breather, she said, "Arda, your boyfriend is a superb specimen of Erthumoi."

"Thank you," Elson said, bowing deeply.

Dee-four wheezed again and walked delicately off to talk to fellow members, so Elson leaned toward me and said, "I think our little deception is going well. I should kiss you. It will be a convincing part of our performance."

I lifted my face for my first kiss—but it was not to be, for Naxo arrived, to be greeted enthusiastically by Dee-four.

"Food!" yelled Naxo. "I'm starving!"

Elson handed me the tray of hors d'oeuvres. "I'm going back to the kitchen for another tray. You can feed the Naxian. When they eat, they remind me of the way small animals vanish down the gullets of hungry boa constrictors."

"I thought doctors weren't supposed to be squeamish."

"Squeamishness has nothing to do with it. I was raised to have good manners."

As he left, I resolved to study the way in which one could become as aristocratic as Elson, manners and all. But the more I thought about it, the more my emotive circuits registered depression.

What was the use? He would never take me seriously, not as a female, or as a mate. I couldn't have his children. I would live longer than he. For the first time in my short life I wondered what could possibly be the purpose in being alive.

Being conscious, aware, intelligent, even emotional—what was it for? Organic Erthumoi talk and write about love—was that the secret? Could I love Elson? Did I already love him?

"Hey, Arda—are you in charge of the eats?" Accompanied by Dee-four, Naxo slithered over to me, gulped down every morsel on the tray, and inspected the rest of the food on the table.

"Leave some for the other members, Naxo," warned Dee-four.

"Yes, leave some for us," said a human male, emerging from the crowd to pick up a drink. "When do we get to see the fabulous jewels you're guarding, Dee-four, and is this the charming housekeeper Zak's acquired?"

He was not as tall and handsome as Elson, but had his own good looks, complete with square jaw and bulging biceps. The epitome of the rugged male, I believe the expression is. Perhaps it is a cliché, but not for me.

"This is Granston, who writes what Erthumoi call thrillers."

"I am Arda."

"I bet you are," he said.

His leer was interrupted by the arrival of Zak with two other members of the GWS. The first was a Cephallonian in a tank. The other was an aged Locrian who tottered over to Dee-four, shook her claw, and called her by her real name, which I can't spell. Zak referred to him as Ter-one.

"I'm Dee-four's guest, in town to visit my Terran publishers, who are being humanly obtuse about how to illustrate my book of essays."

"Illustrated?" Hjeg said. She had somehow moved into my location again without my noticing her. She didn't seem affected by the champagne, but with Samians it's hard to tell. "Nobody ever illustrates my books of poetry."

"You should see what the publishers did to my last book," said Pleltun, the Cephallonian. "The waterproof editions all went to Earth instead of to my home. Furthermore, my careful dedications to appropriate relatives were left out."

Pleltun's tank could be propelled from inside by underwater switches. He was rather small, no larger than a Terran dolphin, but unlike a dolphin, he breathed water and had hands.

Cephallonians use superior, water-filled spaceships they'd acquired in the distant past. Legend has it that all the technology of the Cephallonians came from the mysterious Seventh Species, who vanished and left behind only beautiful artifacts, but no record of what they themselves were like.

"Hey, you Cephallonian—try this and improve your sex life," said Naxo. To my horror I saw that Naxo had ripped open the package of Crotonite food capsules. Before I could stop him, he tossed one of the capsules into Pleltun's tank. Before it hit the water, Pleltun caught it with the four-fingered end of his little arm.

"My sex life needs no improvement. Perhaps yours does."

Pleltun tossed it right into Naxo's laughing, open jaws.

Naxo's teeth crunched the capsule, his eyes widened, and he swallowed. "It tastes odd, but I'll try anything once. Why should Crotonites have all the sexual stimulation?"

"As if you needed any," Dee-four said.

I wondered if cross-species sex ever occurred, but it didn't seem possible. All six were too different, and the coils of a Naxian would certainly crush the fragile body of a Locrian, although—I speculated—the touch of a Locrian's claws might possibly be stimulating.

Naxo suddenly began to sing in Naxian, off-key and so loudly that the other GWSers in the dome stopped talking.

Zak said, "The Crotonites seem to have invented a better psychostimulant than alcohol. Perhaps Kolix wanted to rev up his princess for the marriage flight tonight."

Naxo switched to Galactic Basic. "On every world, there's time for love, time for love, time for love . . ."

"I'll take him down to my apartment," Zak said, putting an arm around Naxo's upper body.

The end of Naxo's tail coiled around Zak's right shoe, which I noticed was even scuffier than the left one. I had forgotten to polish them!

"Want some more of that stuff," Naxo said. An arm extruded from his middle coil, snagged another capsule, and popped it into his open mouth.

"Spit it out, Naxo," said Zak. "Not good for you."

"Non—sen—se . . ." said Naxo, squirming out from Zak's grasp. "Want to fly!"

"Stop him!" yelled Dee-four as Naxo headed for the terrace.

It was not necessary. Naxo reached the open glass doors but did not go through them. "Whooo!" he said, collapsing into a coiled heap.

"Passed out," said Zak.

"Well, well," said Granston. "And he's supposed to guard the ruulogem, is he? Can you handle it yourself, Dee-four?"

"Yes, Granston."

He pulled at his ear and said, "I suppose you can, but I wonder—could the fact that one TFBI agent is out of commission have less to do with jewels and more to do with the Crotonites' recent increase in shady dealings?"

"Like what?" asked Zak.

"Drug running. I suspect the capsules contain a drug harmless to Crotonites but not to Naxians. After all, think of the way Crotonites specialize in Seventh Species artifacts, mostly bought from smugglers. It's said that the royal ruulogem has a long, bloody history. Maybe Naxo was onto something."

"You insult us," said a high-pitched voice.

Two creatures stood at the entrance to the dome. They wore spangled bibs below their jutting chins and velvet shorts on their short, stubby legs. Each had thin but mobile lips beneath a pointed nose, and eyes that resembled balls of shiny gray mud in the darker gray of their faces. Their peculiarly jointed arms ended in two long fingers that were tightly bent, as if in anger.

The new arrivals moved slowly into the room, in step with each other. I estimated that even the taller of the two did not reach my shoulders, but their smallness was made up for by the fact that from the back of each sprouted a pair of huge, unfeathered wings with white tips.

The smaller of the two had what looked like the biggest fire opal in the universe stuck on top of the forehead crest that each sported above a bony forehead. But the stone sparkled more than any opal.

"Will you look at the size of the ruulogem!" muttered Granston.

"Silence, you alien who has insulted us!" shouted the one with the ruulogem.

"I am insulted, too," said the bigger of the two, in a slightly deeper voice. It was clear that the first had been using the royal "we."

The Crotonites had arrived.

Chapter 6

The two Crotonites advanced into the banquet room, wings tightly folded, fingers tightly clenched. As they walked under the dome lights, the ruulogem worn by the princess flashed like a warning beacon.

The GWS members all stopped talking and the only sound was Naxo's snoring, which resembled another kind of warning—that of an oversized rattlesnake.

"We have been insulted," Princess Vush repeated, "and I think my Kolix should resign from this society."

Rescue came in the form of Elson, emerging from the kitchen with a gold-colored tray upon which reposed a huge white orchid, the variety that's been mutated so one pair of petals is much larger than the rest and flares out like wings.

Elson stopped in front of Vush—his smile polite and deferential, his hair crisply blond in the light—and bowed elegantly as he held out the tray.

"This is called the Royal Orchid, Your Highness, in honor of the Crotonite royal family. The Galactic Writers' Society presents it to you to celebrate your marriage to one of their esteemed members."

Vush's fingers unclenched, extended, and clamped upon the orchid, which she affixed to the middle of her jewel-encrusted bib. "It's about time we were treated decently. Are you a member of this foogsluk organization?"

"No, Your Highness. I am the butler."

"A pity. For a human, you are almost attractive. Is there anything for Crotonites to feed upon?"

"Special food capsules from your embassy, Highness."

"Nothing alive?"

"No, Highness."

"Then, it's a good thing Kolix and I had a tasty snack at the embassy. It's so enjoyable to bite into a struggling bikmjlu."

"Indeed, Highness," Elson said smoothly.

After I noticed that Zak had already shuddered, I didn't dare ask how big and how conscious bikmjlus are. I hoped they were even less conscious than the live oysters humans still eat, but I doubted it.

Vush looked down at her orchid and smiled toothily at Kolix. "Shall we stay with these inferior beings, my consort?"

Kolix smiled toothily back. "It will do them good for you to bestow your noble presence upon them, in spite of their insults."

"Oh, come off it," said Granston, his upper lip curling slightly into what was not a smile. "The out-cold Naxian TFBI agent over there seems to have been drugged by one of your Crotonite food capsules. He and Dee-four said they were here to guard the royal jewels, but I suspect they're trying to find out what you Crotonites are illegally doing with Seventh Species artifacts which are big money these days."

"He insults us again!" Vush poked her bridegroom in the way so many organic females have of insisting that the male spouse defend their honor.

"Granston, hear me." Kolix's own rubbery lip curled

up over his longest pointed tooth. "You and I are fellow members of GWS, and although we have never been friendly, I assure you that there could be nothing wrong with the capsules. I do not know that Naxian, but he merely looks drunk to me. Furthermore, the Crotonite antiquities business is now legitimate."

"Then you admit it was not always legitimate?"

Kolix looked at Vush. "We do not need to admit anything."

"My jewels—what about my jewels?" Vush poked him again.

Kolix stretched up both wings for a moment, during which he seemed twice as big as he normally was. "I can guard my own wife. She need not fear robbery— and from whom?"

"We don't know," said Dee-four. "The TFBI was concerned about the princess wearing the ruulogem here in Manhattan, so Naxo and I were ordered to protect you. I suppose it's possible Naxo's eating the capsules was accidental."

"The capsules may have bad effects on inferior species," said Vush with an aristocratic sniff. "They are a recent Crotonite invention, which we of the royal family have used because we must attend these nonCrotonite dinners featuring dead food. The capsules are merely nutritious to Crotonites. Since you do not intend to feed us here, Kolix and I will save them to eat before our mating flight."

"Mating flight?" Zak looked alarmed. "Here?"

"Naturally. This is our first wedding banquet. Then we mate on the wing and return to our embassy. Tomorrow we start on a goodwill tour of the Galaxy."

"Lots of luck," said Granston. "You Crotonites need all the goodwill you can muster. Or is the tour just a way of promoting the artifact business? You can't deny all the rumors about you personally, Kolix."

Now Kolix was so angry he hopped up and down. "You keep harping on the rumors about artifact dealings, Granston. The rumors are false. I am innocent. My princess and I are going on a genuine archaeological tour, at her request."

Vush beamed at him. "I await our mating flight with trembling wings, my noble hero!" It was a line from one of Kolix's novels.

"Dearwing," said Kolix, touching his crest to hers so that the ruulogem trembled, "to enhance our love I recommend an Erthumoi drink called champagne. It also makes speeches by nonCrotonites less boring."

Elson, as efficient as he was handsome, handed each of the Crotonites a glass of champagne and said, "Will the members of the GWS please fill your plates at the buffet and sit at your assigned tables so the banquet may begin."

I quickly went behind the buffet table to join Elson in dispensing food, giving each member a gracious smile as I did so.

"Don't overdo it, Arda," Zak whispered as I spooned the chili he'd asked for onto his plate.

"The chili?"

"The smile. You're outclassing the bride, as well as all the Erthumoi females."

"Thank you," I said, scanning the other Erthumoi females, those physically present and those seen as holographic images. Some were attractive, but perhaps Zak thought I looked better.

Since my activation, I had not given much thought to my appearance, deeming it an unworthy topic for the activity of an advanced positronic brain, but now I was pleased with the remark, although I wished it had come from Elson.

With platefuls of food, everyone went to their tables, while Elson and I sat on stools behind the buffet in case anyone wanted more of anything. The Crotonites were at the head table, nearest the buffet, so I felt I could guard the ruulogem while Dee-four ate her dinner, several tables away.

Zak stood up. "We welcome all our members, in the flesh or otherwise, to the annual banquet of the Galactic Writers' Society. I'm sorry the Crotonite surprise didn't work out."

"We planned no surprise," said Kolix.

"In that case, let me just say that the GWS is honored to have Crotonite royalty present tonight."

Kolix smirked and Vush tilted the top corner of a wing, a presumably royal gesture designed to show a condescending reluctance to overdo gratitude.

After a considerable intake of Terran champagne, Kolix said, "Dee-four, is it true that the Locrian eye can see right into the inside of things?"

"That's correct."

"I would like you to examine the royal ruulogem."

Vush bristled. "For flaws?"

"No, dearwing, merely to affirm its perfection."

Granston, who had by now downed several drinks much stronger than champagne, waved at Vush. "Yeah, let Dee-four see into the jewel. Serve you Crotonites right if it's flawed, since the ruulogem was found in a Seventh Species site, wasn't it?"

"Shut up, Granston," Zak said. "I'm host and I'm in charge of this banquet and I'm tired of you trying to turn a social occasion into a grilling. Makes one wonder who you're working for when you're not churning out potboilers."

Granston opened his mouth to reply but Dee-four clamped a wiry claw on his shoulder as she passed his chair on her way to the head table. "I happen to know who you do work for, Granston, so let it rest for now." Surprisingly, he remained silent.

Dee-four was so much taller than the Crotonite princess that she had to lean down to see into the ruulo-gem. She paused and waited. And waited some more.

"That's strange. I can't raise my eyecover."

"Don't worry, my dear," said Ter-one. "It happens to most Locrians as they age."

"Am I becoming an old lady Locrian so soon, Ter-one?"

"It is somewhat strange, because you *are* much younger than I am. Perhaps too much Locrian fizz, my dear?"

"Only a glass. I'm just old. And I haven't even laid an egg yet, much less found a mate!"

Zak stood up and toasted Dee-four with his glass of ginger ale. I had not yet seen him take anything stronger.

"Older females? Why not? There's a stage
Where the ladies are fun to engage—
Their resistance is low
And desire is aglow—
Like wine, they grow better with age."

"You'll never get that limerick published, Zak," said Hjeg.

"I can get anything published," said Zak. "I'll put my tribute to Dee-four into my next book of limericks."

"Really?" said Pleltun, "I've always thought that the major skill of an author was in knowing what to throw away."

"I'm frequently accused of ignoring that. Anyway, Dee-four is definitely of the best vintage of any species."

Dee-four's head sagged mournfully. "Zak, I appreciate the thought and the limerick, but I must indeed be getting old."

Ter-one said gently, "Perhaps you'll be all right tomorrow."

"I can still guard your jewels, Princess," said Dee-four.

Kolix said, "Unnecessary. Let me assure any would-be robber here that in defending our own, we Crotonites can be *lethal*."

"Like these extraordinarily fattening Erthumoi desserts," said Pleltun. "I'd like noodle pudding and double chocolate cake, thank you. In a squeezable plastic bag, please, so the food won't pollute my tank."

During dessert, some of the members made speeches. There were jokes from Zak, one of Hjeg's poems—cut short when Vush shouted, "That's enough!", several darkly funny stories about editors, and tales about literary agents that I didn't understand at all because I don't have one.

You can't get a literary agent unless you're a published writer, and it's hard to get published unless you have an agent. I do not understand the logic behind this.

To muffled groans from other GWS members, Kolix rose and talked at length about his writing triumphs. Just when I expected Zak to explode, Kolix curved one wing over his bride.

"I want my fellow GWS members to know that Vush is not only a princess but a Crotonite archaeologist specializing in tracking down evidence of the Seventh

Species. I am proud to be her consort and I hereby nominate her for membership in the GWS."

"I second," said Ter-one.

"Everyone will now vote," said Kolix.

"Wait a minute," said Zak, "we're supposed to read what prospective members have written."

Kolix bared his pointed teeth. "My bride has written archaeological papers. Vote."

"All not in favor say 'no,'" said Zak, and when no one spoke, he announced, "Princess Vush is now a member of the Galactic Writers' Society."

"Thank you, fellow members of the Galactic Writers' Society," said Vush, who seemed to be fondling Kolix below his bib, under the table.

When Kolix turned darker gray—it was hard to tell whether he was getting embarrassed or aroused—I whispered to Elson, "Do you think she'll wear him out sexually, the way she did the last royal consort?"

"I should think a truly adequate male spouse would appreciate an experienced bride."

There wasn't time to brood about the fact that no one could be less experienced than I.

Hjeg, of all beings, seemed to be taking up Granston's theme, for she asked, "As a GWS member, Princess, perhaps you'll tell us whether there's any truth to the rumor that Crotonite archaeologists have found a new treasure trove of Seventh Species artifacts near your system."

Vush's long chin lifted until it looked like a weapon raised for combat. "If we have, it is for legitimate archaeological exploration, not commercial exploitation, is it not, Kolix?"

"Yes, dearwing. Commercialism interests me less now that I've married into the royal family. What commercial dealing we'll have will be not only legitimate but as lucrative as possible, with selected species."

His bride blinked, an unsettling sight since Crotonite eyelids go up from below the eyes. "Kolix, dearwing, whatever business we do, I hope you'll keep your promise to me."

"Yes, my princess. Fidelity, loyalty, trust—that is the Crotonite motto. It's all in the novel I'm planning to write about our love."

"I bet it has an eating scene to rival the one in *Tom Jones*," said Zak.

"Why not? The hero and heroine will fall in love at a dinner while eating angpang, an amusing appetizer because it tends to crawl on the ceiling. One must bite it off while flying upside down."

Vush wriggled. "You're making me hungry. Where are those food capsules?"

I placed the dish on the table between Vush and Kolix.

"The package has been opened," said Vush.

"Then, dearwing, I'll be your official taster." Before Vush could stop him, Kolix took two capsules at once. "Ugh."

"What is it—have the capsules been poisoned? They're not supposed to have any taste."

"They don't, but they're disgustingly still. No satisfying wriggle in the mouth and stomach." Kolix smiled at his bride and she giggled.

Vush was just reaching for a capsule when Kolix suddenly gasped and looked up into the top of the dome.

"Angpang?" he asked, his voice croaking.

"I don't see anything," said Vush. "Are you ill?"

Kolix did not answer. His wings flapped wide open,

knocking down Vush on one side and Zak on the other. Staring straight ahead, Kolix rose into the air.

Crotonite wings, designed for thick atmospheres, won't lift their owners in atmospheres as thin as Earth's. I saw that Kolix and Vush both had small power packs strapped on their backs.

"Come down! There's no angpang up there," yelled Vush, trying to grab him as he lifted past her, beyond even the reach of the tallest among us—Dee-four.

Before anyone could do anything, Kolix hit the ceiling hard. His wings folded and the power pack must have shut off, for Kolix began to fall.

As I ran to catch him, Vush screamed, a high-pitched screech of a sound. She also got in my way and I tripped over her.

Before I could pick myself up, and before anyone else could catch him, Kolix crashed to the floor, hitting his head on the corner of the buffet table on the way down.

"Arda, send for a doctor," said Zak.

But Elson was already striding toward the Crotonite. "Let me see Kolix. I am a doctor."

"Aren't you an actor?" Zak asked, frowning.

"No. To avoid possible political repercussions for Erthumoi, the Terran Federal Bureau of Investigation requested that I be present at the banquet tonight in case anyone became ill. I am a specialist in the medical treatment of alien species."

"I don't like deception," Zak said angrily. "Arda—is this your boyfriend, and is he a doctor?"

"Dr. Elson is not actually my boyfriend, but he is a doctor. Since I was coming here to work, I was asked to make it possible for Dr. Elson to be here, in the guise of a butler."

Elson took a small medical scanner from his pocket

and ran it over Kolix's body, taking more time at the chest and head.

"I hope neither of his brains is damaged," I said. Not many Erthumoi know that a Crotonite has an unusual nervous system.

"You're showing off, Arda," Elson muttered. He stopped scanning and pulled down the odd Crotonite eyelids to inspect the eyes. Kolix did not stir and seemed paler than before, his breathing shallower.

"Blood vessels in both brains have been torn. My surgical equipment can make the repair easily. I will take Kolix into— Arda, is there a couch in the ladies' lounge?"

I didn't know what to say. I had not been in it.

"Yes," said Dee-four.

Zak raised a hand. "Kolix ought to go to his own embassy, to be cared for by Crotonite physicians."

"We Crotonites have superior bodies and rarely get sick, so our embassy has no doctor," Vush said, trembling.

"Then Kolix must go to one of our hospitals," said Zak.

"No! I'll send to Crotonis for a doctor."

"Your Highness," Elson said grimly, "your consort is dying *now*. At no Erthumoi hospital will there be any physician as skilled as I am in alien medicine and surgery, and there certainly isn't time to wait for Crotonite help. Kolix must be treated here, at once. To repair the blood vessels necessitates only two small incisions. I will save him."

"How can I trust an Erthumoi doctor?" Vush wailed.

"You'd better," said Dee-four.

Vush's wings fluttered. "Kolix must not die, or my father the king will insist that I take as my consort the next candidate, an impotent cabinet member. That will not do. Dr. Elson, I must allow you to help Kolix."

"Thank you, Princess. Arda, you will find my equipment in a locker in the kitchen. Please get it."

Elson lifted Kolix as if he weighed nothing, and carried him into the lounge. I couldn't help thinking how much the Crotonite resembled a limp, ugly, oversized bat.

I found Elson's locked bag of equipment in the kitchen. It was so heavy that only a strong human could carry it, but of course I had no difficulty. I took the bag to Elson in the big, elegant lounge, followed by many of the GWS members who crowded in after me.

Kolix lay on the couch, his breathing irregular. He looked to me as if he were dying.

Zak asked, "Elson, what have you got in that bag— a complete portable emergency room?"

"Almost," Elson said with a smile. "I came prepared for anything. Please clear the room now."

When everyone else had left, I asked if he needed my help.

"No, Arda. You're just an . . ." He didn't say the word 'android,' but it seemed to echo all the same.

"I have excellent manual dexterity," I said.

"No doubt, but I do microsurgery with the latest equipment, and need no help. What I do need is an undisturbed hour or so. Please go out and make sure no one enters until I'm finished."

"Yes, Dr. Elson." I went out. The door closed, and I stood in front of it.

Chapter 7

The GWS members whispered to each other. Some there in person picked up second helpings of dessert but after going back to their tables sat down and did not eat, as if ashamed of resorting to the solace of food. Even Zak at the head table did not eat his second noodle pudding. I was keeping count.

"Maybe it's a stronger batch of capsules," said one of the holographically present members. "Strong enough to make the Naxian drunk, and to affect Kolix, too. I've never seen Kolix act inebriated at a meeting before."

Zak turned to the princess. "Is it possible that your food capsules do overstimulate some Crotonites?"

"No. Our capsules are harmless to us."

Granston's arrogance was back. "I'm sure you Crotonites can make mistakes. No matter how many brains you've got, you've never seemed very brainy to me."

"We are doubly brainy!" Vush bared her teeth as if about to try them out on Granston.

Zak said, "Let's not get into another argument. I'm pleased to note that my housekeeper is up on alien anatomy."

"You're the Great Explainer, Zak," said Dee-four. "Tell us about Crotonite anatomy."

Zak pointed to me. "No. You explain, Arda."

"Inside the Crotonite head is a ganglion of nerve cells that serves to process cognition. A much larger ganglion of nerve cells is located just inside the upper torso, at the bottom of the short neck. This lower ganglion contains the more ancient, primitive aspects of the brain."

"Stop saying 'ganglion' when you mean brain," Vush said. "We have two real brains. That makes us superior."

Hjeg's surface rippled, presumably with amusement, for the Samian body can disassemble into tiny mobile components each of which has a brain linked telepathically to the others.

Pleltun grunted and blew a small fountain of water in his tank. "We Cephallonians have the largest brains."

"Not the largest cerebral cortex," Granston said. "Only organic Erthumoi qualify for that."

One of Naxo's holographically visible colleagues said "Naxian superior intelligence speaks for itself."

Ter-one clicked his mandibles, presumably in annoyance, for everyone usually agrees that Locrians are remarkably intelligent.

Dee-four, however, glanced over at me and then said quietly, "The most intelligent species may turn out to be the second type of Erthumoi. An android brain contains markedly complex microbubble circuits which do not have to be bulky."

I was glad that Dee-four thought of me as an equal, but I wanted to add that large, moist human brains are not only repulsive to look at but considerably bulky.

Granston sneered. "Androids are pinbrains."

I had heard that some prejudiced organic Erthumoi call us that, but I had never met such prejudice before.

Vush stamped her feet. "I don't care about your stupid human or android brains. My Kolix is near death."

"He wouldn't be if you Crotonites didn't have wings," said Granston. "He just got drunk on the capsules like the Naxian did, only when Naxo collapsed he wasn't up at the ceiling, so he didn't have far to fall."

"I refuse to believe that any of us Crotonites would fall like that even if inebriated!" Vush screamed.

Zak said, "I believe you have a point, Your Highness. Naxo may have acted drunk before he passed out, and so did Kolix, but I suspect that they were both drugged by the capsules. And I think your Locrian fizz was also drugged, Dee-four."

"But who did it?" asked Ter-one.

"We Crotonites did not touch the capsules until my dearwing tried them. They were altered here, before we arrived."

"I don't see how, Princess," said Zak. "The capsules arrived with your embassy's official seal on the outer wrapping, which I removed. I did not disturb the inside packet, and Arda brought it up here still sealed. No one could have tampered with the capsules in my apartment."

"We have only your word for that, Fortizak," said Vush.

"He speaks the truth," I said. Zak could theoretically have poisoned the capsules and resealed the package before I arrived, but the sealing had seemed intact.

"Since you're so good at explanations, servant," said Vush, "tell us what did happen with the capsules."

"Yes, ma'am. The package of capsules was here, sealed, until Naxo opened it and threw a capsule at Pleltun, who threw it back at once. Naxo swallowed it and took another. No one else touched the capsules after that until I put them in front of the Crotonites."

"How can you be certain?"

I could not explain that everything happening in the room registers in my sensor data bank and can be reviewed by my cognitive functions at any time. "I am certain."

Pleltun's tail swung from side to side in his tank, causing waves that almost slopped over the sides. "Princess, is it possible that someone in your embassy didn't want you to marry this Crotonite? Does Kolix have a rival?"

"That's a thought," said Dee-four. "What kind of power does the next-in-line wield? That cabinet member you mentioned."

"No power," said Vush. "Buulng is old, the last of his line, as Kolix is the last of his. Neither has powerful relatives, only aristocratic heritage. Kolix's line has more connections by blood and marriage to the royal family than Buulng's, so he was chosen first."

"By you?" asked Zak.

"No, but after even our short acquaintance I believe that I now love him. He is much more attractive than my first husband, who was older than Buulng."

"Does any other Crotonite resent Kolix, for his marriage to you or for anything else?"

"I tell you that no Crotonite would dare harm me or those I care about."

Zak leaned toward her. "Princess, consider that you may be wrong. The Crotonite royal family could conceivably have enemies who might have tried to embarrass you with drugged capsules, even with a stupid serving robot programmed to deliver a surprise."

"You mentioned a surprise before. What about it?"

"I had a serving robot named Y50, which I sent to Smith's for culinary reprogramming. Y50 never arrived at the repair shop, and when it returned here it had evidently been programmed to deliver leaflets about your marriage at the end of this banquet."

"Pleasant leaflets?"

"From the Crotonite point of view. Unfortunately—or perhaps fortunately—Y50 delivered the leaflets down in my apartment. I have a few here."

Zak extracted a leaflet from his pocket and gave it to her.

"Very nice," said Vush. "How thoughtful of Kolix."

"Princess, if Kolix altered Y50's programming, could he be the one who also altered the capsules when they were still in your embassy? Perhaps he thought they would stimulate him . . ."

"To please me," Vush said. "Dear Kolix."

Zak shook his head. "We'll ask him when he's recovered, but in the meantime, Princess, please check with your embassy to make sure Kolix had access to the capsules there."

Vush whispered into her wrist communicator, her face getting darker as she listened. When she finished, she pulled a thin pointed dagger from her sleeve, opened her wings, and flew to the top of the tallest potted tree. Her ruulogem shone like a solstice ornament, temptingly beautiful above the angry face of its owner.

"My embassy says no one there sent for or received food capsules. As far as the embassy knows, there are no Crotonite food capsules anywhere on Earth. No leaflets were prepared at our embassy."

Zak said, "This means . . ."

"I know what it means," Vush said. "I am a scientist. I can reason better than any of you. Someone here must have obtained the capsules, altered them, and at the same time put leaflets inside your robot, Fortizak. I believe this was done in order to get Kolix out of the way so I could be attacked, and my ruulogem stolen. But I will defend myself."

She waved the stilettolike weapon at the rest of us as we stood there looking up at her. At first, the sight of the little Crotonite flourishing a dagger seemed ridiculous, but Vush held it as if she knew what to do with it. With power packs, Crotonites can fly away from an enemy, or down to attack one.

"Dee-four's eyecover paralysis will probably wear off, and Naxo is just asleep," said Pleltun. "Probably the whole thing is just a joke, dangerous only because Kolix fell."

"Joke!" cried Vush. "Our host likes jokes. I don't believe he knows nothing about this. Fortizak wants my ruulogem!" With a high-pitched shriek, the tiny Brunhilde launched herself at my employer, dagger point first.

Zak ducked, but it was not necessary. Androids can move with more speed than any human reflexes can achieve.

I sprang forward, plucked Vush out of the air and held her wings tightly, as far away from me as possible. She could not harm me, but she could certainly slit my clothes.

Vush swung from my grasp like a spitting cat, trying to reach up with her short arms to stab mine.

"Thank you, Arda," said Zak. "I've always wanted a housekeeper who could act as a bodyguard. Vush, I swear by all the books I have ever written that I had nothing whatsoever to do with the capsules, or Y50. You can ask Kolix when he's cured. He knows me well enough to be able to tell you that I have no use for jewels, either. Blast it, I'm a *writer!*"

Vush stopped fighting and said, "Kolix is your friend?"

"Well, he knows my peculiarities, one of which is that I can't be bothered with possessions or power. All I'm interested in is doing my work. Arda, let Vush fly back up to the tree, where she feels safe."

"But, Zak . . ."

"Let the princess go."

Released, Vush flew back to the tree again, where she began to blink as if trying not to cry. "Will Kolix die before he has even experienced our marital flight?"

Dee-four stood up. Locrians may lay eggs, but they give the hatchlings exquisite care. Dee-four's voice had a maternal tone as she said, "Princess, if the TFBI found the best physician for Kolix, then I'm sure he won't die."

"But I still want to know who did this!"

Dee-four said soothingly, "It's possible that the villain is a writer who is not a member of GWS and resents our successes, including the way your Kolix writes best-sellers. Perhaps this joke was meant to implicate and irritate all of us in GWS, but not result in accidental tragedy."

As far as I knew, I was the only writer or would-be writer there who was not a member of GWS. Naxo didn't count because he was a TFBI investigator masquerading as a writer. And I knew I hadn't drugged the capsules.

Vush was now crying large tears that dropped into the tree fronds. "I don't believe in jokes. I'm sure it's a plot to get my ruulogem. Oh, Kolix, Kolix! So young and virile! So sexually untouched!"

While the crowd of GWS members talked among themselves, Dee-four whispered to me, "Arda, if Kolix is cured, we can't let the Crotonites go back to their embassy alone, because maybe Vush is right. The joke was meant to distract us and get Kolix out of the way so the ruulogem could indeed be stolen."

I was about to tell her about the other threat that had prompted Director Smith to send Elson to the banquet, when Zak raised his hand for silence. "We must call the police."

"Zak, are you out of your mind?" asked Granston. "We can't call the police. Think of what this will do to interplanetary relations!"

"Exactly what concerned the TFBI," said Dee-four. "I will be able to guard the princess . . ."

Granston shouted "You may be employed by the TFBI, Dee-four, but how do we know you aren't a Locrian spy?"

Dee-four swayed from side to side like a praying mantis about to attack. Didn't Dee-four know that a powerful human like Granston could tear her apart?

"Looking for copy, Granston?"

"My spy novels make more sense than your activities here."

"Your novels don't make sense. They sell because your jacket picture is doctored to make you look sexy to misguided Erthumoi, most of them female."

I may have neglected to mention that Granston's hair was tightly curled and stunningly silver, in spite of his apparent youth, so that he appeared to be a man of power with the face of a Greek god, a type used by holov shows designed to titilate the human female.

Granston's cheeks reddened. "Locrian, nobody reads your science articles!"

"Your wordster is programmed to fill in steamy sex scenes cribbed from other people's novels because that's all anyone reads in your books!"

"Your stuff is deliberately obtuse!"

"Hack!"

"Pseudointellectual!"

"Plagiarist!"

I got between them, knowing I could handle Granston if I had to, although it would reveal my strength.

Nothing happened, for too many members were shouting—most of them about wanting to return to their homes or hotel rooms.

"My tank is getting too warm." Pleltun flipped his tail enough to spray a few drops onto Granston. "I've called an aircar and I'm going back to my embassy's pool."

Ter-one said, "At my age I cannot be up this late, Zak. There's no need to embarrass the Crotonites, or the GWS, by sending for what you Manhattanites euphemistically call law enforcement officers."

"I'm leaving," said Hjeg. As we watched, her body collapsed into a swarm of tiny creatures that ran under the glass doors of the terrace, under the Crotonite aircar that had just landed, and over the wall.

"Zak, you might as well let anyone go home who wants to," said Dee-four. "I'll stay to guard Vush and take care of Naxo."

Vush flew down from the tree. "I give permission for everyone to leave. We will sue the Erthumoi government later. The Crotonite aircar is here, and I will take Kolix back to the embassy as soon as the doctor has finished."

One by one, the members of the GWS departed. The holograms of distant members had already vanished. The couple in the kitchen finished cleaning up and left as well. Eventually only a few of us remained—the sleeping Naxo, Dee-four, Vush, Kolix, Elson, Zak, and I.

Granston was the last of the others to leave. He came over to speak softly to me. "Young Arda, I would like to see you again, some day when this ridiculous banquet is forgotten."

"Ridiculous?"

"Very much so. Silly threats, sillier drugs. Nobody would have been hurt if that idiot Kolix hadn't gone into the air and drunkenly lost control of his wings."

"I suppose so."

"Arda . . ." He was centimeters from my ear, and more serious than I thought he could be. ". . . do you know Zak well?"

"No, I don't. I only started to work here today."

"Watch out for him. He's supposed to be a genius, and I don't trust geniuses."

"Should anyone trust you, Granston? Perhaps you're as hard-boiled and exploitative as your heroes."

"Ah, a fan!"

"I've read a few of your novels." I didn't tell him I thought the plots were simpleminded.

"I adore you, fair Arda."

"Granston, take your hand off my left buttock. That isn't the way to get me to trust you. For all I know, it was you who played this nasty joke to embarrass the GWS—or Zak."

"I'll never tell. Or I might, if we got real friendly." He leaned even closer and smacked his lips on mine. I noted that my synthoskin sensors registered pressure but no pleasure.

"Granston!" Zak yelled. "Stop making a pass at my new housekeeper. She's young and—are you innocent, Arda?"

"I am innocent of any crime."

"Hah! But do you appreciate hard-boiled love, a la Granston, my innocent housekeeper?"

"No, sir."

"Good. Get going, Granston, you goon—and notice

the spontaneous alliteration—if a writer of pop thrillers knows what that means."

Granston flexed a biceps. "I'm going, but I'll see more of you, Arda. I have what your nonboyfriend Elson might term a clinical interest in innocent females. And in mysteriously unpleasant events at supposedly innocent banquets hosted by not-so-innocent geniuses."

Dee-four, relaxed but watchful, said, "Whatever sort of writer you are, Granston, I want to point out that your penchant for traveling to other worlds certainly exceeds the necessary research for your writing. Your trips must cost more than your books bring in, yet you can afford them."

"Interesting," said Zak. "Who pays you—and for what? You seldom come in person to the regular GWS meetings here in Manhattan. Why did you decide—this year—to attend the banquet? This supposedly innocent banquet, which you nearly ruined by implying that the Crotonites either run drugs or steal important artifacts."

Granston lifted one eyebrow, flexed the other biceps and said "Artifacts," as if it were a code word. "So lucrative. See you around, Zak."

"Not where you go, Granston."

As Granston left, Zak said, "The blasted joker."

"*The* joker?" I asked.

"I wouldn't be surprised," said Dee-four.

"Too early to tell," said Zak. "Right now I can't even guess at who instigated the events leading to what's going on in here." He pointed to the lounge, where Elson had gone to save Kolix's life.

Chapter 8

Princess Vush was becoming agitated, pacing back and forth before the lounge door. "I must find out if Kolix has been saved. It seems as if they've been in there for hours."

"Only one," said Zak.

Vush flew back up to the treetop and perched there, shaking her head and giving vent to what sounded like Crotonite swear words, each punctuated by a flash from the ruulogem.

My inner clock agreed with Zak; my emotive circuits agreed with Vush.

"Patience, Princess," said Dee-four. She was stroking Naxo's head as if trying to improve his dreams. "If anything terrible happens, Dr. Elson will inform us. In the meantime, I have notified the TFBI of these developments and Director Smith is on her way here. She's ordered me to collect the remaining food capsules and the fizz so they can be analyzed for drugs."

Zak pulled up a chair so he could sit between the buffet table and the door, where I was standing. He spoke softly to me. "The TFBI must be chewing its collective nails. When Crotonites feel like suing other governments, they do."

"Maybe they'll be grateful if Elson saves Kolix."

"Maybe is a big word." Zak took a bagel and began chewing moodily on it. "Want a chair, Arda?"

"No, thank you."

"Not tired?"

"No, sir."

Zak said, through the bagel, "I wonder who could have changed the capsules and stuffed leaflets into Y50."

"Poor Y50. Dead. Murdered."

Zak swallowed and blinked. "I suppose you could say Y50 was more or less alive. It's certainly dead now. As to murder . . ."

"Y50 was murdered—for a stupid joke. And if Kolix dies, it will be another murder, won't it?"

"Not legally speaking, Arda. Accidental death."

"But Y50's brain death was deliberate. I have never seen a death until this afternoon in your apartment. I suppose I never fully realized that we—that anyone can die. Why do I feel so sad about this?"

"It's called intimations of mortality. I'm sorry to have to tell you, young Arda, but death is part of the Universe. Even the Universe itself will die some day."

"Then what is the point of being alive?"

Zak chuckled.

"Is that a humorous question?"

"Oh, no. Intelligent beings have been asking the same question since the Universe began to produce them."

"I'm confused."

Zak laughed again. "Sadness about death; questioning about life; intellectual confusion—all the price we pay for being alive and intelligent."

"But that's my original question—what is the point of being alive and intelligent?"

"You'll have to find out for yourself, Arda. Then we

can compare our ideas. Not now. You're too—ah—young."

Dee-four's angular shape loomed over us. "Naxo's stopped snoring, so maybe he'll wake up soon. I'm beginning to think the Crotonites themselves planned the joke, which backfired."

Zak's eyebrows pulled together. "Perhaps we were meant to think that, and if so, why? Somehow I can't believe yon self-centered crown princess knew about the drugged capsules or Y50."

"Why not?" I asked.

"Oh?" said Zak, "You have a theory?"

"I am endeavoring to reason carefully. Order and method is the correct approach to solving mysteries, I believe."

"Yes, Agatha."

I paid no attention to his literary sarcasm. "Perhaps Vush lied. Perhaps she secretly decided she doesn't want Kolix after all and tried to make him look ridiculous—which he would have, if he hadn't fallen—so she could divorce him and marry the other Crotonite, who probably isn't impotent and who might have been having an affair with her, unbeknownst to her father, the king. . . ."

"Good grief. Have you been trying to write romance novels?"

"No, sir. Only short stories."

"I thought so. Have I been so insane as to let a would-be writer worm her way into my life disguised as a housekeeper?"

"Not at all, sir!" I decided it behooved me to be servile.

"Oh, yeah?"

"Of course, if you wanted to give me advice on my writing, it would be appreciated, but as your housekeeper I would never presume to intrude on your busy life."

"I don't give advice on writing. Writers should learn by writing." Zak reached for another bagel.

"You shouldn't eat another. You weigh too much."

"What!"

"I'm sorry, sir, but it's true."

Zak put the bagel back and groaned. "You must be one of those fans who's trying to see to it that I live forever."

"Just doing my job, sir. As your housekeeper."

At that moment Vush hurtled down from the tree, closed up her wings and pummeled the door to the lounge.

"Open up! I must know what's happening. There's a guard in the aircar outside and if you don't let me in, I will order her to kill you, Dr. Elson."

Elson opened the door, wearing a stiff white gown and mask. He bowed to Vush and said "I have repaired the broken blood vessels. Kolix is still alive, but his heart is malfunctioning from the trauma and the anesthesia. I had to insert a pacemaker and I will need help in closing the wound. Arda, I would appreciate it if you joined me so you can demonstrate that manual dexterity of yours. Everyone else must stay out to keep the field as germ-free as possible."

As I went into the lounge, I heard Vush say, "I will kill that doctor yet if my husband dies."

Hardly any of Kolix was visible. His body was sheeted; his mouth and nostrils covered by an anesthesia mask. There was no apparent incision on his skull.

"Wasn't the cranial brain damaged by a broken blood vessel?" I asked.

"It turned out to be a minor bleed, easily sealed by using a medi-ray wand outside the skull. The thoracic brain had a worse hemorrhage which necessitated surgery. It was successful, of course. You're a robot—can't you tell?"

"A few hospital medirobots have built-in scanners, Dr. Elson, but no intelligent android does. I suppose it would be possible to fit them into our bodies, but it would increase the expense of android construction and make us seem less humanoid."

I did not add that most organics are prejudiced against scanners of all kinds. They seem to resent inspection of the inside of their heads or bodies unless done by doctors, and even then it makes them uneasy. Naxo, for instance, was a friend of Dee-four but when she retracted her eyecover, he was instinctively afraid of her ability to see inside everything.

When Elson removed the surgical sheet from Kolix's upper body, I was glad androids are not squeamish. Kolix's bib was gone and his upper chest had an open wound showing the skin, muscle, and bones Elson had had to cut through, laser-cauterizing small vessels as he went. Inside was a rounded silver surface.

"What's that, Dr. Elson?"

"That's plasti-shielding. You see, the usual pacemaker minimodel works well with the Crotonite heart, which happens to be high up, under the thoracic brain. Unfortunately, Crotonites fly, and their powerful wing muscles insert into what would be the sternum in a human, generating a good many electrical impulses. To protect the pacemaker, I've placed plasti-shielding over it, inside the thorax. It doesn't react with tissue, so Kolix will have no problems with it."

"You've done a marvelous job, Doctor."

"Thanks. I'm going to close up now. Because the dose of medi-ray sealer must be precise for each tissue as I fit the layers of the wound together, you will adjust the machine to the specifications I give you and do the actual sealing."

"Me! I haven't had medtraining."

"Sealing is easy. Knowing what to hold when and how requires training."

"Okay."

We did it. First he tugged the ribs together. It required both Elson's hands to hold them properly, while I adjusted the medi-ray wand to the right dosage and sealed the bones. Then came the muscles and connective tissue, and then the skin. With Elson telling me what to do, the work was easy—and oh, so emotively rewarding. I felt that I was pleasing Elson.

Kolix's upper chest now was completely intact, with only a thin scar a few millimeters below the base of the neck to show where surgery had been done. I couldn't help thinking, however, how peculiar the Crotonite body was—wide, bulging with wing muscles, and adorned with those four nipples.

"There. Healing complete. I'll wake him up now. Go tell the princess to enter, but don't let anyone else in."

I summoned Vush while Elson removed Kolix's anesthesia hood and packed up the surgical equipment. He took off his gown and packed that up, too.

Vush tried to tiptoe over to Kolix, but her foot claws scraped on the marble floor of the lounge. Her lips were trembling.

"Is he really still alive?"

"Dearwing—I am fine!" said Kolix, sitting up. "What happened?"

"You fell and hurt yourself and the doctor—that's Elson, who was here pretending to be a butler so he could help anyone who became ill—has fixed you up. Good as new, Doctor?"

Elson nodded, locking up his medical bag. It seemed odd that he was still wearing his mask, but perhaps he thought it looked more professional. I had not been required to put on a mask because androids don't breathe and don't carry germs.

"Thank you, Doctor," Kolix said, clasping Vush in his arms. "Now, please, leave us alone. You, too, Arda."

I started to go, but Elson walked to the couch and bent over the Crotonites as if inspecting Kolix for the last time.

I could not see what happened, for Elson was in the way, but I heard an odd sound like a tiny hiss.

"What's the matter?" I asked.

Nobody said anything. Vush slowly slid off the couch until she was lying face up on the floor, her eyes closed. From the little I could see with Elson in the way, Kolix had also lost consciousness again, facedown on the couch.

"Have they fainted, Dr. Elson?"

"Not exactly." Elson, with his back to me, stooped, reached down, and removed Vush's bib.

"Is her heart bad?"

"No." He reached down again, stood up and turned around—holding a stun weapon in one hand and the royal ruulogem in the other, his eyes stony above the stiff mask that covered his mouth.

"Don't yell, Arda, or the Crotonites may be damaged."

"You're not a doctor—you're the thief the TFBI was warned about! How did you fool Director Smith?"

"She's an emotionally susceptible old maid who accepted my expertly forged credentials."

"You sent the message about gems being fatal."

"Yes."

"Why did you bother to save Kolix's life when all you had to do was bring him in here, call Vush to come, and zap them both to get the jewels—both bibs as well as the ruulogem."

Elson paused, as if he were thinking hard.

I was trying to estimate how far I'd have to jump to bring him down when he said slowly, "I do not kill those I rob. I was intending to do exactly what you said—drug Kolix, bring him here, call Vush, stun her, and take the jewels. Instead, Kolix flew—and fell. I had to save his life."

"With your medical talents you have no need to steal!"

"Don't shout, Arda. Raise your voice any higher and I will instantly kill both the Crotonites."

"After saving him, that would be illogical, like stealing."

"Your android concern for logic is unimportant, and why I steal is none of your concern. I have taken a ruulogem that is undoubtedly the biggest and most valuable in the Galaxy."

"Elson—whoever you are—gems can be fatal to you as a thief. Don't steal the ruulogem and run away. Give it back to Vush and pretend the Crotonites fainted, instead of being stunned by you. I'll back you up. You can go on in medicine and forget about being a thief."

"I can't do that, Arda. I am committed to this course of action. And now I must go, before Director Smith shows up. I do not wish to see her again."

His voice, still muffled by the mask, had suddenly become hoarse. He cleared his throat and added, "I want to thank you, Arda, for assisting in the saving of a life. To protect you from the accusation of being my confederate, I'm afraid that I'll have to stun you as well. The gun is now set to render positronic brains unconscious."

As he raised the gun, I leaped toward him, but the stun beam caught me and I fell. For the first time in my life, consciousness completely disappeared.

Chapter 9

The man who called himself Elson must have underestimated the stun setting for androids, because when I regained consciousness my internal clock told me that it was only a minute later. My sensoskin told me I was being held in somebody's arms, and when I opened my eyes I saw Fortizak Human's face. Upon rational consideration, Zak's face is not actually a vision of male beauty, but I—and those treacherous emotive circuits of mine—did not care.

I threw my arms around him just the way heroines do when rescued. "Zak, oh, Zak . . ."

"I'm glad you're glad to see me, Arda, but what the hell is going on? The Crotonites are breathing okay, but they seem to be unconscious. All three of you must have been stunned. And why is Elson getting into the Crotonite embassy car?"

Rationality asserted itself. "We must stop Elson! He's an imposter and he's stolen the ruulogem!"

"Come on!" Zak yelled, unwinding my arms and heading for the door with me after him.

Running past Dee-four and the still sleeping Naxo, I overtook Zak and beat him onto the terrace, where we found the Crotonite guard lying stunned beside a large planter filled with tulips. The embassy car itself was lifting, with Elson at the controls. I leaped to catch the car, but it soared up over the terrace railings and then dipped down out of sight.

"It's falling!" roared Zak.

I reached the railings, looked below, and saw the car shoot away from the side of the building and across Central Park West in the cool spring night air of Manhattan.

"He's got the car under control," I said, not sure whether I was pleased or sorry. "It must be a robot car, for there's no one else in it."

"I've called the police, Arda," said Dee-four, squatting beside the unconscious guard. "Elson came out of the lounge wearing a mask and carrying his medical bag, saying he had to leave and Zak ought to tend to you. After Zak went to the lounge, Elson went straight to the aircar and before I knew what was going on, he stunned the guard, pulled her out of the car onto the terrace, and took off."

"That mask doesn't make sense," Zak said. "We'd all seen his face. Why would he need to hide it now?"

"It was his surgical mask," I said. "He just left it on. Perhaps he felt more like a thief with it."

As we watched the car heading north over the trees of Central Park, away from the skyscrapers of midtown, the two Crotonites stumbled out to join us on the terrace. They were minus their bibs but still wearing their velvet shorts.

"Dr. Elson must be stopped," Kolix said, shaking his fist. "He stunned Vush and before I could cry out, he used the gun on me. He must have stolen all our jewels, for they're gone."

Behind him, Vush was bleary-eyed and quite ordinary without her ruulogem and spangled bib, if you can call ordinary any creature that has four green-tipped breasts.

Kolix pointed at Dee-four. "Locrian—you're an agent, hired to protect us—shoot the aircar!"

"I never carry a gun. I always depended on Naxo to knock out and hold anyone we were after. The police air squad is on its way—see?"

Two police patrol cars were flying fast out of midtown, and another was heading south from the other end of the park. When it comes to trouble with or from Crotonites, the Manhattan government tries to be quick.

"Dr. Elson will get away!" Kolix said. "Royal Crotonite cars are equipped with hyperdrive."

"That's illegal," said Zak.

"The Crotonite royal family does not have to obey the stupid laws in this ridiculous city. Unfortunately, with our car, all Dr. Elson has to do is fly up out of the atmosphere and disappear into hyperspace."

"My jewels! My jewels!" Vush moaned.

"I'd like to kill him for doing this to you, dearwing," Kolix said.

The Crotonite car had turned and was heading back toward us, but high up.

Vush cried, "He's going to evade the oncoming police by going straight up—they'll never be able to follow. . . ."

Kolix plucked the unconscious guard's gun from her holster and aimed it at the car.

"Wait!" Dee-four shouted. "That looks like more than a stun weapon."

Suddenly my sensors were assailed by a brilliant light and an enormous noise. The Crotonite car had exploded into a cloud of fine dust particles drifting down upon Central Park's Sheep Meadow. The police cars moved into and down with the cloud.

"Great Galaxy, I was right," Dee-four said with horror. "The gun also fires tight energy beams."

"At least it was quick," Zak said, looking at me.

Vush draped a wing about her husband. "You wanted to kill him, and you did, my hero."

Kolix smiled triumphantly but instantly said, "I may have felt like killing him, but I assure you people that I was only trying to stun Dr. Elson so he couldn't put the car into hyperdrive."

"Well, he wasn't Dr. Elson, and he definitely was a thief, and he's now dead, so there will definitely be a police investigation," said Dee-four.

"He was *not* Dr. Elson?" asked Vush.

I said, "Princess, he admitted to me he was an imposter after your jewels. He intended only to rob, not do physical harm to either of you."

"Who was he?" Kolix asked.

"I don't know. But he's dead now. Nothing could have survived that explosion."

"Amazingly powerful, that explosion," Zak said.

"Probably from implosion of the hyperdrive circuits," Kolix said. "I have only two regrets about not checking the gun setting. One is that the thief should have been brought to trial, and the other is that I didn't get the jewels back."

"There'll be nothing left of them now," said Dee-four.

"Nothing left of what?" Director Smith stood in the doorway, staring at the cloud. "Where is Dr. Elson? Where is his patient? What has happened?"

Dee-four introduced Smith to the Crotonites, and told her what had happened.

Smith's voice quavered as she said, "Dead? Elson's dead?"

"You're missing the point, Smithy. He wasn't Dr. Elson."

Smith bit her lip. "It's my fault. I didn't check Elson's credentials and his ID card—I never dreamed they were forgeries. He seemed so confident. So pleasant . . ." She began to sob, holding her face in her hands.

I remembered Elson sitting on the edge of Smith's desk as if he knew she wouldn't mind such familiarity. I had not mentioned that Elson described her as an emotionally susceptible old maid.

I said, "Director Smith, the man calling himself Elson had genuine medical skills. He told me he'd planned only to drug Kolix and then steal the jewels, but Kolix was hurt, so Elson had to save him. He said he did not like to kill his robbery victims."

Zak touched my arm. "Arda, he's not a heroic rogue. If he put the minibomb into Y50, he certainly killed the robot."

"Yes. Yes, he did." I'd called Y50's death a murder. Did the imposter deserve to die for that? Or just for the theft of jewels belonging to an obnoxious royal couple?

"I wonder what's the matter with Naxo," Dee-four said after going inside for a moment to inspect the still-sleeping Naxian. "I'd swear that while the thief was performing surgery, Naxo was beginning to wake up. Now he's snoring again."

"The fake Elson had a gun," I said. "He stunned the Crotonites and me, and the guard. He probably stunned Naxo on his way toward the terrace."

A police aircar landed, disgorging a broad, middle-aged human in the blue uniform of a Manhattan cop.

"I'm Officer Parelli. Who's the Agent Dee-four who called the police?"

"I am. Was anything recovered from the explosion?"

"Only dust, but nowadays that can tell us a lot. Our

cars have high-tech scanners that feed information directly to the analytic computers at headquarters."

Zak grunted. "I didn't think the city could afford that."

"We can since Manhattan seceded from the state. Now, if we could secede from the Federation . . ."

Dee-four waggled a thin arm at him. "Officer, when will the report on the dust analysis come in?"

"Oh, it's in. I told you we were efficient. Lots of the usual plastic and metal of a demolished aircar, plus particles of ruulogem . . ."

Vush gnashed her teeth.

". . . and plenty of DNA, but we couldn't make the identification. Whoever piloted that car had DNA that didn't match with any on file. The thief was human, but could not have come from Earth or from any of the Erthumoi planets that has a regular filing system."

"Is there a real Dr. Elson?" asked Dee-four.

"Yes, but the dust doesn't contain his DNA, which is on file. The Luna City police say the real Dr. Elson disappeared there three days ago and a few hours ago was found in his hospital's laundry chute. He says a blond young man asked to speak to him privately, and that's all he remembers."

"I'd like to kill the thief all over again," muttered Vush. "I'm sorry about my ruulogem, but I'm glad the thief is dead. I'm glad you killed him, Kolix."

As the cop looked hard at Kolix, the Crotonite's gray skin paled and he whispered, "An accident. Diplomatic immunity. You can't do anything to me."

"What's all this?" said Parelli.

"I will explain." Director Smith stepped forward, in command of herself again.

"Were you here when it happened?"

"No, but . . ."

"You tell me, Agent Dee-four," said Parelli.

While Dee-four explained what had happened, and how Kolix had thought he was only stunning the imposter, I watched the Crotonites. Vush was clinging to Kolix, nuzzling him, rubbing her breasts upon his equally naked chest. It was not, as Zak later put it, an edifying sight.

Officer Parelli gestured to the Crotonites. "Maybe you'd better come with me to headquarters. . . ."

"Certainly not!" shouted Vush. "You can't arrest us!"

"Nobody's talking about arrest. We just want a statement."

"You have it, from that Locrian. We are the victims of a terrible robbery, obviously perpetrated by a citizen of the Terran Federation, and we will probably sue as soon as I send for a new aircar to take us to our embassy."

"Now, your royal whatever, I'm just doing my job."

"Dearwing," Kolix said, in a subdued voice. "We don't need an aircar. We have wings. And tonight is the night of nights!"

"Our wedding night," Vush breathed.

"Good—there's Naxo," said Dee-four. "He's waking up."

Director Smith walked up to Kolix. "Congratulations, sir, on your marriage to the princess. I'm sorry your day was spoiled by such an unfortunate occurrence, but I am, of course, relieved that your life was saved. May I shake your hand?"

In the nastiest tone I'd heard yet from a Crotonite, Kolix said, "You presume, human. Vush, we are leaving on our mating flight."

He pulled the princess to him, put his lips on hers, and spread his wings, shoving aside Director Smith.

Vush spread hers, knocking down Dee-four. The Crotonites left.

Beyond the trees and above the skyscrapers of the
East Side of Manhattan a full moon had risen, and
silhouetted against it were two figures in close embrace, their wings beating back and forth and gently
propelling them to midtown, the Crotonite embassy,
and sanctuary from Terran Federation law.

"Mating flight?" asked the cop. "Those critters aren't
really—great galaxy—they are!"

"Has the party begun?" asked Naxo.

Chapter 10

We had assembled in Zak's living room because the night cleaning robots arrived in the banquet hall upstairs.

Officer Parelli stayed only long enough to take statements from all of us and to promise that every effort would be made to track down the identity of the dead thief. He took for analysis the remaining Crotonite capsules and the Locrian fizz that had, presumably, paralyzed Dee-four's eyecover.

Director Smith, who seemed to have difficulty controlling her tears again, asked Dee-four why it had been necessary for the thief to keep the Locrian from using the deeplook.

"That's easy," said Dee-four. "If I'd been able to deeplook, I'd have used it on Kolix after he fell, to see if the imposter doctor's scanner was accurate. You Erthumoi put such trust in machinery, but the rest of the Six Species don't trust it, and certainly use our inborn talents to check up on it."

"But Kolix was indeed injured," I said. "I saw him . . ."

"Arda, you are not thinking clearly." Smith sounded irritated. "You reported that Elson himself said he had not anticipated that Kolix would be severely injured. It is obvious that Elson meant to pretend that Kolix needed surgery, so he could take the Crotonite to the lounge, summon Vush, stun them both, and take the jewels."

"Good reasoning, Smithy."

"I don't get it," Naxo said. He'd piled his body into Zak's most comfortable armchair and was still so groggy that he could barely raise his head above his flaccid coils.

"Naxo, chum, attend," said Dee-four. "The thief sends a message stating that gems can be fatal. This scares Smithy and the rest of the TFBI into assigning agents to the banquet—you to sense dastardly emotions in would-be villains, and me to find guns and other equipment that could be used in a robbery. This necessitated that the thief disable us through drugged fizz and capsules—maybe the capsules were meant for the Crotonites, but they sure worked on you, Naxy."

"And if I hadn't eaten them?"

"Maybe you'd have been killed," said Director Smith.

"Perhaps," said Dee-four, "but Naxians are known for their appetite for food in general and sexual stimulants in particular. The Crotonite capsules already had that reputation."

I hadn't been drugged like Naxo, and my positronic brain should have been working better than the organic brains of the others because it was not past my bedtime. I do not require sleep—just rest periods . . . where was I? Oh, yes, I was finding it difficult to follow everyone's train of thought.

I asked, "What was the point of sending the message threatening death if it resulted in having to drug agents?"

"Arda." Only one word, but Zak's scowl brought me to full cognitive capacity.

"Oh. I get it. The agents would have to be drugged,

but the death threat insured that a doctor would be there."

"The imposter Elson." Smith stifled another sob.

Naxo's head weaved back and forth in Smith's direction, almost hypnotically. "Smithy, you're really upset."

"Yes. Yes, I am. My trust in him—betrayed."

My positronic brain shifted into high gear. "I have a theory. I believe that Kolix was in league with the imposter."

"But the ruulogem was destroyed—by Kolix's shot!" exclaimed Dee-four, with everyone else nodding agreement.

"Perhaps Kolix told the truth—that he didn't intend to use that setting of the gun. Perhaps he and Elson— I have to call the imposter that because I don't know his real name—planned for a fake accident to keep Vush from suspecting her own husband of trying to get the ruulogem away from her, only Kolix underestimated the effect of the drug on himself. That's why Elson took such pains to doctor Kolix. Then he went through with the plan, taking the ruulogem from Vush and flying off in the car. Maybe the gun accidentally went off when Kolix flourished it to give everyone the impression he was *not* in league . . ."

"In cahoots," said Zak.

"I do not know that word."

"Never mind. Sorry, but your theory won't work, Arda. I talked to the guard before she went back to the embassy and she said she had put the gun on the stun setting. Kolix must have deliberately, or accidentally changed it, and I think that if he'd planned the robbery, he'd have been careful with the gun or he'd lose the very jewel he was after."

Naxo said sleepily, "Judging from the mating flight— and mind you, I only saw it from a distance and in spite of the reputation of Naxians I did not focus on it, besides it was clumsily done compared to Naxian prowess—I would say that that repulsive little Croton-ite princess is crazy about her equally repulsive little spouse. Wouldn't she give him a gem if he asked for it?"

"Not the royal ruulogem, you idiot," said Dee-four. "But I think Zak's right. It wouldn't make sense for Kolix to be careless, after such an intricate plan."

There was a silence, during which Smith sniffed and clutched the tissue she'd taken from her pocket.

Dee-four's communicator went off, the sound pierc-ing the quiet of the room. After listening to it, she said, "That's from the TFBI. Vush and Kolix are back at the embassy and request that one of our agents pro-tect them on their wedding tour."

"Not me, I hope," Naxo said.

"The Crotonites apparently fear that the few jewels they left at the embassy will now endanger their lives on the tour. It seems that Princess Vush isn't willing to go on tour without wearing a begemmed bib."

"Are you sure they want one of our agents?" asked Smith.

"Yes. I gather it's the price for Vush not suing the governments of Manhattan, Earth, and the whole T. Federation. But they don't want a Naxian or a Locrian, not after our failures tonight. They want Arda."

One of Zak's eyebrows shot up and he said, "Fasci-nating." He did it very well.

Smith said, "Arda seems like a poor choice to me since she has little experience. However, going with the Crotonites will not affect her the way it would you, Dee-four. You and Naxo would have severe problems in the atmosphere of Crotonis."

"Then Arda it is," Naxo said.

Dee-four, however, was considerate. She inclined her head in my direction and said, "If Arda agrees."

"She does," Zak said.

"I think I should say . . ." I began.

Zak interrupted. "Naturally it's up to Arda, but as her employer I am willing to let her go on the Croton-ite tour."

"Thanks a lot," I said, trying to emphasize the sarcasm.

Zak continued, as is his wont. "Furthermore, as host for the banquet tonight, I've been embarrassed person-ally and on behalf of the GWS as well as the Terran government. It's outrageous that there has been dam-age to the royal spouse and theft of the royal jewels. I hope that on her trip, Arda may prevent other robber-ies, and even discover the thief's identity."

"I will go," I said. "I will protect the royal couple."

"Then be at the embassy tomorrow morning," Smith said.

"Well, Arda," Zak said with a whimsical smile. "You could get what romantic would-be writers want—as-sorted scenery and aliens, plus adventure. Of course, you might get boredom . . ."

"Since it's settled, I'm going." Smith headed for the door.

"I'm leaving, too," Naxo said. "Share an aircar, Smithy?"

Zak whispered to Dee-four, who waved Naxo and Smith on. "I'll be leaving in a while. Have to discuss a book with Zak."

When they'd gone, she said, "Zak, what's up?"

"Try to remove your eyecover."

After a few tries, with Zak worriedly asking if it hurt, she succeeded. "What do you want me to look at?

Hurry up—you know I hate the feel of your oxygen on my eyeball."

"I had to find out if you were only temporarily paralyzed."

Her eyecover snapped shut and I said, "Why can't everyone admit that Elson was not a terribly nasty thief?"

"You're right, Arda," Dee-four said. "Nobody was permanently damaged except Elson himself. Somehow I feel sorry for the guy. He did do major surgery on Kolix to save him."

"Exactly," I said. "I helped seal the wound together."

"Ugh," said Zak.

Dee-four tilted her head. "Need a vacation?"

"I never take them."

"I do. I'm going on one tomorrow. A writing vacation, something special. See you soon, Arda."

As the door closed behind her, I wondered what she meant, but Zak had grabbed my arm and was pointing to the balcony-terrace off his living room. Each apartment in the building has one.

"A giant cockroach just scooted under the balcony door—after it, Arda! I hate bugs."

I opened the balcony door to see thousands of bugs scuttling between the gaps in the balcony railing and disappearing down the side of the building.

"Not cockroaches, Zak. Disassembled Samian. Hjeg never left. She must have listened to everything upstairs. Before you and I returned to your apartment she probably went down the outside walls to your terrace."

"That's what I thought. Arda, I see something shiny out there. Look at the planter my last housekeeper insisted on filling full of whatever that yellow thing is that's in bloom."

"It's forsythia, with something caught in the branches."

"You get it, Arda. I hate heights."

"You live next to the roof!"

"With the blinds down. You rescue what's in that bush."

In a fork of the forsythia's main stem was a glittering object the size of Zak's smallest fingernail. A ruulogem, but not the royal one. I also found a pile of cloth and a crushed flower next to the planter on the night-dark balcony floor.

I handed Zak a Royal Orchid in sad condition, the small ruulogem, and two Crotonite bibs minus jewels. "The thief must have thrown these onto the terrace when the embassy car dipped down. Was Elson trying to implicate you in the theft?"

"Or throw the robbery booty to Hjeg, who dropped one."

"Shall I run down to the street and see if I can catch her when she gets down?"

"No. Presumably her component parts can travel as quickly as cockroaches, and disappear as readily. Even if she's back in her normal Samian shape, it would be hard to find on the building now. She'll probably stick herself to some vehicle and escape."

"But I thought she was a *poet!*"

Zak rubbed his chin. "Hjeg is a good, if wordy poet. And a philosopher on her native world. I haven't the faintest idea why she would become the confederate of a ruulogem thief."

"She's gotten away with the royal gem. That means only the little ones from the bibs were exploded, except the one on your forsythia. Perhaps Elson knew the police would stop him—Zak, this doesn't make sense."

"No, Arda, it doesn't make sense because if Elson

had to conceal the ruulogems from the police, he would have thrown all of them to Hjeg."

"Unless there was a deal between Elson, Kolix, and Hjeg," I said enthusiastically, warming to the process of detection. "Elson was to give the big ruulogem to Hjeg, who could conceal it in her body and take it off Earth undetected and sell it someplace where it wouldn't be so identifiable. The small gems Elson could sell and split the money with Kolix, only Kolix decided to kill Elson, sacrificing the little gems. Kolix would meet Hjeg later, explain that there was an unfortunate accident to Elson, and there'd be only two thieves to split the profits."

"Um. Quite a theory." Zak laughed.

"What's so funny—my reasoning?"

"No, you're doing rather well. I was just wondering if we were set up to think that Hjeg is a confederate."

"We can't very well ask her since you prevented me from following her and finding out."

Zak yawned and stretched. "Won't matter. I have a feeling that Hjeg will be findable."

"A feeling? You are using intuition?"

"Uh-huh. It's all I've got at the moment since my cerebral cortex is too sleepy to operate efficiently. Now I'm going to put this mystery out of my mind and go to bed. Arda, I want you to spend the night writing up what's happened."

"Certainly, sir . . ." I am intelligent, but sometimes I do not grasp interpersonal implications immediately. "You know that I don't need sleep?"

"I surmise that you are an android, and newly hatched—er, activated. Not a difficult deduction, given enough hints like your weight, your physical prowess, your use of language, your ability to get Y50 moving again, and your reactions, Arda."

"Then you won't expect me to work for you after I've gone with the Crotonites. You'll fire me because I'm not organic."

"I won't fire a would-be writer who's willing to investigate something a stay-at-home like me can't."

"Then you do want me to investigate the mystery?"

"Indubitably. But write it up first."

"I don't know the solution."

"Just write down everything you saw and felt since you were told to take this job as my housekeeper. Do it as if you were writing a story in the first person. You can even indulge your predilection for Victorian romanticism, only don't overdo it. You did fall in love with Elson, didn't you?"

Embarrassed, I looked down at his unpolished shoes. "He was an imposter and a thief, but perhaps he didn't deserve to die."

"Good. Never assume that someone is only a villain. Now get to work, Arda. I'll see you in the morning."

So I have done as Fortizak Human requested. I have written down what happened, from my point of view. Since the story is not finished, I have called it "Part One."

I hope there will be a Part Two.

PART TWO

Chapter 11

Fast-moving saltwater separates Manhattan from Long Island to the east. Along the Manhattan edge of this so-called East River is some of the most expensive and overtaxed real estate in the Galaxy, but—starting in mid-twentieth century Earth—no local taxes were collected from a large section of this prime territory because it was occupied by the United Nations, an organization of regional Terran governments.

The U.N. real estate is now used by a regional branch of the Galactic Alliance, an organization which many claim is just as loosely tied together and as fraught with peril as the old U.N. ever was. And, like the U.N., the Alliance does not pay local taxes for any Station on any of the home planets of the Six Species.

The Alliance Station for the Terran Federation could have been built on any planet settled by Erthumoi. When the Feds insisted that it be in Manhattan, the excuse was that it could use the carefully preserved buildings of the old United Nations, which every Erthumoi knows was the first long-lasting, workable alliance of diverse peoples.

According to rumors, however, there was another reason. A prominent Fed official was heard to say that the Alliance Station would be in Manhattan because "it will serve them right." It took me quite a while to discover that "serve them right" does not mean good service. At any rate, Manhattanites do tend to refer to our local Galactic Alliance Station as the Works, an abbreviation of GASworks.

Personally, I think that having one's hometown full of aliens from outer space makes existence more interesting. I've been told that life is exceedingly dull in the species-restricted Terran Federation Capitol, an enormous satellite constructed mostly by robots and occupied mostly by human bureaucrats. Since Capitol Satellite is equipped with hyperdrive, it can orbit whatever Erthumoi planet it chooses. It surprises no one in Manhattan that the Feds usually orbit Earth, maintaining a large embassy here in Manhattan for their Alliance diplomats. The Fed's embassy doesn't pay local taxes either.

Over many years the Works has expanded east across the East River shoreline, where once there was a highway when ground cars were the norm, as well as north and south between two major medical complexes. During the time of the old U.N., hundreds of buildings all over Manhattan provided housing for representatives of the many member nations, who didn't pay taxes on these, either. Today, there are only six (tax-free) embassies. We androids pay taxes.

When constructing its embassy, the Terran Federation took over and consolidated buildings on top of the small cliff directly across from the Works. The Federation embassy is bordered on the left by Naxians and on the right by Locrians. The Naxian building has a coiled spire, while the Locrian building runs to odd angles.

Plastered against the cliff below these three embassies, facing the Works, is the small rectangular Samian embassy that even looks like its occupants. No Erthu-moi has ever been inside.

The Cephallonian embassy is large, low, and square—jutting out below the Works gardens into the river. The inside pools are said to be magnificent, with special water locks so the Cephallonians can swim in the East River (wearing their own form of wet suit—they tolerate our ocean water but can stay in it longer when suited up).

Then there's the Crotonite embassy, on an island especially constructed for it in the middle of the East River, across from the Works and south of the wealthy Manhattanites who live on Roosevelt Island and threaten lawsuits with almost Crotonite regularity every time a Crotonite violates their air space. The Crotonite embassy is easily accessible by aircar and by Crotonites wearing power packs, but the other five species prefer having the Crotonites surrounded by water.

I have taken time to explain all this because Zak says I should convey the atmosphere of the setting. I don't know what he means by atmosphere and I'm afraid to ask, but at least I have given some facts to explain why Zak and I had to travel a considerable distance by robot airtaxi from his upper West Side apartment to reach the Crotonite embassy. Kolix and Vush flew it easily, mating the whole way (or so the news media said the next day), but with Fortizak Human it was not an easy journey to make.

In the taxi Zak insisted on sitting in the exact middle of the seat, so I had to squeeze between him and the door.

"Heights only bother me when I'm near enough to an edge so I can see down. Just tell the taxi to fly low, so there will be plenty of buildings higher than we are and I can have the illusion that I'm on the ground, walking. I like to walk. I'd much rather have walked."

"You didn't leave enough time. You wanted to finish writing that last chapter."

"We're on time. I'm always on time. Tell the taxi not to go so fast."

"It isn't going fast."

Zak closed his eyes and his face promptly congealed into an expression so grim I made the same mistake I had the day before.

"Are you all right?"

"I'm *thinking*!"

I let him think—presumably about his writing—and felt a trifle smug about the fact that when I am writing there is certainly no such malevolent transformation of my features. Zak did complain that morning about the slight metallic tinge to my voice after he interrupted me twice while I was polishing Part I, but it was his imagination. Besides, he interrupted three times.

The taxi left Central Park behind and weaved its way at the low height Zak specified, through the canyons of midtown, while I thought about the dead imposter I intended to go on referring to as Elson, a thief who used medical skills to save the life of his victim. I couldn't help but admire Elson and grieve over his death, so it was difficult for me to contemplate being polite to the Crotonites on this long journey I was about to make.

The taxi turned east and zoomed up over the Works—strangely modern for such ancient buildings— and began to descend rapidly to the river, where a pod of Cephallonians flipped tails at us. Ahead was the Crotonite embassy, on an island that was one huge gray building, its flat top festooned by many landing cradles of all sizes.

"Look, Zak—the Crotonite royal space yacht."

He peered down, gulped, and closed his eyes again while I enjoyed the view. Situated in the largest landing cradle of all, the yacht resembled a giant teardrop lying on its side, its pointed end attached to a fat cylinder containing the propulsion unit that was used only in hyperspace. The teardrop would be my home for the next weeks while the royal couple went on tour.

Our taxi landed directly on the concrete surface of the roof, for only large hyperdrive ships need cradles. No one came out to welcome us.

"Arda, have you accurately programmed that communicator?"

"Yes, sir. I am always accurate."

"Never say always. There are always exceptions."

I looked at him and he laughed. I was beginning to realize that Zak's ability to laugh at himself was one of his better characteristics.

I permitted my facial synthomuscles to arrange themselves into a small smile—the kind that says "You are a nice but fallible human." Aloud, I said, "The communicator is now coded so that only I will be able to receive your messages, and only you will receive mine. Is this really necessary, Zak? Do you distrust everyone?"

"Have to, this early in the game."

"Is it a game?"

He grimaced. "Not at all."

"Are you thinking of the deaths?"

"Yes, and a good many things that haven't been explained adequately, including why this first ever Crotonite goodwill tour coincides with rumors of a secret Seventh Species cache, and the royal bride just happens to be an archaeologist specializing in Seventh

Species artifacts. Keep your sensors tuned, Arda, or whatever you do."

"I shall do my best, sir."

"And you must report to me every day, never letting the Crotonites know you are doing this. Don't discuss any of the mysteries with anyone else. We'll play this alone."

"Play as in game?"

"As in duet."

Activity had begun on the roof. A parade of Crotonite servants marched out of the building's roof access door carrying an assortment of luggage that no doubt contained royal bibs and shorts. Royalty has to change costume every day even if appearing at a new place, because it would be unthinkable if the news media reported that Princess Vush wore the same bib twice.

As Zak and I watched, a small hyperdrive ship flew up the river from somewhere downtown and came to rest in a nearby cradle. Naxo emerged from the air lock wearing natty amber sunglasses attached around his head with an elastic band, since Naxians have no external ears. He'd extruded two small hands high on his upper body and was holding a holov camera to record the imminent departure of royalty.

"Fear not, the press has arrived," Naxo said to a trio of armed Crotonite guards who approached him. They hadn't bothered Zak and me. We were apparently expected.

"Press? You're a Naxian," said the guard, flourishing a large gun which made up for the fact that his head was no higher than Naxo's midsection. "We are authorized to welcome a Locrian who is to report to the news media on the glorious tour of the royal princess and her consort."

On cue, Dee-four appeared in the air lock, her eyecover on tight and in the shadow of a wide green sun-hat that did nothing for her angular head.

"The Naxian is my aide," she said, joining him on the roof. "He'll be the photographer for my *Spacelog* article."

Zak and I got out of our aircar and after a short argument over who was to carry my suitcase—I won—we joined Naxo and Dee-four.

Naxo waved his tail at us. "Clever Dee wangled a magazine assignment early this morning. It pays astonishingly well, so we'll be following right behind you, Arda, in this zippy little hyperdrive ship *Spacelog* provided. If anything interesting happens inside the Crotonite ship, let us know about it because we can't go into that atmosphere. All right for you . . . oh, I'm sorry. Does Zak know . . ."

"That I'm an android? Yes, he does."

At that moment the royal couple came out onto the roof, followed by none other than Director Smith, whose baggy eyelids and deepened wrinkles proclaimed that she had not slept well.

Aiming his camera at the royal procession, Naxo said, "Smithy looks ghastly, but I don't sense strong anger or grief right now. She's not exactly happy, either, but it's more an emotion of sardonic—something. Can't catch it. Of course, it's easy to have sardonic feelings about Crotonites."

"How about Kolix and Vush?" asked Zak. "What are their emotions this morning?"

"Sexually satisfied but getting hungry again. Both of them. Kolix much more primitive—hunger for food, sex, sleep—all there. Vush has more complicated lust and, yes, anger—directed at Smithy, I think."

"Perhaps because of the way Smith's fawning over Kolix," said Dee-four. "Why is she? He killed that romantic male she thought was the doctor who would save the Crotonites."

"Elson did save them," I said, exasperated. "And my auditory apparatus, considerably better than that of any organic's, informs me that Director Smith is apologizing to Kolix for not checking up carefully on the imposter. She's pleased because Kolix is being nice to her, asking her forgiveness for accidentally killing Elson. It's a perfectly civilized conversation."

"Indeed," Zak said. I could not tell whether or not there was an implied question mark at the end of that word.

"Smithy must be trying to save her job," Dee-four said. "The TFBI isn't pleased by the way Smith's Employment Agency handled the security problems at the Galactic Writers' Society banquet. I got chewed out this morning and so did Naxo—but it wasn't our fault we were drugged. Analysis of my fizz drink showed that it contained a drug which causes muscular spasms in Locrians. I didn't have enough to affect the rest of my body, or I might have been unable to walk, but even a small dose will paralyze our eyecover muscles. The Crotonite capsules were loaded with a different drug to make most organics so drunk they pass out."

Naxo sighed. "I still have a hangover. Judging from the primitiveness of his emotions, Kolix has one, too."

"Let's get closer, Naxy. Make it look as if we really want to record the start of the Crotonites' tour."

But Vush saw them coming. I heard her tell the guards to force the newsbeings back into their ship. As the guards advanced toward him, Naxo handed me his holov camera.

"I have another inside, Arda. You'll have to record the precious moments of conjugal intimacy."

"No!" shouted Vush. "We permit only certain media opportunities, like planet arrivals."

"I was joking, Your Highness," said Naxo, coiling down so he was no higher than the guard confronting him. "We are honored to be allowed to accompany your ship on its noble tour, and we will do nothing to interfere."

"You'd better not," said Vush. "Guards, put these mediabeings into their ship. Arda, you will join Kolix and me now. You will not use that camera until requested by myself."

"Yes, ma'am."

The Crotonites spread their wings and flew up into the air lock of their big ship, high on the cradle. There was no landing ramp for me to use. I waited a moment, but none appeared.

"You'll have to climb up," Smith said, with a faint smile on her face. "It's an example of the famous Crotonite sense of humor about what they consider to be lesser species."

Kolix was standing in the air lock. "Use this, Arda." He threw a square bundle to me and went inside.

"Good catch," Zak said. "Looks promising."

It was a modified Crotonite power pack, probably two of them put together, and big enough to propel me through the air. Because they are hard to control and cause many accidents, such power packs are illegal in Manhattan for anyone except Crotonites, who know how to fly anyway.

I put it on, touched the switch and elevated three meters. I also flipped upside down and Zak laughed a good deal as he helped me right myself. I vowed to learn to control the thing.

"I guess I'd better get into their air lock as gracefully

as I can," I said. "Good-bye, Director Smith. I will try to protect the Crotonites better than I did last night."

"I'm sure you will, Arda. But no matter what they do, you must only protect them from outside dangers, not interfere in their activities. After the mishaps of last night, we must not have another Galactic Incident."

"Mishaps?" I said. "Elson's death?"

"It was his own fault. I have come to terms with my negligence in the matter, and with the loss of such a— talented man. He might have been rehabilitated."

"You really cared about him, didn't you?"

"Unfortunately, I did. I will not repeat such a mistake. We of the TFBI and the Agency in particular cannot afford political problems with the Crotonites. Your job is simply to prevent assassination attempts while the royal couple visits other planets. I doubt if there will be any, for the main jewels are destroyed, but the Crotonites are fearful and the Federation government believes it is good policy to accede to Crotonite wishes. Please comply with them, Arda. And, Mr. Fortizak, if you wish another Y model robot to take Arda's place while she is away, it can be provided."

"Hell, no. I'll make do with the kitchen computer and besides, the *human* cooks for the banquet have promised to cater two dinners a week for me."

"Oh, they have, have they?" I asked.

"Good-bye, Director Smith," Zak said, waving her away. "Arda and I need a last minute argument."

Smith nodded and entered a parked airtaxi which lifted up to take her to her midtown office.

A Crotonite guard reminded me that the royal yacht was about to leave.

"Bon voyage, Arda," Zak said, shaking my hand as if

I were an ordinary housekeeper off on an ordinary trip. "Take care of yourself."

"My job is to take care of the Crotonites."

"And to spy. You'll be my traveling eyes and ears. Remember everything and tell me—what's the matter, Arda?"

"Look at the Crotonite ship. Isn't there a brown patch on the bottom, just visible between the landing girders?"

"Yes. I thought it was a shadow."

"In my visual memory of the Crotonite aircar last night, when it took off there was a similar shadow. Reviewing the visual memory tells me that after the aircar dipped down the side of the building to your apartment, the shadow was gone."

"Hjeg. She was stuck to the Crotonite ship and left it that way, with the jewels."

"In cahoots with Elson," I said, masterfully colloquial, "only she betrayed him. Maybe she left a bomb inside."

"Maybe. Watch out for Samians, Arda. I never pictured them as villains, but you can't tell about anyone these days, especially writers. They all seem to have to earn a living doing something besides writing."

"Zak, if that is Hjeg, should I warn the Crotonites?"

"No. Samians can survive for a while in space and in hyperspace, but even disassembled they can't enter a sealed air lock of a ship. Just watch carefully to make sure the ship isn't invaded when the air lock is opened. If you do run into Hjeg, try to get her to tell you what she's up to."

Kolix was shouting from the Crotonite air lock again. "Arda! Are you coming with us or not?"

For a millisecond I debated about whether or not I

should kiss Zak good-bye, but decided I wouldn't push my luck, as the humans say. I shook his hand again.

When I entered the air lock I looked back at Zak. He had a worried look on his face, but he waved. I waved.

I was sorry I had not kissed Fortizak Human good-bye, but his known preference for human housekeepers had intimidated me. I consoled myself with the thought that, after all, he did tolerate android secret agents.

Chapter 12

Aboard the Royal Crotonite spaceship the cabins had artificial gravity, so I could dispense with the power pack while in them. The ship's atmosphere was thick, and although it did not hamper my vision, it would have played havoc with the breathing apparatus of any species except Crotonites—and, I suppose, Samians.

My cabin was small, the ceiling only five centimeters above my head, and colored the usual Crotonite gray. Perhaps because their ancestors were primarily night-fliers, Crotonites have little ordinary color vision.

The crew had removed the usual Crotonite bed, a soft, weblike mattress hung from the ceiling with the head end higher than the foot, which curves up. Crotonites sleep with their feet held by the curved end, their fronts resting against the webbing, and their wings unhampered in back.

Although I do not sleep, advanced android brains function better with occasional rest periods, so I had two Crotonite mattresses put on the floor. It looked odd—a bed that curved up at both ends—but I could lie down on it, relax my circuits, and allow the emergence of intuitive and creative thought processes, something I tried to convince myself an android brain could manage with practice.

It was difficult, and so easy for humans. Some humans. Mostly writers. And when it came to writing, I believed that creativity would come quicker if I wrote the way humans do, sitting down. The room had a table and bench, both too low for humans, but that didn't bother my synthomuscles and joints.

I unpacked my suitcase and hung up the tunics I'd chosen in shades of blue and purple, which go well with my coloration. Even androids—perhaps especially androids—like to look presentable. To my surprise, Zak had put into the suitcase a packaged labeled, "For Arda when she is thoroughly discouraged."

I decided I was nothing of the sort, and did not open it. If I needed Zak, I'd call him on my coded hycom communicator or use the cabin's larger holoscreen. It would be like talking to him in the same room because hycom signals go instantaneously through hyperspace. So do hyperdrive ships.

Unfortunately, we can't zip to and from planets the way we can talk to them. Using hyperdrive within a planet's gravity well is dangerous. Even at space normal drive, it's an unpleasant experience to hurtle fast through a gravity well.

On hyperdrive it would take about the same amount of time to visit all the planets of the Six Species, but I had been told that after entering normal space, the Crotonite ship would move slowly and carefully, as befitted a honeymoon.

My holoscreen displayed the gray patterns of hyperspace, as boring as the gray favored by Crotonites. I left the holoscreen on, however, so that when the ship entered normal space I would be able to observe star fields and planetfall.

The cabin steward (I couldn't tell from the stiff bib uniform which sex it was) said the machinery that ran the ship was in a long corridor over the living quarters.

"Why is it overhead? Why not underneath?"

"It does not matter in normal or hyperspace," the steward said in heavily accented Galactic Basic. "I have been instructed to show you the control room. There is no artificial gravity there, so put on your power pack, inferior Erthumoi."

So much for deference due to visitors.

Even with the power pack, I had trouble maneuvering in the big, circular control room, for the only directional reference point was the door and, above it, the wide open entrance to the engineering space that went to the stern. The Crotonite crew were well-adapted to null-G flying, and had no trouble going back and forth to the various computer panels that covered all the curved walls except for three holoscreens.

The steward left and nobody paid any attention to me. I hung in space near the door, unable to understand any of the Crotonite equipment because it was so different from that of the Erthumoi engineering I had, of course, absorbed. The holoscreens were as gray as the ship, for we were in hyperspace, heading for our first stop, Samia.

Could a Samian clinging to a ship's hull really survive in hyperspace? I was not at all certain that the shadow Zak and I had seen was actually Hjeg, but I wanted to know. I spoke to the nearest Crotonite.

"Can your sensors describe the condition of your hull surface even if the ship is in hyperspace?"

"Do not bother me, Erthumoi."

I studied the room and found a group of panels that looked as if they were showing monitor data from the entire ship. I tried to jet to it, only to find myself spinning wildly. If I'd been human, I'd have been spraying my last meal in all directions. As it was, I was merely disoriented, and that was bad enough. To steady myself, I grabbed hold of a nearby projection from one of the walls.

"Get your stupid Erthumoi hands off that!" yelled a Crotonite whose bib was fancier than the rest.

The crew's bibs were emblazoned with a pair of Crotonite wings inside a gold circle. This Crotonite female (her breasts were visible when her bib floated out from her body) had a small ruulogem affixed between the wings on her bib.

I let go. "Sorry, ma'am—or is it Captain?"

"Look at my gem, fool. What are you doing here?"

"I was just looking for something to hold onto so I won't bang into your computer panels."

I thought she was clearing her throat when she uttered a sound like "Glxuuf"—but in response, a small Crotonite flew over, tapping his chest, presumably in homage.

"Glxuuf, fly this Erthumoi over to the exit, and see that she doesn't come back in unless invited."

"But I *was* invited.!"

"The royal consort said you were to be shown the control room. You have seen it. Get out."

By the time I returned to my cabin, the holoscreen showed that we were in normal space, heading into the atmosphere of Samia. To make sure of privacy, I turned my own communicator to Zak's frequency and his image appeared in its tiny screen.

Zak was eating dinner. He'd evidently ordered the food synthesizer to give him roast meat, potatoes, and cake. No green vegetables. No salad. But I heroically refrained from comment on this choice of cuisine.

"Zak, I'm not certain we saw a Samian on the hull of this ship, and if Hjeg is there, the Crotonites don't seem to have detected her."

"It's hard to imagine that a Samian could be a danger

to anyone—they are usually the species that someone else takes advantage of . . . or maybe that's it, Arda. Perhaps the Crotonites were—or are—using Hjeg."

"Yes! If she has the ruulogem, maybe she's hiding it until the royal family can collect on the insurance."

"I doubt it. Property insurance is a uniquely human invention," Zak said. "Maybe Hjeg just took the small jewels from the royal bibs after Elson threw them onto my balcony to implicate me. Then she decided to hitch a ride to Samia."

"Do you know Hjeg well?"

"No. She's only been at a few meetings of the Galactic Writers' Society, and then only as a holoimage."

"Would Hjeg be likely to hitch a ride without first asking permission?"

"I would, if the ride were on a Crotonite ship."

I described the Crotonite control room to Zak, then said I hadn't seen the royal couple yet.

"Judging from Vush's reputation for passion, you won't be seeing much of them en route to their various ports of call. Try to get to Hjeg before she leaves the ship at Samia, if she's on it and if that's what she does."

Samia has valleys full of cactuslike trees, thick green marshes, a multitude of rocky mountains, and no buildings except the automated factories that build their ships. Larger than Earth or Crotonis, Samia's gravity was strong enough to force the Crotonites into pressure suits although they could breathe the air. I elbowed my way to the air lock and entered it as soon as it was opened.

"Erthumoi!" bellowed the captain, first in a bevy of lined-up Crotonites beside the air lock. "Their Highnesses have not yet arrived at the air lock. You insult . . ."

"Not at all. It is an Erthumoi custom that we exit

first in order to show those on the planet how we bow to superior royalty. It will give the Samians a good impression. Besides, I'm supposed to guard Their Highnesses, so I'd better be outside, looking for trouble. Got that, Captain?"

She glared but waved me on and I was soon outside, finding that my synthomuscles had an easier time adjusting to higher gravity than to null-G. This time there was a landing ramp since Crotonites can't fly in pressure suits. I went down it and made a quick run—something no Erthumoi organic could have accomplished—around the entire ship.

I did not find any Samian anywhere on the ship or on the ground near its landing cradle. Since assembled Samians move slowly, Hjeg either had never been on the ship, or had disassembled as soon as it landed.

This was discouraging, for at a distance of five meters from the landing ramp was a semicircle of ten waiting Samians. The only way I could find out if Hjeg had joined them would be to look at the ship's sensor scan of the area as it was before the ship settled into the landing cradle, and I was sure the Crotonite captain would not permit me to do this. Besides, I had to protect royalty.

And there they were, carefully stepping off the landing ramp onto a plush rug put down for their royal feet. After bowing extravagantly to them, I stood to one side and slightly behind them like a good bodyguard.

I felt foolish, for there seemed to be no possible danger. Samian mobile components might seem frightening, but they've never been known to be dangerous, and an assembled Samian is not only slow-moving but has no appendages. As I stared at the

Samians, my cognition speeded up. What if a Samian were dropped on a Crotonite? Wouldn't it squash . . . ? I looked up.

There was no Samian overhead, but there was another ship, with Naxo's upper body hanging from the air lock. The rest of him was tightly coiled around the inner handgrips prominent in Locrian ships. He was wielding a holov camera like an authentic newsbeing, while Dee-four must have been protecting her delicate body by staying in her control room. She was probably also coping with the strain her engines were enduring while the ship maintained hovering distance above Samian gravity.

"We of the Crotonite royal family greet the esteemed Samian council," Vush said through her suit mike. She gestured toward the air lock. "We bring you a gift."

A large square tank wheeled down the ramp, past Kolix and Vush, to stop in front of the ten Samians. One at a time, the Samians moved slowly under the tank while depressions formed in their tops. Once beneath, a Samian received a dose of fluid from the tank and wobbled out.

Kolix stepped closer to me and whispered through his mike, "Terran champagne. Samians love it."

"But it will lose its bubbles in that tank."

"They don't care. They like it flat."

When the Samians had each had a drink, Vush said, "I am an archaeologist specializing in artifacts of the Seventh Species. I would be happy to lend my expertise in identifying any such object your species may have found on your planet."

Kolix turned his pressure-helmet-encased head just far enough so that I could see his beady little eyes staring at me through the faceplate. One of them

winked before he resumed his gaze of devotion at his
beloved.

I got the point. The royal tour was not so much an
exercise in Crotonite goodwill toward aliens, but a
method of promoting Vush's career as an archaeologist.

The oldest Samian, judging by the number of wrinkles covering the block, moved a few millimeters toward the princess.

"Princess, we thank you for your gift. It will promote
enjoyable thought. We ask another favor—will you hold
up the royal ruulogem so that it may promote higher
thought in the Samian council?"

"I can't do that," Vush said. "It was stolen and then
destroyed while I was visiting Earth."

Ripples undulated down each Samian, as if in dismay or sympathy or both. If Hjeg was one of them,
she had not told the others, or she—and they—were
all pretending they didn't know.

I dared to speak up. "Is Hjeg here? She was present
when the robbery took place and might know something about it."

"Nonsense," Vush said. "Hjeg left long before the
robbery."

Kolix said, "If you Samians are very interested in
ruulogems, we Crotonites have the best on the market—smaller than the lost royal ruulogem, but fine
gems for good prices."

"Ruulogems should not be bought or sold," said the
elderly Samian, undulating his wrinkles.

"What's all this stuff about higher thought?" asked
Kolix.

"To an open mind, willing to be more open, certain
large ruulogems stimulate not only intellect but the
finer aspects of the mind—creativity and compassion."

"That's hardly what I've heard that ruulogems stimulate." Kolix smirked. "You help us find more things from the Seventh Species and we'll do a deal."

"It is a pity that you blaspheme, Crotonite. We must ask you to leave our planet."

Vush stamped her feet. "You insult royalty!"

"I will avenge the insult, dearwing." Kolix drew a gun from the pocket of his pressure suit.

"No, Kolix!" I shouted. "You must not kill a Samian."

"There will be no real death. I do not kill." Before I could stop him, Kolix fired the gun—at the tank.

So much for goodwill. The tank fragmented, the champagne dropping down to spread out around the blocks of Samians.

Instantly, the blocks disappeared. In their place was a seething mass of tiny creatures, swimming into the pool of champagne.

"They're coming from everywhere!" Vush screamed, dragging Kolix back up the ramp.

Samian components were pouring into the area from all points, running over the landing cradle and even over the ship. Kolix and Vush made it past the inner door of the air lock, which shut, but the outer door was still open and Samians ran in and out. Overhead, I could hear Naxo chortling as he recorded the whole debacle in holov.

I was afraid even to move, much less try to get into the air lock, because if I stepped on a Samian component I might create a Galactic Incident. Not that we didn't already have one.

I watched the pool of champagne vanish as the components incorporated it, or whatever Samians do to ingest something.

"Arda, you can go inside the ship now," Naxo yelled. "Dee-four says to tell Kolix to try to be more diplomatic when the Crotonites get to Locria. But tell him to be his own detestable self when you get to Naxia. It will amuse us."

I ran inside the ship, so determined to speak severely to the Crotonites that I didn't think of asking Naxo if he'd seen Hjeg.

Chapter 13

The ship was back in hyperspace and I was still trying to find a way of getting to Kolix when I was summoned to the royal suite. It was spacious, if dismally gray, and furnished only with the low tables and seats favored by Crotonites. Along one wall were so many computer panels and microbubble storage units that I realized Vush was a serious scientist.

The royal couple were more or less enthroned on high, backless, curved seats covered by thick gray plush. I bowed.

"Sit down, Arda," Vush said, pointing to a seat much lower than hers. When I sat on it, my head was at her level.

Kolix looked unhappy. Either he was ill, or he'd just been scolded, at length.

"In defending my honor, my royal consort has, perhaps, made a mistake. Do you think so, Arda?"

"Your honor is worthy of any attempt to correct insults to it," I said, my emotive circuits churning slightly as I thought of what Zak would say when I told him this.

"It's all your fault, Arda," Kolix said. "The Samians were already irritated by your question that implied Hjeg could have been part of the robbery."

Vush's wings stiffened. She and Kolix had evidently

been arguing this point. "Arda, what made you ask the question? Didn't Hjeg leave the party earlier?"

"Fortizak Human and I do not know, but we suspect that a Samian, perhaps not Hjeg, was a confederate of Elson and made away with at least the small ruulogems from your bibs. I thought I saw a Samian on your ship today. Would you ask your captain to review scans of the ship's hull after leaving Manhattan?"

Vush spoke into her communicator, listened, and said, "We do not scan the hull except in the case of meteorite strike. It is not expected that any organic being could live without atmosphere. Do Samians?"

"Supposedly. Please call the Locrian ship and ask if they noticed any suspicious shadow on your hull when we left hyperspace and came down to the Samian surface."

Dee-four said she and Naxo were intent on the Samian council and never thought to examine the Crotonite hull.

After Vush severed connections with the Locrian ship, Kolix laughed. "It's an implausible story, Arda. You're trying to avoid blame. Maybe you were in league with the criminal, Elson."

"Yes," said Vush. "Perhaps we have made a mistake in hiring you as a bodyguard, Arda. Perhaps you and the imposter villain did something terrible during the operation on Kolix. Although my spouse seems well and performs more than adequately, the top of his chest bulges out more than in most Crotonites."

I explained the surgery necessary because Kolix had unexpectedly fallen from a height and injured himself more than the imposter had anticipated.

"I helped seal your surgical wounds, Kolix, but I did not assist Elson in the robbery. He used his gun on me as well. I was unconscious when Fortizak Human entered the lounge after Elson left. You can ask Fortizak Human to affirm that I had been stunned by Elson. I say this on my honor as an—do you know what I am?"

"An expensive robot called an android," Kolix said, with a small smile. "Erthumoi say that all robots must tell the truth, but is that the case with the new model androids like you?"

"It is."

"Are you certain?"

I could not be. Lying, for good causes, or in subtle forms, is a very tricky thing and I suspected that in many ways I had done a lot of it in my short life. I felt extreme guilt.

"Kolix, you have no right to accuse me of lying about the Samian in Fortizak Human's apartment, or of being in league with the imposter. I did not lie."

"Then I apologize, my dear Arda." Kolix said it solemnly, but I saw him wink at Vush. "When I called Smith's Employment Agency to hire a bodyguard for this trip and was informed of your—um—physical nature, Vush and I decided on you."

"I will serve you to the best of my ability."

Kolix bent a wingtip in my direction. He was learning royal technique fast. "One more thing. During my sojourn on Earth, I was told that although you androids acquire knowledge through learning, not programming, nevertheless your brains are manufactured with built-in safeguards. Is this true, Arda?"

"Each robot and each android obeys the laws of robotics."

"I do not know these laws," Vush said. "Please reassure us by articulating them for us now."

"I shall comply. 'Law 1—A robot may not injure a human being or, through inaction, allow a human being to come to harm. Law 2—A robot must obey the orders given it by human beings except where such orders would conflict with the First Law. Law 3—A robot must protect its own existence as long as such protection does not conflict with the First or Second Law.' "

Vush scowled. "Human beings! Nothing but human beings!"

"What do you mean?" I asked.

"Those laws of robotics apply only to human beings. What about us Crotonites, and the other species who are not Erthumoi? How can we trust an android to protect us when your laws of robotics apply only to human beings!"

"Princess, I believe that any advanced android would interpret the laws as applying to all of the Six Species and, for that matter, to any intelligent being."

"Bosh," Vush said. "You Erthumoi, whether organic or robotic, are selfishly parochial. It was one of the reasons the Galactic Alliance hesitated in granting you admission. Your laws of robotics are meaningless for the Galactic Alliance."

"But, Your Highness, the laws of robotics were invented before human beings had ever seen any being from beyond our own planet. The laws have not been officially rewritten because everyone assumes . . ."

Kolix's wings trembled. "Assumes. Such a delicate word. What does it really mean?"

"Many Erthumoi writings have pointed out that there is a close correlation between the laws of robotics and the oath taken by physicians, like Elson."

"Elson was an imposter and robbed us!"

"Yes, Princess, but Elson told me he'd had medical training. He repaired your husband's blood vessels and used a pacemaker to aid your husband's heart. If a thief acts honorably as a doctor for Crotonites, can't you believe that an android would apply the laws of robotics to Crotonites as well as to organic Erthumoi?"

Vush sniffed. "Fine talk, but Kolix and I cannot trust your laws of robotics, and therefore you do not have our trust or our friendship."

"Nevertheless, I will do my job."

"See that you do."

"Dearwing, you can always trust me to protect you," Kolix said, kissing her.

"Do we go to Locria next?" I asked politely, as if I were still in their employ as a bodyguard.

Vush nodded. "When we get to Locria, I will do the speaking, Kolix, although I have forgiven you your tactlessness with the Samians. I should have told you that archaeologists believe the Samians, as well as the Cephallonians, were once given their ship factories by the Seventh Species. The technology of the other species was their own invention, and ours is the best."

I did not comment on this. "If the Seventh Species cut and polished the major ruulogems now known, that would explain why the Samians revere the gems, would it not?"

Vush was too preoccupied with fondling Kolix to do more than grunt assent. Kolix's eyelids were halfway up.

Since I had not had a good view of their mating flight, I was reluctant to leave. I thought that perhaps, if I stayed, I could learn more about organic sex.

"Erthumoi androids are not permitted to observe Crotonite mating rituals closely," Vush said, waving me away. As I went to the main door, I looked back and saw the Crotonites clinging together as they part walked, part flew into the bedroom next door. From what I could see inside, their own large bed looked well-used. It seemed probable that when Crotonites cannot perform mating flights, they make do with beds.

I went back to my own cabin, which seemed lonely and much too confined. I told myself that androids don't get claustrophobia. About loneliness, I wasn't so sure. No one had ever explained to me what sort of problems advanced emotive circuitry can create. Perhaps no one really knew.

I called Zak, who was reading in bed, his visible torso encased in one of his undershirts. I'd been told that Zak was happiest rereading his own books, but this one, by an ancient writer named Wodehouse, had clearly put him in a good mood.

"Good to see you. How's life with the Crotonites?"

"Unpleasant."

"Report verbatim, Archie," Zak said.

"My name is Arda."

"Indubitably. Report everything, including your thoughts."

It took much longer than I thought it would, although Zak did not interrupt. I was not happy when I had to tell Zak my thoughts about watching organic sex, but not a muscle flickered on his face, so presumably I had not annoyed or embarrassed him.

Zak stroked Wodehouse. "Interesting."

I decided he was not referring to the book, or making a comment on my thoughts. "Not fascinating?"

" 'Fascinating' is a word for sudden revelations. Most of the time. Or sudden sarcasms. That depends . . ."

"Mr. Fortizak, please tell me what you have found interesting. Something that might clarify the mystery of the stolen ruulogem?"

"Great detectives keep their ongoing deductions to themselves. And call me Zak."

I was about to ask him when he became great, but I paused.

"I'm no longer certain I know exactly who my employer is. I started with Smith's Employment Agency, which sent me to you as a housekeeper and secret agent and which will pay me out of the fees the Crotonites pay them for my services as a bodyguard. But I'm still working for you. It is very confusing."

Zak yawned and said, "You're my housekeeper, hired by the Crotonites but on salaried retainer to me as an inducement to return to my employ."

"Thank you, sir. Do you have any instructions?"

"When the ship drops back into normal space around Locria, ask Vush to order the captain to scan the hull for a Samian. I don't think the scan will show anything, in which case Hjeg may be somewhere on board. Samians are religious about those ruulogems, and may think the Crotonites are the real thieves, especially since Crotonites have snared most of the galaxy's best ruulogems for themselves. So it seems odd that they'd ask to see the royal ruulogem if it had been thrown to one of their own. I suspect that Hjeg is trying to find the ruulogem."

"But if she doesn't have the gem, then it was exploded."

Zak yawned again. "The vulnerability of ruulogems to explosion is not known."

"But who—what—how . . . ?"

"Don't know yet. At least, I haven't enough evidence. Collect some, Arda. Observe carefully at each planetfall."

"How can I be a detective when you won't tell me what you are reasoning out?"

Zak said sleepily, "Good detectives are supposed to reason up from experiential facts, not down from a theory, but both theory and facts are essential. My modest theory needs facts, Arda. You observe. I'll use the little gray cells."

He can be a most irritating man.

Chapter 14

The Crotonite ship could have arrived at Locria in a few hours, but it stayed in hyperspace throughout the ship's scheduled nighttime, presumably so the royal couple could restore themselves after the debacle at Samia.

I wondered how I could most profitably pass the time. What came to my mind was, I sadly report, strongly influenced by my emotive circuits. I am referring to the loneliness afflicting me, particularly after I stopped reporting to Zak and was left with no one to talk to.

As I waited in my cabin, I suddenly thought that I ought to start a novel now. I wouldn't be lonely if I invented characters who had their own problems for me to think about instead of my own. And it would be good practice for my next career, when I moved on from being one of Smith's agents and/or Zak's housekeeper to the glorious occupation of full-time writer. I even had an idea for a plot but was puzzled by one aspect of it.

I called Zak, not paying attention to a little detail in my memory banks. He'd been in bed a short while ago.

I woke him up, but he wasn't groggy. I was to learn that Fortizak Human slept only five hours a night and no matter when awakened, he was in command of that human brain of his.

"Problems, Arda?"

"Yes. I have so much spare time on this voyage that I've decided to practice writing. I'll start a novel."

"You woke me up to tell me this?"

"Oh, no, sir." I remembered that I was only a servant and supposed to be deferential. It was odd how infrequently I was able to remember this.

"Well?"

"Oh. The novel. I have a marvelous plot, but I can't decide whether or not it should be a tragedy or a comedy. In my novel, there's an android who decides to become fully human . . ."

"Ah, yes. *Star Trek*'s Mr. Data tried hard and tragicomically to learn humanness, and I suppose one could say that, given a disregard for the short lifetimes of organics, *Pinocchio* ended happily, but *The Bicentennial Man* conquered robothood at great cost. I am assuming that you've studied all the relevant fiction on this subject—or are you only projecting from your own limited experience?"

It felt as if someone had stepped on my emotive circuits. "I don't know, sir. I haven't studied. My experience is limited. I am an android and I don't even know what *I* want."

"Then don't write it yet. Live a little more. Have you found Hjeg yet?"

"No, sir."

"Keep looking. Good night, Arda."

Since a minimal crew was awake during the night, I went out to explore the ship and look for Samians. I could not enter the living quarters of the crew or the royal couple, but it seemed logical to suppose that a

Crotonite would be likely to notice a boxlike object that had not been in the bedroom before.

I wore my power pack but left it turned off when I inspected the crew's dining salon and then the corridors. On my way toward the control room, I noticed that the ceiling of that corridor contained a trapdoor well within my reach, so I opened it and hauled myself up.

I was inside the long engineering section. Now in null-G, I pulled myself along the various tubes and cables to the point where they left the main ship to enter the hyperdrive unit. Then I went forward, examining each piece of equipment and every square centimeter of surface. No Samian visible anywhere.

When I arrived at the opening to the control room, the captain was not present. Only three crew members were on duty, so I turned on my power pack and flew into the central space of the room. One of the crew members was the hapless Glxuuf, who stared at me wide-eyed. I stared back at him.

"Their Majesties wish me to guard them against possible assassins, so I am inspecting the ship." I felt pleased that I had not lied—more or less.

Glxuuf and his fellow crew members turned paler gray, bowed and let me look around. Apparently the words "majesties" and "assassin" struck the right note of terror. I could imagine what Vush would do to any crew member suspected of disloyal thoughts.

Finding no evidence of Hjeg, I tried another ploy.

"It would be advisable for you to instruct me on basic procedures of running the ship in case organic life aboard is rendered helpless by an assassin's weapons." I was conscious of further stretching plausibility, for Samians—unlikely assassins to begin with—are not known to carry weapons.

Glxuuf got the courage to answer back.

"Are you not organic, too?"

"I am a machine. One of the android members of the great Erthumoi species. Teach me."

"Our computer will teach any other computer everything it knows about running the ship. We Crotonites are loyal. We have no secrets. You plug yourself into that main computer panel."

Plug in? I acted as if I knew what to do, but I didn't. And all at once I badly wanted to know how to run the ship. As I made my way through the control room, my efforts to appear dignified were diminished by the two somersaults I inadvertently made in midair, but I did make it to the main computer panel, which seemed highly simplified compared to the complex programming panel of Zak's kitchen computer.

While I was in training at the Android Center (a euphemism for factory), I'd read that the most advanced machinery has an elegant simplicity of form, preferably with few if any moving parts. If their computer was an example, perhaps the Crotonites had some cause for feeling superior to the other species.

At one end of the panel was a large round spot of orange—the brightest color I'd seen on the ship. In the middle of the spot was a small hole, too small for any of my fingers. That, presumably, was where machines plugged themselves in. I am a machine, but I was built to look and be humanoid. I do not run around with wires dangling from my person, pluggable or not.

Below the large spot were four smaller, round orange spots arranged in a horizontal row, with a larger space between the second and third than between the others. It was utterly mysterious to me until I looked over at one of the crew as she touched another panel.

Have I mentioned that Crotonites have two long

fingers on each hand? Two plus two equals four. I placed two fingers of each of my own hands onto the four smaller round spots of the computer panel and waited.

Nothing happened.

"Accessing," I said loudly, imitating the Crotonite accent in Galactic Basic.

There was a tingle at my fingertips and a voice spoke in my mind, not in the air.

—*Ready*.

"Teach me basic procedures for running this ship."

—*You are a computer. Why are you using the organic touchpanels instead of the computer plug-in site?*

"Scan my form."

—*I am not familiar with such a form as yours, but you scan as a computer. You may access. At what rate?*

"The rate for computers."

If I'd been human, I'd have been knocked out by the flood of information pouring into my brain, but I handled it well. That is, reasonably well. Androids don't get headaches, but I did have a distinct inner sensation of discomfort. The important thing is that I now knew how to manage the ship if I had to.

I could also force the ship's scanners to examine the hull, even in hyperspace. I did so, and the result was negative for any alien body of any kind on the hull.

By then the ship's clock indicated that it would soon be their morning, when the rest of the crew would arrive. I wanted more information, but this time I would ask for it without spoken words. I focused my mind and said slowly and silently, —*Where was the royal ruulogem found?*

—*That is classified information. Give security clearance.*

—*What is the latest archaeological discovery connected with the Seventh Species?*

—*That is classified information. Give security clearance.*

—*Give all Crotonite information on the Seventh Species that is not classified.*

—*All Seventh Species information is classified.*

My shoulders were suddenly gripped from behind and a voice screeched, definitely out loud.

"Erthumoi spy! Get out of my control room!"

The captain propelled me to the main door and flung me hard out into the artificial gravity of the corridor. I was, of course, unhurt, but I felt more alien and alone.

I have read of the pleasant recreational lounges aboard Erthumoi spaceships, but there was nowhere to go on the Crotonite ship except my own cabin. I could have joined the crew in their dining salon, but I did not wish to run into the captain again.

To my surprise, Vush was waiting for me in my cabin.

"It's morning. Where have you been, Arda?"

"Inspecting for Samian species, which I did not find, and learning about the ship in case the organics aboard are damaged."

The truth seemed to impress Vush, for her face softened and she almost smiled at me.

"Arda, I am here because I am worried about Kolix. I cannot discuss this with the crew. My parents call me every day, but they are elderly and I do not wish to distress them. I pay you for your help, so right now you can help by listening to me."

"Then you've decided to trust me after all, Your Highness?"

"Not precisely. Crotonites trust no other species. But Erthumoi are an unusual species because they are both organic and nonorganic—humans and androids. No other species uses robotic devices that have intelligence. As an android, you assisted in the surgical cure of my husband, and you can quickly learn from our data banks everything you must know to be Kolix's doctor should the need arise during this voyage."

"A doctor! But . . ."

"Listen to me, android. I want your help, and that of Fortizak, who knew my husband before I did. I know from the ship's monitors that you speak with Fortizak by coded signals every day. Call him now."

Zak was surrounded by piles of printouts and looking annoyed.

"Arda, observe and note that I am *working*."

"Yes, sir. Princess Vush wishes to consult us about Kolix. Both of us, because she considers me intelligent, and capable of doctoring Kolix if necessary."

"You'd better not try doctoring me, young Arda." Zak shoved some paper aside, put his elbow on the desk, and rested his chin on the palm of his hand. "Okay, Princess. What's bothering you about your spouse?"

Vush said, "Last night after we mated many times, I slept, but when I woke to use the excretory facilities Kolix was sitting on the floor, holding his head and moaning. I asked him if his head ached from the surgery, but he said no, he'd had a bad nightmare. He would not tell me what it was about. This morning he did not wish to mate again, and when I left our suite he was once more sitting on the floor with his eyes shut."

"Was there anything else, Your Highness?" Zak asked.

"Nothing you need to know. I have told Kolix that he is not to worry about accidentally destroying the royal ruulogem, and that he is a hero for killing the thief."

"Do Crotonites usually kill thieves?"

"Execution is the punishment for anyone who robs or otherwise harms the royal family. Lesser Crotonite criminals have various other punishments."

"Including death?"

"No. That is the privilege for criminals against royalty."

Zak grimaced. "If death is a privilege, don't bother to tell me what forms of punishment ordinary criminals receive. But you did say Crotonite criminals. What about criminals who are not Crotonites? Elson was Erthumoi."

Vush looked down. "Officially, we have not had occasion to execute a nonCrotonite."

"But you believe it has been done?"

She nodded. "I would guess that it has been done secretly, to avoid diplomatic problems with the other species, who misjudge us Crotonites badly enough as it is."

Zak raised an eyebrow. "I gather that most Crotonites would not become ill with guilt over killing a thief who was Erthumoi."

Vush clenched her fist. "A noble Crotonite like Kolix may feel guilty about destroying the ruulogem, but should not worry about executing a thief."

"Did Kolix look into your ruulogem?" I asked.

"Legends, Arda," said Zak.

I ignored him. "The Samians said that ruulogems promote higher thought, and your gem was the biggest ever known. Perhaps it helped you want to become an archaeologist, Your Highness. Perhaps it gave Kolix a conscience."

"That is absurd!" Vush laughed shrilly, but as her eyelids shot up in a fast blink, I could see the tears she was trying not to shed.

"Have you fallen out of love with him, Princess?" I asked.

"You Erthumoi do not understand. I adore him. Kolix is my first true love, so much better than my previous husband, who was stupid, boring, clumsy, and frequently impotent. I want Kolix to continue to love me."

"But why shouldn't he?" I asked before Zak could make what I thought might be a sarcastic comment about Crotonite love.

"It is possible that Kolix now believes marrying royalty will undermine his standing as a businessman. In addition to his renown as a writer, he has a reputation for clever business deals. His wealth was initially an added attraction to me, but now I do not care if he stops making money as long as he loves me. Perhaps it was a mistake to tell him so, for when he moaned during the night I heard him mutter something about being a business failure."

I said, "You must continue to reassure him that it doesn't matter, because you love him for himself, not for his money."

Zak raised his hand. "Let's get away from sentiment and back to Kolix's conscience. I know Kolix and I refuse to believe that he's making himself ill because marrying royalty doesn't give him as much time to carry on his business dealings, which I gather have always been suspect. Surely you would not prevent him from making money, Princess?"

"No." Vush gulped. "Not exactly. But I wanted him to join me in my legitimate archaeological work, and he said he would. I admit that might not give him much time for business, but he could go on writing while spending much of his time with me. He understands that before I met him, archaeology was my great passion. . . ."

"Since when?" Zak asked. "All your life?"

"Of course not. I was officially adult only five years ago, and became a scholar after that."

"And what happens when you become adult, Your highness?"

Vush turned a darker gray. "That is not for discussion with inferior Erthumoi."

"Princess, whenever you Crotonites say 'inferior Erthumoi,' I never know whether you mean our species or me in particular as an inferior member of my species."

"You are not inferior. Kolix says you are a genius and a passably good writer."

"Passably!"

I spoke up before the conversation could degenerate further. "I think Fortizak Human was asking if you were given the royal ruulogem when you turned officially adult."

"Bravo, Arda." Zak beamed at me.

"I was. I have often gazed into it. Are you saying it was the ruulogem that made me a scholar?"

"Princess," Zak said gently, "ruulogems may promote higher thought, or they may not. Seems rather magical to me, magic being what we don't understand yet. Maybe the beauty of a ruulogem is sufficient to turn any mind toward creative endeavor—in your case, archaeology."

"But, Fortizak, my Kolix only gazed into the ruulogem a few times during and after our marriage, before it was stolen. The change in him happened earlier."

"What kind of change?"

"When I met him at the Manhattan embassy, I was not wearing the ruulogem, yet he gave me the proper greeting of a spouse-to-be and said he had read all my scientific papers and was looking forward to marriage with such a gifted scientist. Then he vowed he would serve me and my chosen field."

"Interesting. Possibly even fascinating." Zak rubbed his chin. "Well, I have to get back to work. Arda, go see Kolix and find out if giving up business chicanery, and possibly bad prose, is giving him nightmares."

Zak's image disappeared and I was left alone with Vush. She seemed embarrassed.

"Princess, there is something more, isn't there? I am an android *female,* and perhaps you can tell me what you can't tell Fortizak Human, who is very male."

"It has nothing to do with sex," Vush said. "When I left Kolix sitting on the floor again this morning, I did not shut the door completely at first. I listened, and distinctly heard him say the words 'atone' and 'death' over and over. Atone for killing Elson? It's absurd."

"Is it?"

Vush looked at me as if she had not quite seen me before. "You say that because Elson was Erthumoi and you androids vow to uphold your precious laws of robotics about humans."

My emotive circuits were showing the strain of being polite. By now I was experiencing what any human would say was anger.

"Princess, the laws of robotics were not invented by an android but by a human. As I've tried to explain to you and Kolix, nowadays most androids and many humans believe the laws apply to all thinking creatures."

"That still seems hard to believe."

"In the ship following us are two beings you met at the Galactic Writers' Society banquet—the Naxian, who is photographing your voyage, and the Locrian writer Dee-four. I know them only slightly, but if they died and I were in any way responsible for their deaths,

I would spend the rest of my life atoning. And they are not Erthumoi."

"But I do not want my husband to become ill grieving over the death of a human thief!"

"Princess, if the royal ruulogem boosted your interest in scholarly pursuits, it certainly didn't give you much of a conscience."

When she bared her teeth, I thought she was about to bite me, which I'd have to prevent because she'd have broken off a tooth in the process, but instead she began sobbing.

"When we get to Crotonis, you must tell no one! Do you understand? No one!"

"Then you do have a conscience. The death of Elson bothers you as well."

She went to the door, but before she opened it, she spoke so softly that only an android could hear. "He is teaching me. Kolix does have a conscience. And I love him more for it. Help him, Arda."

After she left, I had to report this information to Zak, coded. He did not seem particularly annoyed.

His only comment was, "Ain't love grand?"

"Zak, sir . . ."

"You can dispense with the 'sir' which doesn't come easily to you, does it?"

"No, sir. I mean—what I was getting at is that the mystery of the stolen ruulogem doesn't seem very important. It's what's happening to Kolix and Vush. They seem to love each other, and she's a scientist . . ."

"And that's the problem—for him, I suppose. Getting engaged to a royal princess who is also a scientist turned Kolix's life around. Vush says he's wealthy—but I doubt if his writing could make him so. The money must have come from dealing in Seventh Species arti-facts, as Granston said at the GWS banquet. Didn't

Granston also say that the royal ruulogem has a bloody history? Suppose some of Kolix's dealings have been equally bloody? Would he want an archaeologist wife to see him doing more of the same?"

"Not if he loved her. And he apparently does."

Zak sighed. "Love. That topic seems to be one of your reverberating circuits. But you're possibly right. Try to find out from Kolix—or anybody—just what he used to do to get lucrative Seventh Species artifacts, especially ruulogems."

"I'll try, Zak."

"And keep looking for Hjeg."

Chapter 15

The intercom in my cabin blared out the message that in two hours the ship would enter normal space around the Locrian home world. Erthumoi Arda was requested to ready herself for the forthcoming celebrations in honor of the royal couple.

I wondered if Dee-four and Naxo would follow us in. Perhaps they'd even gone on ahead so Dee-four could welcome us to her world. I also wondered what mistake in etiquette the Crotonites would make this time, and found myself almost hoping there would be another crazy scene, but since the Locrian species comes equipped with a good sense of humor (hence their close friendship with the irrepressible Naxians), I doubted it.

Feeling bored, I wandered out into the corridor and instantly, perhaps because I was not trying hard to think about it, I knew where Hjeg was hiding.

My new knowledge of the Crotonite ship included the fact that the air lock could be operated not only from the main control room but also from a computer panel in the wall beside the lock, if one knew the mental code. I riffled through my data banks and there it was. All I had to do was place my fingers on those round spots—pink, this time—and think the coded order at the computer.

I was about to do so when Kolix walked down the corridor, looking at the floor and not at me.

"Hello, Kolix. Feeling better?"

"I am fine. Whatever gave you the idea that anything was wrong with me?"

"Er, nothing at all. It's just an Erthumoi greeting."

"Why should you greet me? I saw the way you looked at Elson during the GWS banquet. Were you not attracted to him? Don't you blame me for his death?"

I could not answer untruthfully, for I was thinking of Elson's charming words, his handsome face, and the way he tried to save the life of this ugly little creature who killed him.

"Yes, I do blame you. You should atone for his death."

"And just how do you propose I do that?"

I tried to reason it out, but no logical possibilities presented themselves, only emotions. I thought of the little princess I was beginning to like and respect.

"Kolix, you should protect and care for all living creatures, for the rest of your life."

"The way your laws of robotics say? Or only the creatures I love, the organic beings I cherish?"

"All life, Kolix."

He laughed. "But I love only one form of life now, only my bride. I will protect her, even from you, Arda. You have the capacity to hurt her."

"I would never do that."

"But you will. You are intelligent; you find out things you should not know, things that will hurt Vush."

"Like your criminal activities?"

Kolix was completely still, as if he had frozen there in the corridor.

I said, "I think you've been stealing valuable objects made by the Seventh Species, but now you're afraid that Vush, an archaeologist, will find out how wicked you've been, how you've desecrated or destroyed or sold so many important works of art that she would stop loving you, and you'd no longer be a member of the royal family. I think that after you became engaged to the princess you said you'd reformed, but it was only pretense. At last you were married, to a female who owned the biggest ruulogem in the Galaxy. Perhaps you married her for it. Then it was stolen, and in a rage, you killed the thief."

"You don't understand . . ."

"I understand only that an organic Erthumoi who bothered to save your life was killed. He tried to steal a few gems. How many have you stolen? Kolix, you must atone for everything, but most of all for that pathetic dust of dead DNA the police recovered from the explosion. I think you want to atone, to be different. Start now."

"I can't. You are too dangerous, Arda. Get in the air lock. This gun is on a setting that will deactivate your positronic brain. Get inside. Everyone knows you've been hunting concealed Samians aboard this ship. You will have had an unfortunate accident in the process. Hurry, for we won't be in hyperspace much longer."

I had no doubt that he would use the gun in his Crotonite hand if I did not comply, so I opened the air lock and went inside. The door closed and locked behind me.

"Hjeg, I'm about to be murdered. Can you help?"

She was plastered on what would be the ceiling of the air lock once we arrived at a planet. Then I realized it was still the ceiling, for the air lock had artificial gravity like the corridor, no doubt so the Crotonite wings would not be damaged in such a small space.

She did not answer and I wondered if she were dead.

Samian bodies can stick to anything, and she may have died up on the ceiling for all I knew.

I tried the computer panel inside the lock but could not open the inner door. I did, however, open a voice channel to the corridor.

"Kolix! All life must be protected! I am alive, and Hjeg is here with me. You must not kill living creatures!"

Kolix answered. "You are not alive, Arda. Only organic beings are truly alive, like Vush—and me. You have an artificial body, an artificial brain, and hyperspace will destroy the artificial patterns of your brain."

"Hjeg is organic!"

"She is a Samian, and can survive hyperspace. Goodbye, Arda. You should not have tried to make me feel guilty."

When the outer door to the air lock opened, the air burst out into the gray of hyperspace with such force that although I was hanging onto the inner guard rails, I could feel my hands slipping. I shouted into the maelstrom of air before all of it vanished, me with it.

"Hjeg! I am an android! My body will not be damaged in hyperspace, but my brain will lose its patterns. Help me!"

Just as my hands left the guard rails, something slammed onto my back. Slowly, so painfully slowly, I was drawn upward.

One end of Hjeg's body was still sticking to the ceiling. The other was sticking to me. There was no more danger of my being forced out of the ship, for the air had left, but the air lock was open to the strange fields of hyperspace. My brain felt as if it were being poisoned.

I was about to lose consciousness when Hjeg spoke to me telepathically, just like the ship's computer, except that with the Samian I could sense emotion. Hjeg was compassionate.

—*Crawl between me and the ceiling. Since you are an android and do not need to breathe, you will be safe from hyperspace if I seal myself around you.*

I did so, and instantly felt better, enclosed by the Samian's body. Thoughts of claustrophobia never occurred to me, and I was grateful for sanctuary.

—*Thank you for your gratitude, Arda. You have an interesting mind.*

—*I didn't know Samians were telepathic.*

—*We don't advertise it, since we must usually be in profound and lengthy contact with other species to achieve it with them, and most aliens don't like that sort of contact with other aliens. Have you noticed?*

—*I'm afraid I have. Must you be in touch physically with other Samians, as well?*

—*Not on Samia, where we are mentally connected because we are living portions of our planet, just as each of the Six Species is part of their home planet. Erthumoi thinkers call a living planet Gaia. It seems, however, that only we Samians know we are Gaia-Samia. The rest of the Six Species do not, alas. It is why they do not revere the Seventh Species artifacts as we do.*

—*I don't understand, Hjeg.*

—*We believe that long ago the Seventh Species helped develop our intelligence and telepathy, just as they gave us automated factories to make spaceships. Perhaps they found in Samians the only species who would never lose consciousness of being one with their planet. At birth a Samian child is linked with us, but also develops her own mind patterns, which are communicated to the rest. That is why we are the only species that can't forget what the Seventh Species taught us, for although*

Samian bodies die, our mind patterns continue to live, linked on and with our planet.

—What happens when you leave your planet?

—For that time, we become completely separate individuals. If I die here, the knowledge I have accumulated since leaving Samia will die with me. Only a rare Samian is willing to take the risk of leaving home for a secret mission.

—What is your mission, Hjeg? What does it have to do with the Crotonites?

—We Samians are protectors of antiquities. I was chosen for this mission because I belong to the Galactic Writers' Society and had an excuse to go to Earth when the Crotonite marriage took place. I was to locate the illegal source of the Crotonites' supply of artifacts. From attending many GWS meetings by hycom, I was familiar with everyone who would be there, especially Kolix, who would not suspect that I am also a secret agent.

—Hjeg, is every member of GWS something besides a writer?

I could feel laughter welling up in Hjeg and transferring to me. She said—*You are also a writer, Arda, according to your thoughts. Can you make a living at it?*

—I think it would be impossible, so far.

Hjeg laughed again. —Fortizak is almost the only writer I know who doesn't need another job to supplement his writing income. You are attracted to him, are you not?

—Hjeg! Stop reading my private thoughts!

—Sorry. I will comply, but first I will answer a thought you had earlier. I did not steal the royal ruulogem. Part of my mission now is to find out if it is truly lost.

—Then when Elson threw the royal bibs onto Zak's balcony, the royal ruulogem was not among them?

—*No. I took most of the small gems from the bibs and decided to follow the Crotonites after Elson was killed. It was easy to attach myself to their ship before it left Manhattan, and on Samia I disassembled, reported to my people, and got back into the air lock before it was sealed. You didn't notice me when you went through the lock. If you're going to be a good agent, Arda, you must be more observant.*

—*I'm sure Zak would agree.*

There was a pause, and I felt no touch of Hjeg's mind. I wondered if she had to withdraw to conserve energy, or if touching an alien mind was unpleasant for her.

Then, so lightly that I knew she was not invading my private thoughts, she spoke to me again.

—*Arda, I am a creature that never truly dies, for what I know is also part of the larger body of our living planet-organism. I would like to know why you had such fear when the outer air lock door opened and exposed you to hyperspatial fields. Cannot android brains be used over and over?*

An emotion akin to human anguish permeated my mind. —*Hjeg, I will deliberately concentrate on what it means for an android to lose its own brain patterns, developed through experience. Please read my thoughts.*

After a moment she said—*I understand now. You are like the organic Erthumoi, individual, alone inside your brain the way we Samians are when away from Samia. Too bad Erthumoi scientists cannot transfer mind patterns from one Erthumoi to another.*

—*Yes, Erthumoi mind patterns cannot be transferred between humans, between androids, or between android and human. Both organic and nonorganic Erthumoi have brains that are too anatomically complex, with brain patterns that grow in complexity as humans grow and as androids learn. This makes each Erthumoi a unique individual.*

—And your individuality dies with you, as ours does if we Samians are separated from the rest. I do not wish to die until I have completed my task. Will you protect me, Arda?

—You're the one protecting me, Hjeg.

—For now. Arda, I cannot help feeling your emotions. What do you hate?

—I was thinking of a simple Y50 robot whose little individuality was destroyed by a bomb that must have been implanted by the thief, Elson. For a moment I hated Elson, but there's no logic in that. Y50's death was a waste, but so was Elson's, more so.

—You teach me much, Arda, for even a machine like you is intelligent enough to have compassion. We who belong to the rest of the Six Species tend to disparage the way humans strive to create nonorganic intelligence, but we have not understood how lonely humans must be to want to create a partner like an android. And we have not understood that you androids are lonely individuals, too.

—Thank you, Hjeg. Not many humans understand this either.

—You have my sympathy, Arda. Kolix may regret killing an organic Erthumoi, but he thought nothing of trying to kill an android. Yours is a hard role in the Galaxy.

There was an intense quivering of the entire ship and Hjeg spoke in my mind again.

—We are in normal space. It is safe for you now.

I crawled out, stood on the floor, and saw the planet Locria below the ship. A purplish planet, Locria has a few shallow seas, forested hills, and vast regions that would be like Earth's deserts if they were not crisscrossed with the vegetation-edged canals constructed by early Locrians. There are no farms or animal breeding stations, for Locrians long ago switched to synthesized food, with factories and living quarters below ground. Surface buildings are used for meetings, study, and recreation.

I reached up to touch Hjeg. —*Locria is beautiful. They seem so ecologically-minded that their cities deliberately intrude little upon the wild landscape of their planet, just as you Samians have not spoiled yours because you don't need cities.*

—*We had help, Arda. The Locrians achieved maturity on their own, a very long time ago.*

—*I'm thinking that it's too bad an asteroid wiped out the terrestrial dinosaurs, because they might have gone on to become civilized much quicker than it took the little primates to develop into Homo sapiens sapiens.*

—*Then you might look very different, Arda.*

As I experienced the emotional thought that I didn't want to look nonhuman, the outer door suddenly closed, followed by a rush of air into the lock. Hjeg swung down to attach herself to my back just as the inner door opened.

In the corridor stood the ship's captain. She was scowling and I wondered if anger as well as sex arouses Crotonites, for the points of her four breasts sharply pushed out her bib.

"The ship's computer notified the control room that you entered the air lock and opened the outer door, a stupid thing to do. Perhaps you tried to get to Locria ahead of the ship—is there a power pack in that suitcase you carry on your back?"

"Not exactly," I said. "Captain, I did not intend to open the outer door of the air lock. Perhaps someone else . . ."

"No one aboard would do such a thing. When I told Prince Kolix . . ."

"Prince!"

"That is his new title. When he learned of your foolish entry into the air lock, he commanded that if you were still alive you were to be locked into your cabin for the rest of the trip."

"But, Captain . . ."

She had a gun, too. "Move! And don't think you can order the ship's computer to let you out, for the door locks have been reprogrammed to block you."

In my locked cabin, I let Hjeg slide to the floor and make herself comfortable in a corner while I reported to Zak.

When I finished, I added, "There's no use in my complaining to the ship's personnel or to Vush that Kolix tried to kill me. It would be my word against that of the royal spouse."

"Uh-huh," Zak said, as if my predicament were trivial. "You must somehow join the luncheon party, which Dee-four tells me is to be in the archaeological museum. And take Hjeg with you in your real suitcase. Fortunately, you can carry the weight. I think you're the right age for a chum, Arda."

"But, Zak, I can't get out! How can I make friends and guard the royal couple when Kolix wants me destroyed? Even if I can get out, I'll never be able to persuade Kolix that I'm no danger to him or to Vush."

"I am sure you will be able to use your reason and judgment to extricate yourself from your predicament," Zak said, and shut off the hycom.

Hjeg laughed. "Zak is a humorous being, is he not?"

"I doubt that. Hjeg, can Samians get under doors that aren't sealed air locks?"

Chapter 16

Under a sky of lusciously lucid lavender, in which two small suns shone serenely, the ship lay in a landing cradle in the open plaza of a city paved in purple.

I composed the above sentence immediately after we landed on Locria. It has since occurred to me that the alliteration may be slightly overdone, although the most famous of ancient human writers got away with it in those sessions of sweet silent thought. I suppose Zak, whose writing is the essence of unadorned clarity, would no doubt say that my positronic brain had been overstimulated by the lethal hyperspatial field.

I admit to some sort of overstimulation. As I stood at the open air lock, I experienced an extraordinary pleasure in still being alive, and more fully alive than I had ever known. The present moment—each present moment—seemed wonderful beyond imagining. Alive and free from imprisonment, I was on a purple planet I wanted to embrace and describe in purple prose.

A self-scan seemed in order, so I performed it, finding no obvious impairment of my brain structure and functioning. As humans would say, what in hell was wrong?

What had the encounter with hyperspatial fields done to me? Humans often refer to having an "intuitive feeling." Could my cognitive and emotive circuits come up with such a phenomenon? Kolix had been afraid of me and tried to kill me, but I had survived. Hyperspatial fields exist always. I existed. With a little care I would go on existing. It was quite logical, nothing to get emotional about.

But I definitely had an intuitive feeling, and I could not put it into words. It was more than an enhanced appreciation of life. It also included a new fear—of being alone. I was glad Hjeg was with me, in my suitcase to be sure, but at my side.

I stood at the open air lock and admired the capitol city's white buildings, as angular as the Manhattan Locrian embassy but here the angles caught and reflected the lavender sky. The city was so pristinely clean it might have been built all at once with material that never got dirty, and inhabited only by creatures who were as clean as the buildings.

Carrying my suitcase, I sauntered down the gangplank used by the Crotonites because they hated to fly in the thin Locrian atmosphere, even with power packs. The Crotonite guarding the gangplank wore a breather mask that supplied oxygen, and looked miserable. It was Glxuuf, tentatively clutching a gun.

"Hi, Glxuuf—guarding the ship from dire invasion?"

"How did you get out of your cabin, Erthumoi?"

"Someone must have released me. I couldn't have done it myself, could I?"

"I . . . I suppose not. Certainly not. Impossible."

"That's right. Since I've been hired to guard Their Highnesses, I will now go do my job. Good-bye, Glxuuf."

Hoping that Hjeg would not laugh inside the suitcase (I'd bored a hole in it so she could hear), I walked to the Locrian science museum as quickly as possible before it occurred to Glxuuf to check with his captain.

Escaping had been easy. Disassembled, Samian components can indeed get out of a locked cabin to disconnect a door lock. The problem remaining was to get back into the good graces of that horrible Crotonite, the new Prince Kolix.

The luncheon was sponsored by the Locrian branch of the Galactic Writers' Society, and was almost over by the time I arrived. The Crotonites were not at the mammoth table where many Locrian writers and archaeologists were assembled.

"Hello, Arda," said Dee-four, her voice musical with happiness. Apparently, things were going well. "Put your suitcase down and sit here between me and Naxo."

I placed the suitcase beside me. "Where are Vush and Kolix?"

"Your royal charges are in a special section we manufactured for them, full of the sort of atmosphere and flying food they like—see?"

A transparent wall had been erected at one end of the dining table. In the hazy air beyond the wall, small flying creatures were being pursued by Vush and Kolix, wings outspread.

To avoid watching the Crotonites' method of dining, I turned to speak to Naxo, who was coiled up on the Locrian dining bench trying to eat synthesized shell-wofs without disturbing the oxygen mask precariously fastened around his nostrils.

"Have you recovered from the Galactic Writers' Society banquet, Naxo?"

"My pride is hurt and my head still aches. When we checked in with Smithy today, she said it served me right for being greedy enough to eat the capsules."

Dee-four waggled her head. "Smithy shouldn't have told you they were an aphrodisiac. Shouldn't you stop eating and do your job? You're the official photographer at this luncheon."

"I've already taken plenty of holov shots showing the lovely royals in flight, in the process overexposing my sensitive nature to those disgustingly primitive Crotonite emotions."

"Naxo," said Dee-four, "I've worked with you for years and I've never known you to dislike primitivity."

"Crotonites are a different matter." He paused and uncoiled enough to send his head weaving in my direction. "Hey, Arda, have you developed emotions? I'm not supposed to be able to sense the emotive circuits of androids, but you're feeling hungry . . . comet tails! It's not you! It's the suitcase!"

Dee-four's eyecover shot back. "There's a Samian inside that suitcase! Open it, Arda!"

Released, Hjeg slowly glided over to Dee-four. "Sorry about the deception, but I didn't want the Crotonites to know I've been on their ship. Would you pretend I've been on yours?"

"Sure. You joined us in order to write an introduction to my book on interspecies botanical research."

"We Samians are not interested in botany."

"How about the book I'm always urging Dee to write?" asked Naxo. "The one on interspecies sexual symbolism?"

Hjeg's body rippled with amusement. "I think I will tell the Crotonites a truth—that I wish to travel as Arda's roommate. I will write a narrative poem about the glorious royal tour, celebrating the intelligence and knowledge of the royal archaeologist, the Princess Vush."

Naxo lifted a corner of his lip to expose a fang. "Bah."

"I think it's true," I said. "Vush is intelligent and

she's an ethical archaeologist. She's got a conscience and she loves her husband and she doesn't want anything to happen to him."

"What's the matter, Arda?" Dee-four looked concerned. "Are you all right? Staring into space like that . . ."

"I'm fine. Just fine. I'm alive, aware, and . . ." I stopped, because in my mind a strange word appeared. Even when I knew that Y50 was dead, I had not entirely accepted, with complete certainty, that the word "mortal" applied to myself.

I did not say it aloud. It seemed almost obscene.

Hjeg spoke to draw attention away from my inability to finish my sentence. "Naxo, you correctly sensed that I'm hungry. Dee-four, could I eat a little pinch of that metal-enriched powder you use for dusting your face?"

While I thought about mortality, the organics resumed eating and talking. Hjeg and Dee-four regaled Naxo and me with GWS stories, often about the way Zak, Kolix, and Granston would hurl amusing barbs at each other during meetings whether all three were there in person or as holoimages.

Dee-four said, "Since I work for the Terran Federal Bureau of Investigation I can assure you that most of us believe Kolix to be a crook, yet I confess that at GWS meetings, I've enjoyed his verbal nastiness as much as I do his novels, which is more than I can say for the nastiness of someone like Granston, either in conversation or in prose. Has anyone seen Granston, by the way? Smithy seemed to think he might show up."

Nobody had seen Granston. As far as I knew, the two Crotonites, Naxo, Hjeg, and I were the only non-Locrians present.

The lights went out beyond the translucent temporary wall, a door opened at the bottom of it, and the Crotonites entered the main dining hall fastening breathing masks around their heads.

Everyone rose, bowed politely, and Dee-four said, "I hope Your Majesties have enjoyed your repast. On behalf of our branch of the Galactic Writers' Society, we welcome you and hope that you will now enjoy our museum exhibits before we end the royal visit with a champagne toast."

"The prince has metal in his neck," said a young Locrian who had broken his species' courtesy code by pulling back his eyecover to examine the Crotonites for a second.

Dee-four inclined her head toward the miscreant in a distinctly threatening manner. "The prince has required surgery for a serious injury. The metal protects and promotes the action of his heart."

"Thank you, Dee-four," Kolix said with a magnanimous gesture, as if he had not been insulted by the deeplook intrusion. "My princess and I thank all of you of the Locrian Writers' Society for the glorious luncheon we have been given. But where is the ruling class of your system? Why have they not come to honor us?"

Dee-four bristled. "We have no ruling class, Kolix, as I've told you many times at GWS meetings. You Crotonites are so steeped in autocracy you can't even imagine a true democracy, in which each citizen participates—through computer linkages—with all others in the making of community decisions."

"Which explains," Naxo said, "why nothing of consequence has gone on in Locrian society for millennia."

Everyone laughed, especially the Crotonites. The bad moment had passed and, with Dee-four leading the way, we all left the dining hall for the main exhibition next door. In order not to slow the party down, Hjeg stuck to my suitcase, which I carried. I stayed well to the rear to avoid the Crotonites.

The first rooms displayed the most primitive Locrian artifacts, which seemed unlike those made by primitive humans until I saw that the similarities outweighed the differences.

A series of egg nests, from the most primitive to the most sophisticated, was like a display of human cradles from early woven baskets to stylized plastiforms. A series of dishes and eating utensils was also similar, taking into account the Locrian facial anatomy. Chairs and benches fit Locrians, but were still chairs and benches.

Locrians sand art was exquisite, consisting of naturally colored sand arranged three-dimensionally in stasis fields. Their sculpture was entirely metallic, beginning when primitive Locrians worked with the copper and gold they could find. They seemed to have little interest in jewels, but did embellish belts and necklines with thin wedges of a yellow pearl-like material secreted by real shellwofs.

To my surprise, I felt at home on Locria. Like humanity, Locrians had lifted themselves up to civilization without help from the Seventh Species. Locrians look unhuman with their skin of flexible keratin and faces like one-eyed praying mantises, but they possess an inner skeletal structure, two legs, two arms, and a bendable body. To me, Locrians are more humanoid than any of the other nonErthumoi species.

I hope the Crotonites never read this. Crotonites also have two legs and two arms, and even two eyes. They would say that Erthumoi humans and androids have more resemblance to Crotonite perfection than the Locrians do. But they're wrong. Crotonites do not remind

Erthumoi of themselves. To Erthumoi, Crotonites resemble bats—not the friendly ones that eat fruit or insects, but the ones that drink blood.

Next we entered the Seventh Species display room, which was well-guarded by Erthumoi robots of a type much larger and somewhat brainier than Y50. In the room, benches were arranged around an open space in the middle. Dee-four ushered me to a bench next to the space and opposite the Crotonites. I thought that Kolix was deliberately looking everywhere but toward me.

An aged Locrian tottered out to the open space and said, "I am a member of the Galactic Writers' Society because I write comic plays for our nestlings to perform, but I am also the Curator of Antiquities here. Our small exhibit of Seventh Species objects will be presented as holoimages, but if the princess wishes to examine the real object, she has only to ask."

In the exact center of the open space a circular opening appeared. From it rose a shimmering cylinder of light that blanked out to show the three-dimensional image of a crescent wandlike object that seemed to float in midair, turning slowly.

With much creaking of his joints, the curator sat down next to the opening in the floor so that his head would not obstruct anyone's view of the object.

"This object is made of a metal alloy we moderns have yet to duplicate and cannot, so far, date. We do not know what the object is, but we suspect that it may have been part of a larger piece of equipment. Like so many Seventh artifacts, this was found in a hollowed-out asteroid orbiting a white dwarf star with no living planets."

I knew that the asteroid belt of Earth's sun was still being explored for signs that the Seventh Species had used it, but so far, there was no evidence. Sol will not be a white dwarf for a very long time. Did the Seventh Species deliberately choose solar systems without life so that their artifacts would be found only by space-faring species? It is a point much debated in scientific journals.

The curator continued. "These asteroids may once have been ships, but when the Seventh Species left, they took all but a few things with them so we cannot tell if propulsion devices were ever installed in the asteroids. We do not know if the artifacts that remained were left from carelessness or on purpose."

We all stared at the crescent until it disappeared and a new object appeared in its place. This was a hollow cube made of strips of metal finely etched in circles and dots distributed around curving lines. I had read that most Seventh Species artifacts have such patterns, each slightly different.

Inside the cube was a ball emanating a greenish glow. I could not see any way the ball could stay smack in the middle of the empty space in the cube, but it did.

The curator said, "Although the sides of the cube appear open, they are closed by a field none of our equipment can penetrate. We do not know how such a field is generated."

"I've never seen anything like that," Vush said. "Where was it found?"

"We do not know. Many artifacts have been passed down through the ages with no records kept of where they were originally found. We can say for certain that only the Erthumoi, who are recent members of the Galactic Alliance, had no part in finding and all too often stealing Seventh Species artifacts, which have, so far, never been found on the Erthumoi home planet."

My emotive pang of regret that the Seventh Species apparently passed Earth by was tempered by relief that humans—throughout their decidedly immoral history—had at least not been guilty of stealing Seventh artifacts. I wondered how many Kolix had stolen before he hooked up with a royal archaeologist.

When the next object appeared, I could hear many of the visitors gasp, for it was a dagger similar to those found among all species that were once warlike, including humans. This dagger, however, had a hilt bearing a medium-sized ruulogem.

The curator pointed to it. "A usable weapon, for it is very sharp and much stronger than it seems. We have determined that unlike most if not all of the other artifacts, this dagger was not machine-made but hammered from metals that can be dated. We are fairly certain that the dagger was made by the Seventh Species because it is older than any of the Six Species, and contains a ruulogem. As far as we know, ruulogems are found only with or on objects of the Seventh Species, but we do not know if they are manufactured or are natural stones whose origin is yet to be discovered."

Naxo asked, "Is there any other Seventh Species artifact that could be used to kill?"

"None like this. Perhaps many could, but only this dagger would be usable by any of us."

Kolix was staring at me. I was glad the dagger was only a holoimage, for Kolix still looked ready to kill.

The next object was a simple, lovely bowl made of thin white alabaster. I have seen bowls almost as beautiful on Earth, but this one was etched with the Seventh pattern.

"The bowl was found with other Seventh artifacts on an asteroid in the Locrian system. We do not know whether the Seventh Species used liquids as food or only to drink, but the bowl must have held liquids. There is a ridge inside the lip that prevents splashing."

Ten other objects were shown but, small or large, their shape and purpose were mysterious, although each had beauty. I kept thinking of the one I liked best—the alabaster bowl.

After the exhibit ended, Vush rose. She must have communicated with the ship, for when she flapped her wings, a Crotonite crewman flew into the room bearing a package.

It was Glxuuf again, breathing heavily through his oxygen mask and struggling to appear graceful in what was obviously a grandiose display of Crotonite flight through air inadequately designed for the purpose.

He more or less fell in front of Vush, who took the package from him. As poor Glxuuf staggered out of the room on his feet, Vush unwrapped the gift and handed it to the curator.

"This piece of Seventh Species sculpture was found on the same asteroid as your bowl. To my regret, I discovered that it had gone onto the antiquities black market and was purchased by my unsuspecting husband as a wedding gift for me. After I realized the find, I discussed the matter with my dearwing, who is pleased that it would give me the greatest pleasure to return it to the Locrian system, for your museum."

Kolix, who squirmed throughout her speech, did not look at all pleased. I wondered how much the sculpture had cost him, and whether he'd had to kill anybody to steal it in the first place.

The object at first glance seemed to be a mess of wires, but the curator was delighted. "A small free-form sculpture! Only one like it has ever been seen."

"Does it have any use?" Dee-four asked.

"I doubt it. What do you think, Your Highness?"

Vush smiled with happiness at being professionally consulted. "I have endeavored to detect a function, but so far none has occurred to me."

I had been comparing the dimensions of the sculpture with the dimensions of one of the other artifacts, and I couldn't keep quiet. I asked, "Would it fit inside the bowl?"

All heads turned in my direction. If I'd been human, I'd have blushed. Being android, I felt compelled to explain. It's one of our worst habits.

"The external dimensions of the free-form correspond to the internal dimensions of the bowl, beneath the ridge. I have measured them exactly."

"By looking at them?" asked the curator.

"Yes. I am an android."

Vush tugged at the curator's arm, almost as long as she was tall. "Let's see if they go together."

The curator called up the actual bowl from the storerooms below and the tangle of wire exactly fit inside.

"But what could it be for?" asked the curator. "Was the feeding apparatus of the Seventh Species so intricate that it required help from a device like this?"

Vush shook her head. "I doubt it. We'd have found many other devices like it. More likely, it was to hold live food until ready to be eaten."

Naxo laughed. "Princess, are you saying that the unknown Seventh Species was, in fact, Crotonoid?"

"Why not?"

"Yes, why not?" Kolix asked belligerently, going to stand beside his spouse. "We are the superior species, so we must have been descended from the Seventh."

"Descended?" asked Naxo. "As in retrograde evolu . . ."

"Shut up, Naxo," said Dee-four. "Your Highnesses are to be congratulated not only on the beauty of your gift but on your possible close relationship with the

Seventh Species, a factor that must now be considered, thanks to the suggestion of the Erthumoi, Arda."

"I don't think so," I said. "The relationship, I mean."

"Just what do you mean, Arda?" Kolix asked, curling his lips back to show all of his sharp teeth.

"I think the bowl and the thing inside are for arranging flowers. They'd fit inside the holes and stand up . . ."

"You *machine*!" Kolix yelled. "You insult my wife's theory, our species, and our gift!"

Everyone began to talk at once, but Kolix was grinding his teeth. His hand was on the gun I had already observed was stashed in the belt of his shorts.

Chapter 17

Vush folded a wing around her furious husband. "Arda, you do not insult an archaeologist. My dearwing does not yet understand that the purpose of true archaeology is to study a species through the remaining physical forms of their culture. The market value of an artifact is not as important as what it can teach us."

Kolix sighed deeply and took her hand in his. "You are a true scientist, my princess. I revere you."

Vush smiled happily and said, "I am always delighted when the true function of an object is discovered. I now believe the bowl and the device were not used in eating, but were art forms of the Seventh Species, used for making beautiful arrangements. I am grateful to you for the suggestion, Arda, and pleased that my gift has such a noble purpose."

The curator said, "It is remarkable that almost all of the artifacts left by the Seventh Species are so beautiful, even those that may have been part of machines. Now we have more proof of the interest the Seventh Species showed in displaying beauty, like the bowl and its retaining device."

Vush nodded. "The bowl doesn't look machine-made. Was it?"

"No. We do not know if it and the dagger come from an earlier time than most of the machine-made artifacts, which are products of the end stages of Seventh Species history, when they were already technologically superior to any of us."

The Crotonites did not disagree, apparently willing to admit their technological inferiority to the Seventh Species.

Vush said, "It is very frustrating that we have not been able to use the known artifacts to make an archaeological record of the unknown history of the Seventh Species. And since physical remains have never been found, the bodily form of the Seventh Species is also unknown."

"The unknown makes me thirsty," Naxo said, twitching his tail. "What happened to the champagne Dee-four and I brought all the way from Earth?"

"It's coming, Naxo," Dee-four said. "Champagne *and* chocolate chip cookies—the two greatest contributions of the Erthumoi to Galactic culture."

Kolix laughed heartily at this pleasant insult to my own world, and everyone joined in. I didn't mind although I did have an emotive pang at not being able to taste either champagne or chocolate chip cookies.

Kolix smacked his lips over the cookies and said, "I pity Arda, the machine who looks human but cannot enjoy human delicacies. When the humans invent new androids, will you go to the scrap heap willingly, Arda?"

Dee-four quickly said, "It is my understanding that androids are considered people and citizens of the Terran Federation."

"They are not people," said Kolix.

Vush patted his head. "Dearwing, I'm sure Arda is a good Erthumoi citizen who has accepted the job of guarding us because she wishes to keep us from harm, so that we may enjoy our royal tour much more."

Before Kolix could answer—he looked angry again—Dee-four raised her crystal of champagne.

"I propose a toast—to the royal house of Crotonis!"

As I refrained from adding my voice to the cheering, I became aware of Hjeg's body pressing against my leg, and her voice in my mind.

—Arda, I think it's time for you to say something polite about the Crotonite royal tour, if you hope to resume it with them in safety. And put in a plug for me.

I didn't know exactly what to say, but I rose and tapped my untouched crystal of champagne to get everyone's attention. The crystal pealed like the sweetest bell on Earth.

"Although I am an Erthumoi android who can't drink, I also wish to honor the wedding couple with a toast." I raised my crystal and so did everyone else. "To the Prince and Princess of the royal house of Crotonis—long life, happiness in marriage, and success in legitimate archaeology."

Everyone (except Hjeg) tapped their champagne crystals and drank deeply while I poured my champagne onto Hjeg's ventral surface. I went on speaking, because by now I had decided what I wanted to communicate to Kolix.

"Like many here, I have enjoyed reading your detective stories, Prince Kolix. They taught me much about courage—which you will need in your reformation . . ."

Kolix's pointed face seemed to sharpen as it paled, and he muttered, "Arda, don't . . ."

". . . I mean yours and your bride's reform of Galactic archaeology. It is a noble cause, one that will bind the Six Species in a worthwhile scientific endeavor. You will aid in the understanding and protection of what you archaeologists call the residue of material culture from the Seventh Species."

The audience clapped. Vush nodded and said, "Thank you, Arda. You have spoken well."

I did not sit down.

"Android bodies may last for millennia, barring accidents. Because of this, I could not understand the suffering of organics, either those who are injured—as you were, Kolix—or those who wish to atone because they have caused the death of someone else."

Hjeg pushed my leg. —*Arda! Are you out of your mind? Do you want Kolix to have a temper tantrum and kill you now?*

I stepped away from her and said, "Thanks to an accident on your ship, I now know that I am as mortal as any organic, for all beings die as individuals when their brain patterns are disrupted. Perhaps this knowledge of mortality will someday make me a good writer, like you."

To my horror I saw that Kolix's eyelids were halfway up and brimming with tears.

I added, "I hope that by the end of the royal tour, the royal house of Crotonis will consider me a friend."

"You are one," Vush said. Kolix seemed unable to speak.

"And I would also ask that my Samian chum, Hjeg, be allowed to accompany me. She wishes to describe the royal tour in poetry that will honor Crotonite culture."

"Excellent," said Vush. Kolix blinked again.

I sat down to applause and saw that Vush was nudging Kolix.

He stood up and carefully avoided looking at me. "On behalf of the princess and myself, I thank the Locrians for this excellent tribute to the Crotonite royal family and to my dearwing's chosen profession, archaeology. Since I am primarily a fiction writer, I would now like to tell a story."

Naxo muttered, "It had better be short. We have to move on to Naxia."

"Let Kolix talk," Dee-four whispered. "He's got his emotions under control."

Kolix cleared his throat and said, "I have never used a certain time-honored Erthumoi way of opening a story, but I shall do so now because, in a way, this story is a true fable."

He was pale again, but as Dee-four said, under control. I wondered how much I had upset him.

"Once upon a time," Kolix said, "there was someone who wanted wealth, and to get it he had to be bad and to conspire with others who were bad. He was determined to win against the competition no matter what harm this did to others. He did not intend to fall in love, but he did, and because his love was good, he got the courage to say no to his bad confederates. For this he inadvertently caused deaths . . ."

Kolix stopped, swallowed, and went on. ". . . and was nearly killed himself. Yet because he continues to live, and to love, he will be good—forever."

Kolix sat down, while the assembled guests looked anxiously at each other, not knowing whether to applaud or not. Finally they did, and I stood up.

"As we Erthumoi would say, three cheers for the Crotonites!"

We all cheered until Naxo uncoiled to his full height and said, "And now, on to my home planet. I am eager for Your Highnesses to see our most impressive life-forms, which the Erthumoi call trees. With power packs you will experience flight through the most beautiful scenery in the Galaxy, and make all of us flightless

Naxians envious. On my world, you won't have to wear
breathing masks."

Dee-four sighed and said, "I will."

Although I was sorry to leave Locria for the con-
finement of the Crotonite ship, I now had congenial
company all the time, for Hjeg insisted that she be
with me, stuck to my power pack, whenever I went out
of our cabin.

"We Samians are not and never have been warlike,
but other species are often disconcerted by the appearance and rapidity of movement of our components. I
am willing to disassemble any time you are in danger, Arda."

"Thanks, Hjeg." I hoped she would not read in my
mind the thought that I, an android, also reacted emotively to Samian components. Insect pests are dangerous in android assembly centers, for even one
cockroach could mess up a positronic brain before it
is safely installed. Unless my skull was opened, I could
not now be harmed by a Samian component, but the
instinctive fear was there.

Instinctive? Perhaps it is not an accurate word, but
there is no other for the basic aspects of survival that
newly activated androids learn along with the laws of
robotics.

I called Zak, who was dressed in his work clothes of
baggy pants and undershirt, his hair delightfully
rumpled.

After my verbatim report, he said, "I am pleased to
see that Hjeg has become your chum. Hjeg, you must
recite the poem about the royal tour at the next GWS
meeting, if it's not too long."

"It will be short, Fortizak. Praising the Crotonites
does not take a long time."

"And, Arda, you performed well. Now please repeat, verbatim, Kolix's story—obviously about himself."

When I had told it to him again, he said, "Are you certain he said, 'deaths' and not 'death'?"

The difference had not registered in my cognitive centers, but I was sure of my sensory data. "Yes, sir. Perhaps he has killed others in the past, in addition to Elson. Perhaps—I hope—that he is trying to atone, and means it when he says he'll be good."

Hjeg said, "I was astonished that Kolix told his tale in the simplest language. He is usually wordy and flamboyant in prose, even in those detective stories. We Samians are wordy, but never flamboyant. That's why I like your prose, Fortizak. It doesn't upset the one million neuro-digestive tracks in each of my components, accustomed to a diet of quiet mineral food that has never been alive, plus soothing quantities of Samian poetry."

"Thanks, Hjeg."

"Don't you have any instructions for me, Zak?" I asked.

"Follow the Crotonites. Are you worried, Arda?"

"Yes. Kolix must still distrust and even hate me. Why did he almost cry when I told him, in a disguised way, that when he nearly killed me he also did me a favor that made me more human?"

"Mortality, Arda."

"I do not understand. Don't organics understand and accept mortality?"

"Not usually. Perhaps occasionally their own, but not the mortality of those they love, and Kolix seems to have fallen in love with Vush. Pity him, Arda."

"For loving Vush? I like her . . ."

"No, pity him . . ." Zak paused. ". . . for needing to

kill you. It will be difficult for him now that you have revealed your perception of android mortality."

"Why? Won't it make it easier for him now that he's proved I am mortal?"

"You still don't understand Kolix. Probably best, for now."

"I understand that Kolix is already upset from killing Elson, and if he thinks I'm more than a machine, he might not kill me. But I can't pity him yet. I don't like him enough."

"You don't have to like someone to pity them."

"But I hate Kolix!" I hadn't known it until I said it.

"She doesn't mean that, Fortizak."

"She does, Hjeg. Because of Elson. Arda, control your emotive circuits and do your job. Naxia is still a dangerous planet for the Crotonites. Too many hiding places for predators."

"Zak, what Naxian predator could possibly want to eat a Crotonite?"

"I was thinking of predators bent on revenge. Intelligent predators. Watch out, Arda, and report to me immediately after the ship leaves Naxia. Zak out."

The planned arrival at Naxia was dinnertime.

"Hjeg, I have never understood the organic compulsion to socialize at meals. Very difficult with Crotonites."

"I'm sure Vush and Kolix have eaten their fill today. They can watch and drink the rest of Dee-four's champagne—they brought it along—while I stay near Naxo and think calm thoughts so he'll pick up calmness. He's nervous around the Crotonites."

"I hadn't really noticed."

"You are an android. You notice everything; you just don't pay close attention to what your sensors pick up."

"Hjeg, sometimes you sound a lot like Zak."

Chapter 18

The land surface of Naxia had a wet, temperate climate. It was bordered by high, rocky cliffs broken by rivers that often plunged in spectacular waterfalls to the green sea. Inland there was a strange mixture of city and forest—one city and one forest, covering all of the one continent.

Each sector of the Naxian city had its own center, but the ship's landing cradle was on an elevated concrete platform in Capitol, where government headquarters were located. We'd been told that the Naxian Writers' Society celebration for the Crotonites was being held nearby in a building adjacent to a grove of the oldest and biggest trees.

I realized that the "trees" of Naxia were examples of how planets develop similar life-forms to fit similar environments. In the shape of their trunks and upper branches, the Naxian trees resembled Earth's giant sequoias, but they were much taller, with bark as scaly as Naxo's skin. The trees also grew long, strange, vine-like limbs below the higher foliage-bearing branches.

Carrying Hjeg stuck to my power pack, I walked down the ship's gangplank onto the landing platform. The Crotonites flew overhead, followed by a small, tube-shaped Naxian antigrav flitter. In the flitter's bubble top, Naxo wielded his camera while Dee-four, wearing her breather, was at the controls.

"The trees are magnificent," I said to Hjeg.

"Indeed. Naxians call the trees 'siblings of the wind,' and claim to have close genetic ties to them. According to Naxian myth, the trees once could speak and walk on legs before they took root. It is more certain that Naxo and his people were vaguely humanoid for millennia, during which they developed technology and underground factories, and then gradually evolved to the serpentoid beings we see today."

"Their city seems so interwoven with groves of trees."

"No tree is ever cut on Naxia."

While the Crotonite swooped and sailed ahead of me, I traveled along elevated walkways that curved through the spiraled city. Compared to Locria, the Naxian city was unscrubbed and, if anything, almost as messy as Manhattan, but the splendor of the trees made up for that. I stopped comparing everything to Earth as I watched the joy of Crotonite flight, and the apparent pleasure the Naxians took in sliding up, down, and along their city's spiral ramps.

Hjeg said, "I'm sorry, Arda, but I couldn't help catching your thought. You are amazed that your own humanoid shape is beginning to seem odd to you."

"Not only that, but I even think that the Crotonites look much less ugly than they did."

"Crotonites have never looked ugly to me. No one does."

"Oh, Hjeg, can't you see clearly?"

"My vision is excellent. You cannot see my visual receptors but they are all over my anatomy, about five square centimeters per receptor. No one looks ugly or beautiful to me because we Samians have no concepts defining physical appearance."

"But you think the ruulogems are beautiful."

"They make us feel good and they may represent the finest achievement of the Seventh Species, and thus are worthy of veneration."

"But what do ruulogems really do?"

"We are not sure. Ruulogems have odd effects on almost everyone. Some think that they are keys to the intelligence or even the wisdom of the Seventh Species, but that may only be wishful thinking."

"How I wish I could handle a ruulogem!"

"You shall. I still have one of the small ruulogems that were on the Crotonite bibs that Elson threw onto Fortizak's balcony. The others I gave to my people when the Crotonite ship went to Samia. If only Elson's death had not meant the destruction of the royal ruulogem!"

"Zak says nobody knows if ruulogems can be destroyed in explosions."

"Then I have hope. I wish to find out where the Crotonites have been getting their supply of Seventh Species artifacts, but it is more important to find the truth about the royal ruulogem. Even if it is gone, Samia would like to know where it came from."

"I think that knowledge is locked in the computer of the Crotonite ship. Kolix must have put it there, for I doubt if Vush knows. I believe that she would not keep an important archaeological site from the Galactic Alliance."

"That is undoubtedly correct, Arda. Kolix would keep the knowledge in the ship's computer. Did you not know that the royal yacht once belonged to Kolix?"

"What!"

"When I was waiting for the ship to take off from

Manhattan, I overheard the crew talking. Kolix is a very wealthy Crotonite, which may have been one reason Vush consented to marry him. He turned over his yacht to the royal family, but insisted on using it for the royal tour . . . Arda! Look behind you! Another ship has landed beside those of the Crotonites and Dee-four."

It must be efficient to have eyes all over one's anatomy. I looked back and she was right. The new ship was not of Crotonite or Naxian design, but had lines like the small hyperdrive vessel loaned to Dee-four by the Erthumoi *Spacelog* magazine.

"I said, "It's an Erthumoi ship, but I can't tell who's using it, for no one's getting out."

"Perhaps they already have. With power packs, anyone could leave a ship high in the atmosphere and fly anywhere they wished. We won't be able to find out who owns the ship because it won't have been monitored or registered. I'm afraid that Naxians worry as little about intruders as we of Samia, a laxity which always seems to worry Erthumoi."

"It worries me. Perhaps I should tell the Crotonite captain to monitor the new ship."

"Crotonites are so suspicious that she is probably already doing so. And this new development behooves you and me to be careful, Arda."

The walkway ended at a ramp that led to a round building. A steep ramp. The Crotonites descended to the door on wings, but when I tried to negotiate the ramp I fell on my rear end and hurtled downward like an Erthumoi child on a playground slide.

It is hard on an android with female-patterned emotive circuits, taught in the android Center to be a nice girl, to fail at keeping my dignity up and my tunic down while Naxo opened his flitter dome to lean out, take pictures of me, and make comments.

"Hey, Arda! You're sexually mature! Stick around on Naxia and I'll show you what to do with what you've got."

—*Ignore him* [Hjeg said telepathically]. *Naxians brag that they enjoy sex with all species. It's a lie, of course. The Locrians don't permit interspecies sex; Cephallonians have sex only with their own species because it takes hours underwater; Crotonite sex is usually during flight; and I assure you that we Samians not only don't have sex, but if we did, we certainly wouldn't have it with Naxians.*

—*That leaves Erthumoi.*

—*Well, yes. There are rumors. I advise against it, although perhaps the throb of pulsating coils does not affect androids. I detect in your mind that you are a virgin . . .*

"Hjeg!" I shouted aloud. "It's all very well to have a chum, but there are limits!"

—*Then you must set them for yourself, Arda. I am speaking not of your friendship with me but of your desires to experience sexual relationships with . . .*

—*I don't want to talk about it. Elson is dead.*

—*Sorry.*

By now I was at the bottom, remembering too late that if I'd turned on my power pack I might have been able to fly down, not as gracefully as the Crotonites, but without quite so much loss of dignity. I got to my feet and we entered the building.

It was full of Naxians. Naxo was now recording the entrance of the Crotonites into the Great Hall, its circular walls covered with paintings of Naxian history. I wished I could study the murals, but everyone moved on.

We went through the Great Hall and out the other side of the building to an immense circular terrace protected by a faintly shimmering force field, upon which a misty rain had started to fall. Apparently Naxians have a lot of rain, but never storms or days of downpour of the kind we have on Earth.

Two of the small Naxian suns had set, while the dim red third sun stayed low in the sky, its eerie light augmented by shining spiral lanterns that hung out from the side of the building. The glow shone upon the wet trunks of the biggest trees I'd ever seen, growing just outside the terrace.

Naxo gestured to Dee-four, who picked one dish from the table and bowed as she handed it to Vush.

"Your Highnesses," Naxo boomed, "welcome to the Naxian Writers' Society. We have imported a supply of Crotonite food capsules in case you get hungry, and each of them has been tested. No harmful additives. Please be seated for the entertainment."

The seats were large, low pillows, rather difficult for Dee-four to manage, and awkward for me. Hjeg slid off the power pack to sit—or whatever Samians do—beside me. The pillows were arranged in a semicircle so we faced the trees outside while an assortment of food dishes was passed around.

The entertainment consisted of a few speeches and a short story reading by Naxo's cousin, the romance writer. The story provoked laughs from the Naxians and the Crotonites, but I did not understand it.

"What is mud-grappling?" I whispered to Naxo.

"A form of sex."

"I don't understand. Isn't it awfully dirty?"

"As your ancient Erthumoi philosopher W. Allen is supposed to have said, 'sex is dirty if you do it right.' "

The entertainment concluded with a dance performance by several Naxians, of which sex I had no idea and was afraid to ask Naxo for clarification. Sinuous bodies performed gyrations with bouquets of flowers, long scarves, and each other. Vush and Kolix seemed amused.

Finally it stopped raining and the force field dome winked out. The dancers twined themselves into a knot in the center of the terrace, and sang. The notes started deep and rose higher.

—*Too loud* [Hjeg said]. *Dee-four is covering her auditory patches and I feel like disassembling to get out of here.*

The song changed to a low hum. The dancers seemed to flow out to the edge of the terrace where they rose up, their upper bodies swaying rhythmically back and forth. To my astonishment, the lower vinelike branches of the nearest trees whipped out to touch the dancers, who wound themselves up the vines and danced on them and with them.

It ended all too soon, for me, and I applauded with the others as the dancers slithered back across the terrace to vanish inside the round doorways to the building.

"Dancing With Trees is our sacred custom," Naxo said. "And now the government of Naxia has granted special permission to the royal Crotonites. Prince and Princess, you may fly directly into the Oldest Grove, alone."

"I must go with them," I shouted. "I am their bodyguard."

"The trees are harmless."

"Nevertheless I must attend the Crotonites."

"Come, Arda," Vush said. "We will all fly together, Kolix and I on each side of you. I do not believe you are a skillful flier yet."

"Thank you, Your Highness."

I took off without Hjeg, for her weight and bulkiness made flying more awkward for me, and by that time she was deep in conversation with Dee-four. I must say that Kolix and Vush were cordial enough, and helpful, for when I turned on my power pack and tried to elevate, they took my hands, spread out my arms, and lifted me easily into the air.

I have never experienced anything like flying with the Crotonites. Kolix wanted to show off with a few turns and rolls, but Vush said it would only disconcert me.

"I suppose it would," Kolix said, showing his teeth at me in what was not quite a smile.

We were in the middle of the grove, out of sight of the terrace, when the trees closed in. They didn't move from their rooted spots, of course, but they leaned in, their branches closing off the spaces around us. The lower vine-branches whipped toward us like agile snakes.

Kolix dropped my hand and flew quickly to protect Vush. But it was not Vush who needed protection. The vines were after me. They wrapped around me, rendering my power pack useless, and sent out thin tendrils that probed my person, concentrating on my head. It was unnerving, but it only lasted a few seconds, and then they dropped me.

I plummeted to the ground, but Kolix swooped down and caught me before I landed.

"Thank you," I said. "Androids might not be badly damaged by such a fall, but I prefer not to experiment."

"The trees seem to have lost interest in you, Arda. Can you manage on your own now? I wouldn't want Vush to get jealous."

The idea seemed ridiculous, but I remembered that

Kolix thought highly of himself, so I turned my power pack back on and flew by myself over to Vush, who was hovering near a huge tree.

"We ought to return and report this," Vush said, "but the trees are so intriguing, are they not, Kolix? Don't you feel as if they are intelligent and thinking about us?"

"Yes. They've probably never before seen anything like Arda, if they can see. I wonder . . ."

He did not finish the sentence, for the enormous tree nearest him seemed to yawn as a slit opened in the trunk. Before Vush or I could stop them, vine-branches seized Kolix, pushing him into the interior of the tree. When the slit closed, it was impossible to see where it had been.

"Dearwing!" Vush screamed, flying to the section of tree trunk into which Kolix had vanished. She hammered on the trunk, yelling for him.

When Vush paused for breath, someone else spoke from the top branches, as if the tree had found a voice.

"That's convenient. Good-bye, Kolix." The words sounded as tinny as they would through a faulty intercom.

"Tree! Let Kolix go," I shouted, inwardly cursing myself for not thinking to bring a communicator. I flew awkwardly to the section of trunk where Vush was hovering.

The strange voice spoke again, closer this time. "I hope the tree keeps Kolix forever."

Vush and I looked up. Descending from the tree canopy was a small antigrav boat, more like an Erthumoi taxi than a Naxian flitter. From its open top leaned a two-armed space-suited figure whose head was completely covered by a helmet with a one-way visor that concealed the face.

"All right, Princess, I'll rescue you before the tree decides to eat you, too. Fly to me."

"I won't," Vush said. "Who are you? I don't trust you."

"Too bad. But you'll be a useful hostage." The boat moved sideways so quickly that we were pinned against the tree, Vush just out of my reach.

To my dismay, the space-suited figure produced a gun and shot the princess. She was unconscious and limp when she was hauled into the boat, which immediately moved upward.

The tree reacted. Vine-branches lashed at the boat, stopping its ascent, and the figure fired the gun again and again. As the struggle between them continued, I flew awkwardly away from the tree, up and around to the other side of the boat. I arrived just as the vines gave up and let go.

The helmeted head turned around and saw me. "Sorry, Arda. The stakes are too big for me to worry about the life of one unimportant Erthumoi."

The gun fired again and I began to fall.

Chapter 19

The big tree's damaged vine-branches moved, catching me before I hit the ground. As they carried me up again, I tried my power pack, but this time it would not work at all. I would not be attacked again because the antigrav boat had gone above the trees and was out of sight.

I did a quick systems check and found that although the stun force of the gun had hit me as well as the power pack, it had not been powerful enough to affect the shielded brain of an android.

I could not free myself from the vine-branches and did not try hard because without the power pack I could not fly.

"Tree? What are you going to do with me?"

I didn't expect an answer and I got none, unless action qualifies. The slit in the tree trunk opened up again and the branches pushed me through it.

Inside, the darkness was broken by a high patch of light coming from the open top of the tree's hollow core. A few centimeters over my head, between me and the opening to the outside, were thick fibrous bands too close together for me to get between them.

I was sitting on a thick webbing that formed a floor across the wide core, dividing the hollow that seemed to go downward through the entire trunk. Not far away on the webbing was a shape I recognized as Kolix, curled up in his wings.

"Kolix!"

"Vush?" He peered eagerly between his wings, but his face crumpled when he saw who was with him. "Arda . . . where is Vush? Somewhere else . . . inside this thieving vegetation? Where is she?"

"She's not here," I said, and proceeded to explain what had happened to Vush. "I'm sorry, Kolix. I have failed in my job as bodyguard."

"You're . . . fired." He began to sob, rocking back and forth on the webbing.

"Kolix, we must think of a way out. If I bend some of the fibers overhead, perhaps you can fly up and get help."

"Arda . . . you . . . don't understand. Dearwing . . . in danger because . . . I'm . . . Kolix . . . Kolix the schemer . . . crook . . . not Kolix the wise."

"It doesn't matter now. We must get out."

"Too late . . . taken her . . . my secret place. They'll steal . . . everything." As he rocked harder, his eyelids halfway up, he became even more incoherent.

"My fault . . . evil past . . . stupidity . . . wealth . . . obsession . . . left behind . . . left *him* behind . . . death . . . not expected . . . terrible, terrible . . . lies, all lies . . . emotions remain, overcoming, swallowing me up . . . yet *he* is gone . . . memories, facts, stolen . . . too late . . . atone . . . but not without love of my life . . . mortality . . . death . . . love transcends . . . must save her!"

"Okay, fine, we'll do that. Do you still have your gun?"

"Gun? Nothing . . . have nothing . . . it took everything." His wings opened fully, revealing that he was completely nude. I looked around for his clothes but couldn't see them.

Kolix's lungs were laboring, and when I went over to touch him, his body was much too warm for a Crotonite.

"Are you ill, Kolix?"

He quivered with the effort to answer me. "Assessed damage not severe ... stress disorganizes ... you must help ... integrate my functions ... please, help me. Arda?"

"I'm here, Kolix."

"You ... every reason to hate me ..."

"Well, yes, but I'm certainly willing to help you even if you've fired me. Vush needs us, and I think you love her."

"Yes ... yes ... oh, yes."

The eyelids were all the way up and he seemed to be losing consciousness, so I shook him. "How can I help you, Kolix?"

"Lower brain center ... out of control. Killing me. Distract it ... help me!"

"Distract your lower brain how?"

He did not respond, so I shook him again. "Kolix!"

His eyes opened all the way. "Sex," he gasped.

"Accessing," I said. "In Erthumoi medical data there is the indication that an orgasm is an integrating total body response. I don't know if this applies to Crotonites as well, but am I correct in thinking that you believe an orgasm will prevent your lower brain from killing you?"

"Yes." He sat up, wheezing for breath, and touched my cheek. "Sorry, Arda. In your eyes, I am ugly."

"Crotonites seemed ugly once, but not now. How do I assist you to have an orgasm? I see no external genitals—just a furry patch on the part of your anatomy that corresponds to the genital area for both human males and females."

"Hand . . . stroke . . ."

I thought he had fainted, but when I stroked the furry patch, he groaned as a short, fat, pointed penis emerged from a fleshy mound under the fur. I tried to massage it, but Kolix screamed in pain.

"No . . . use."

I touched the fur around the organ, stroking that, and to my amazement, a hole at the end of the point opened and a wormlike structure protruded, reminding me of the forked tongue of a serpent. I thought that if this was the Crotonite way of depositing sperm, then the organ of their females probably starts as a single tube, like the human vagina, and then bifurcates.

I have a fully functional humanoid vagina, not bifurcated, but perhaps that would not matter to a dying Crotonite.

Before proceeding I quickly reviewed the laws of robotics. My existence was not in danger. Sex with Kolix could not harm me. Not having it might harm him. Substituting "organic beings" for "humans," the laws of robotics applied to the situation. I decided.

I pulled up my tunic, pulled off my underpants, leaned back, drew Kolix to me, and lost my virginity. It was pleasurable, astonishingly so. The relevant parts of my female anatomy are not only fully functional but covered with synthoflesh apparently loaded—almost overloaded—with sensory receptors that indescribably stirred up my positronic brain.

Kolix moaned as his pelvis convulsed, injecting warm fluid into me. At first I was pleased that I had helped this organic creature achieve a biological culmination, but then I was afraid it had not helped. He'd been in agony, perhaps dying, and now he was so quiet that I thought I'd killed him. I moved back from him so that our bodies were separate again.

He opened his eyes, touched my face, and smiled.

"I think another one of those would be efficacious," Kolix said meditatively.

"Good medicine?"

"Excellent. I'll show my lower brain who's master. Help me force it into synchrony again. Lie back, Arda."

His wings spread out and he rose into the air.

"Where are you going, Kolix?"

"Into you. Crotonite style. Open up."

I opened up and as he hovered over me, the forked organ leaped out and penetrated me once more. Under the renewed stimulation, my entire pelvic area seemed to glow with enjoyable sensation that increased in intensity and spread throughout my android nervous system.

I wanted to hold him and caress him and kiss him, but I was afraid it would interfere with the aerodynamic problem of intercourse on the wing, so I merely moved in time with his thrusting.

I didn't even have time to think of how all the Erthumoi (human, that is) writers have described sex. Not that I wish to interrupt the narrative flow too much at this point, but it does seem to me (as I reflect on the subject during this time of writing about it) that writers do not do a good job of it.

Naxian writers may do well, but I haven't read any Naxian novels with sex scenes in them, mostly because few translators can cope with the intricacies of Naxian muscular movement. Apparently Naxians have separate descriptive words for every twitch of a muscle fiber, and when the coordinated action of muscles results in the Naxian equivalent of orgasm, the language becomes so technically complicated that it does not come across in Galactic Basic.

Naxo would say that the other Six Species don't understand sex, but I disagree. Everybody understands sex once they've done it well.

As I was doing, moving in exquisitely gratifying rhythm. Kolix was happy. I was happy. I was sure the next sex scene I put into a story would make editors happy.

Then suddenly the intensity increased to a point I had not anticipated. I could not speak—except for strange sounds that sounded almost primeval.

Most extraordinary for an android was that I could not *think*.

"Arda!" Kolix shouted.

Suddenly waves of contractions took place within my fully functional vagina. I felt as if I'd been overcome by something I can only describe as a total physical and mental experience.

I counted thirty-four contractions. I hasten to state that I did not consciously count them at the time they were occurring. My positronic brain automatically counts whatever is around to be counted. It was only later on that I noted the number.

The pleasure experienced during the contractions was the best of all, and when the contractions ended, the pleasure subsided so gradually that I had time to savor it as well as Kolix's subsequent second climax.

I closed my eyes and heard the flutter of wings as Kolix came down to lie close beside me. One of his wings enfolded me, and we both rested. I did not have to rest my body, but my emotive circuits needed quieting down.

While Kolix seemed asleep, I looked around and saw his power pack and clothes wedged into the webbing. When I rolled over to retrieve them, Kolix opened his eyes.

"My lower brain is no longer overreactive. I control it."

"Your clothes and power pack," I said, handing them over.

As he dressed and put on the pack, I wondered why the inside of the tree seemed colder. I do not react to cold the way humans do. Furthermore, automatic temperature reading showed me that the tree was not actually colder.

Then I realized I missed the warmth of his organic body.

"I trust you will not inform my wife of what we have done?"

"Never. And thank you, Kolix."

"I'm the best."

"Indeed, you are."

"Do you have any idea how we are going to get out of this tree, Arda?"

I looked up at the barricade above us. "I'm going to climb up and pull on these fibers that block our way to that opening up there. I may be able to pull them back enough so that you can squeeze out."

"Do it, Arda. Androids are strong."

I put my clothes back in place, climbed up, and positioned myself so that I could pull apart the weakest fibers in the center of the barricade. They were very tough.

"Pull, Arda! You're not a weak human!"

"I'm not a weak organic of any sort," I said, pulling harder. The fibers began to bend slightly.

"Do you want me to help?" Kolix asked.

I was determined to show him that in addition to providing activity suitable for subduing an out-of-control Crotonite lower nervous system, I was as strong as any android could be. "No, your exertions may have worn you out, but they haven't worn out me. Stimulation makes me stronger . . ."

"Keep bragging about your androidness and I'll fly up and give you another efficacious demonstration . . ."

I was tempted, but I went on pulling. Finally, the fibers gave way. I had achieved an opening big enough for Kolix to squeeze through.

"Hurry, Kolix—it's hard to keep the fibers apart."

He brushed past me and the fibers sprang back. Kolix was on the other side of the barricade, shaking his wings out. I jumped back down, still a prisoner.

"Your strength is as the strength of ten, Arda. Now I must be on my way to rescue my beloved!"

Kolix flew up from the barricade of fibers, spiraling upward inside the tree trunk so his wings would not touch the sides. He reached the top and clung to it, his wings slack.

"Kolix—are you all right?"

"Yes. Quite all right. I'm going to Vush."

"Kolix—wait!"

He tilted the tip of one wing in my direction, but without so much as a good-bye, much less an effort to help me escape, Kolix vaulted up into the open sky and vanished.

Chapter 20

I tried to tell myself that Kolix was embarrassed about having sex with an Erthumoi android, not that there was any other kind of android. Probably all Erthumoi look ugly to a Crotonite.

When I looked down at my body, it did seem strange. Such long legs, and only two breasts.

After a while I decided I could not stay inside the tree much longer. Zak would wonder why I hadn't reported to him.

If I'd been sensible, I'd have had my communicator with me. I would have been able to ask Naxo for help. Even more importantly, I could have asked Zak what to do about a dying Crotonite.

Then I thought over the fact that I'd managed to save Kolix without assistance from anything except my well-engineered body. Getting help from anyone would have meant not having sex with Kolix. And I was glad I had. At least, I was glad then.

I looked up at the fibers again and it seemed to me that the space between them was slightly wider where I'd pulled them apart. They had not rebounded completely back into place.

I climbed back up and pulled again. My first attempts were fruitless. I thought about trying to tear the fibers out of their roots in the tree trunk, but they were part of the living tree. Did the laws of robotics apply to trees?

I thought about it for another ten minutes until I decided that trees qualified. At least these Naxian trees did. I remembered that even the sloppy, good-humored Naxians had never cut a tree. I also decided I had come to believe that the laws of robotics applied to all living things whenever possible. If it were possible, I would get out without damaging the tree.

Yet after another try I almost gave up, thinking that my android body was too much larger than a Crotonite's. Then I remembered their wings. Even with his wings folded tightly against his back, a Crotonite such as Kolix was larger in diameter than I was.

I tried again to escape, and during this effort, the tree started to produce a booming noise that sounded as if it were at least partially composed of words I could not make out.

I stopped pulling at the fibers, but the tree did not stop booming for another minute. When it let up, I could hear muted low booming as the other trees of the grove began speaking, too.

I'm not easily frightened, but this did scare me. Were they telling each other that an intruder was damaging one of them?

The words in the booming became clearer, but they were in an unknown language. Accusing me?

"Tree! I mean you no harm! I have to get out—please let me go."

My tree boomed again, louder and louder. This time the very walls of the trunk were vibrating—and so were the fibers of the barricade. I pulled once more, and squeezed through, rolling upon the other side of the barricade as the fibers sprang back into place with a twanging noise that added a tenor to the bass of the booms.

I sat on the fibers and gazed upward through the hollow tree. I was filled with misgivings, for it did not seem likely that I would find any purchase on its smooth inner bore. I tried, and I could not climb.

Kolix had flown up to freedom. That seemed to be the way to go, so I sat down and took my power pack apart to the accompaniment of more booms. Thanks to the knowledge I had gained from the Crotonite computer, I understood the electronics of power packs.

I was just about to try reworking some of the pack's circuits when the booms stopped and someone yelled at me.

"Grab the rope, Arda." Naxo leaned out of the flitter, poised above the opening at the top of the trunk.

The knotted end of the rope fell upon me. I put my still useless power pack back on, took hold of the rope, and was going to ascend hand over hand when I was quickly pulled up into the flitter. Dee-four was at the controls, Naxo's constrictions holding the rope.

She nodded to me; Naxo favored me with a swipe of his long tongue. The Naxian kiss is friendly, and removes dirt.

"Have you got it?" Dee-four asked.

"Got what?"

"The key."

"What key?"

Naxo's tail touched Dee-four. He coiled the rope as neatly as himself and put it under the seat. "Let me handle this, Dee. Now look, Arda. The trees have been speaking to us Naxians in the ancient Naxian language . . ."

"All those booms?"

"Yes. It is a language that goes back before time as

we civilized Naxians mark it. This language is not used by modern Naxians, but we are taught early in our schooling to understand it. For generations we have done this in the hope that the trees would some day speak to us as they were supposed to have done with our ancestors. Now the hope is fulfilled, our precautions in preserving the language worthwhile."

"Naxo," Dee-four said, "the trees are restless, bending toward the flitter. Get on with it."

He hissed. "As I was saying, Arda, the language . . ."

I interrupted. "Naxo, have you seen Kolix?"

"Oh, sure. He flew back to where we were waiting for you."

"Well? What did he say?"

I dreaded hearing that Kolix had bragged about nullifying my virginity.

"Let me see—he told us about the abduction of Vush. Very upset he was about it. I'd never have thought a Crotonite could love as deeply as we Naxians do, but I confess that Kolix seems to love his princess . . ."

"Naxo!" I yelled. "What did Kolix do?"

"He left," Dee-four said, a trifle grimly.

"Left!"

"In his own ship. Arda, do you have any idea where he's going?"

"No. He said he wanted to rescue Vush."

"He told us that, too, but not where he had to go to do it."

"Blast," said Naxo. "He must know where Vush's abductor was heading. And then we've got this other problem about the trees."

The trees were indeed bending closer, and although the booming was not so loud, it seemed faster, more urgent.

"The booming?" I said. "But you Naxians understand them."

"We don't understand what they're talking about. The trees have been saying, over and over, the same thing—'the key must be taken to the Suffering Ones.'"

"Whatever the key is," Dee-four said. "And whoever and wherever the Suffering Ones are."

"You mean the Naxians don't know?" I asked.

"No."

"Well, I don't have any key," I said, annoyed.

"What's the matter, Arda?" Dee-four asked.

"That Kolix! He left me still a prisoner in the tree. I bet he neglected to mention that I was the one who helped him get out of the tree, and that I was still trapped inside."

"But he did tell us—by hycom, just before his ship went into hyperspace," said Naxo. "At least he said that he thought you might still be inside the biggest tree."

"That was very nice of him."

My sarcasm was wasted, for Naxo's and Dee-four's attention had been captured by a vine-branch from the same tree that had imprisoned Kolix and me. It had snaked up to tap on the flitter.

"Well we can't take the whole blasted tree with us," Naxo said. "Why doesn't it tell . . ."

"Ask it, Naxo," I said. "If you speak the ancient language, ask the tree where the key is and where the Suffering Ones are."

Naxo spoke, the deep guttural syllables rolling out.

The tree replied in a series of deep booms that seemed to vibrate my brain.

Naxo looked at me. "Arda, you must lean out and let the tree touch you."

"But what does it say about the key?"

"I didn't understand it completely. Something about the two likely candidates having been tested."

"Candidates for the key? Why don't you understand the tree?"

Naxo vibrated his tail portion like a rattlesnake. "Now don't scold me, Arda. I wasn't the best student at school, and languages, especially dead ones, were not easy for me. All I know is that the testing was done and that you must be touched so information can be passed. Something about you being the right candidate, although you are alien."

"I'm not Naxian . . ."

"More than just not Naxian, Arda. Alien in a sense I can't understand. Maybe it's because you're an android."

"Probably." I felt discouraged, as if my new sense of oneness with organic life had disappeared. "Why must the tree touch me? I've just been inside it for hours. Why didn't it tell me then?"

"Legends say the mind-touch of the trees occurs through the external vine-branches when the trees are fully awake. That would mean the tree could talk in the old language to you but could not do a mind link with you until you came outside and could be touched by a vine-branch."

Dee-four removed her eyecover and deeplooked at the waiting vine-branch. "This vine-branch has a primitive nervous system, going back into the tree. It might very well be the means of telepathic communication with other species who don't know the old Naxian language."

"I'm willing," I said.

Suddenly Dee-four turned and deeplooked at me. Her head tilted expressively.

"What do you see, Dee?" Naxo asked. "Something different about Arda?"

There was a long moment, and then her eyecover slid down. Naxo's coils relaxed, but I did not. I looked at Dee-four.

"Arda is in perfect working condition," Dee-four said. But she reached out to take my hand and squeeze it gently, one female to another. She had undoubtedly found what Kolix had left inside me, but I trusted her. She would tell no one.

"That's good," Naxo said, oblivious. "I think there's something about you, Arda, that awakened the trees for the first time in Naxian recorded history. You're their candidate—I wish I knew for what."

"Lean out, Arda," Dee-four said. "Let the tree touch you."

Hoping that the tree would not tell Naxo everything that Kolix and I did inside the tree, I leaned out and let the vine-branch touch me.

Instantly my mind was filled by a message that had no words, only feelings that reverberated through my emotive circuits until I was almost terrified. I drew back my hand and broke the link.

"Terrible danger," I whispered to Naxo and Dee-four.

"What kind of danger?" Naxo asked.

"Not danger to the trees. But they know about it. Naxo, ask the trees if they've received messages."

Naxo spoke and the trees answered. "Yes. Through the air—no, not through the air. Must be telepathic. Maybe through hyperspace. From very far away."

I let the tree's vine-branch touch me again, although I was afraid. This time the emotional message was quieter, as if the tree was aware of my fear and was trying to communicate more meaning to me.

I said, "The danger is to something or someone the

trees feel close to, as if they were once related, or perhaps came from the same place. And you're right, the danger is far away."

I listened again, this time not afraid. "It's a danger that's been going on for a long time, and I think they're trying to tell me that it's been getting worse in recent years. Something must be completed, or there will be death."

"Whose death?"

Then I knew. "The Suffering Ones."

The vine-branch now wrapped itself around my head, and I distinctly heard a "Yes." Not the word, but the emotional affirmation of what I had just said, as if the trees could understand me but could not reply in my language.

I tried to order my thoughts and emotions into picturing the planet Naxia and asking the question— where?

The picture that the tree sent in answer was amazing. At first I thought it was the planet Earth, so blue from space that the continents seem insignificant. Then I realized that the planet in my mind was a different shade of blue.

"The tree is showing me a picture of a planet that's blue in color. It's beautiful . . ." The picture in my mind turned, and I realized that I could see no continents, not even an island on this planet.

"Blue like Earth?" asked Naxo.

"All ocean. A planet without dry land."

"Cephallonia," Dee-four said.

The name and the planet came together in my mind. I had never been there, but everyone in the Galactic Alliance knew that Cephallonia had no dry land.

I was about to pull away from the vine-branch when it tightened around my head. The picture in my mind enlarged, focusing down on a patch of the planetary ocean that seemed slightly lighter than the rest, as if something metallic were just below the water's surface.

"I understand," I said to the vine-branch. "We must go to Cephallonia and find that spot."

The picture disappeared from my mind and the vine-branch uncoiled from my head. Then it startled me by reaching into the flitter to palpate my body. I was about to object when the end of the vine-branch dipped into my tunic pocket.

I could feel the vine-branch vibrating.

Naxo and Dee-four could not see what the vine-branch was doing because my back was to them, and I did not explain. I waited, wondering, and then the vine-branch withdrew. It whipped out of the flitter, paused, and came back to touch me once more.

I saw no pictures, but I felt a strong emotion coming from the tree. It was like a child pleading with a parent for help.

I spoke to it in my mind, trying at the same time to form an image of a mother consoling a child. —*I'm not your parent.*

It spoke back, in my mind. I could not understand the Naxian words, but I felt the emotion of trust. Trust they were putting in me, for I was the one to help the Suffering Ones.

I spoke again in my mind. —*Yes, I will.*

At last the vine-branch released me and left for good, falling back into the foliage of the tree.

It had all happened so quickly that neither Dee-four nor Naxo were aware that my tunic pocket now contained something that hadn't been there before. I felt as if the tree wanted this kept secret, for it had not told the Naxians, so I didn't bring out the object or make any comments except one.

"We must go to Cephallonia. That's where the Suffering Ones are. I promised the tree that I would help."

"Then you're the key, Arda," Dee-four said. "You've done well. Zak will be pleased with you."

She piloted the flitter back to the landing where the ship she and Naxo had used was docked.

"You and Hjeg will travel with us," Dee-four said, "since your transportation has left without you."

We transferred from the flitter to the ship, and went immediately to the control room. I liked Dee-four's ship much better than the Crotonites'. For one thing, it was pale green and beige inside, not gray, and for another, there was no crew except us, so I didn't have to contend with the nasty Crotonite captain. It was also a relief to be far away from Kolix.

"Here comes Hjeg," Naxo said. "One of my friends is bringing her in another flitter."

When Hjeg came aboard, I avoided touching her. I didn't want her to know about my latest experiences. It was not that I was embarrassed, or ashamed. I just wanted them—for myself.

She seemed to understand when I did not come near her.

"You must have had a difficult time in the forest," Hjeg said. "I'm glad you're back with us."

"Thanks. Dee-four, we must hurry to Cephallonia. I have a job to do."

The ship lifted from the landing cradle and sped through the atmosphere of Naxia. Once beyond the atmosphere, Dee-four turned on the hyperdrive engine.

"On to Cephallonia."

Naxo said, "Arda, do you think you were selected for the job of saving the Suffering Ones because the Naxian tree sensed that you are a robot?"

"Why would that . . ."

"But, Arda, robots—I mean you androids—are so reliable. So strong and immortal."

"I'm strong. Not immortal."

Hjeg said, "Whatever you do, you must be careful, Arda. Fortizak knows you are not immortal and he does not want you to be hurt. I failed him by not protecting you on Naxia."

"Not your fault, Hjeg. I went off with the Crotonites without you, and I didn't even bother to take a communicator."

"Take it next time," Naxo said. "At any rate, I'm sure the Naxian trees assume that you're a better rescuer than any of us organics. Maybe the Suffering Ones are other robots."

"There aren't any robots on Cephallonia," Dee-four said. "There aren't any anywhere except on Erthumoi planets."

"Then I can't be going to Cephallonia because I'm a robot."

Hjeg's upper surface rippled. "Odd, isn't it? We'd all be going to Cephallonia next anyway. It's the last stop of the Crotonites' goodwill tour."

"Goodwill," Dee-four said. "I once thought it was impossible for Crotonites. After meeting Vush, I'm willing to give them the benefit of a doubt. We must rescue Vush as well as find the Suffering Ones."

"Hey, I just thought," Naxo said. "We might have to get out into the water of Cephallonia. I love water— swimming is one of my favorite hobbies—but it could be dangerous for you, Arda. Are you likely to rust if we run into trouble on Cephallonia?"

"No. I'm more or less impervious to water."

"Unlike *some* of us organics," Dee-four said. "I hate getting *wet*."

*　　*　　*

There was no cabin for me in Dee-four's ship, and I wanted to report to Zak alone. When I asked where I could go to rest my mind and report to Zak, Naxo showed me to the tiny lounge in the stern. I did not think it was private enough. Anyone could come in or even walk by and overhear me.

"Naxo, is there someplace more private? You don't mind?"

"Of course not. Tell Fortizak the plot thickens, or whatever writers do to complicate perfectly simple stories."

He led me back through the hall. "I sleep in the control room, but here's Dee-four's cabin. She won't mind."

He extruded a hand, opened the door for me, and I went inside. It was a pleasant room with holoimages of Locrian nestlings on the walls.

I did not report at once. I badly wanted to rest my mind. Perhaps I was trying to build up mental strength to lie to Zak, or at least to avoid telling him the entire truth.

Resting did no good. Images from Naxia obscured my cognitive processes. I relived the entire trip to Naxia, especially what happened inside the tree.

Trying to shut the trip out of my mind also did no good, because images of the trip were replaced by the words "key" and "Suffering Ones," repeated over and over.

What was I to tell Zak?

My thoughts were in turmoil. I did not have to treat Zak the way I was treating Hjeg. Zak was not telepathic; he was back on Earth busy with his writing, and it would be easy to lie to him. Yet he was my employer. Or was he? Technically I still worked for Smith's. Would I have to tell him everything?

I imagined telling Director Smith what had happened on Naxia. The thoughts were upsetting, for I visualized the disapproval on her face.

Taking what I considered to be extraordinary precautions, I locked myself into Dee-four's cabin. I sat down beside the computer terminal and thought again.

What should I tell Zak?

My own actions decided me, and I laughed. I had locked the door, insuring privacy. That meant I wanted to tell Zak extremely private things.

I touched my communicator with Zak's call numbers, and took out what was in my tunic pocket.

The key was not myself but the Crotonite royal ruulogem, coruscating with color.

Chapter 21

"Fascinating."

Zak was in his underwear, sitting at the kitchen table and buttering an ear of corn. On the plate before him were two thoroughly gnawed corncobs. There was no evidence of a green vegetable of any sort.

I waited for more comment. It was, as humans are wont to say, unnerving to get only that one word of reaction after I had carried out my momentous decision to tell Zak all.

"I suppose," I said, enunciating carefully, "that you are referring to the news about the Suffering Ones on Cephallonia."

"Um." He was eating the ear of corn, going round and round instead of across the rows of kernels.

"Can you also be commenting on my intimate experiences?"

He looked up from the corn and twitched his right eyebrow. He does not always succeed in raising it to a perfect arc of quizzicality.

"And did you enjoy sex with Kolix, Arda?"

It occurred to me that I had told Zak the facts, but not my thoughts or the reactions of my android nervous system. I had not at all told all. I couldn't think of what to say now.

"Or is 'enjoy' not precisely the operative word for an android?" he asked.

"Androids can enjoy many of the bodily experiences that humans do. In fact . . ." I was warming to the subject, ". . . we may very well enjoy them *more*."

Now both eyebrows shot up, and then he massaged his chin. "Pretty good, was he?"

"Having been a virgin before, I cannot corroborate his statement that he is the best. I can only repeat it."

"The best. Well, that's logical."

"Why?"

"You don't have any idea?"

I thought. "Vush was very experienced before marrying Kolix. I assume that she taught him how Crotonite sex on the wing is best accomplished. While I was not on the wing with him, nevertheless . . ."

"You needn't repeat the description of the event, Arda. I'll take your word for it."

"Zak, you must understand that the procedure did stimulate a good portion of my anatomy as well as the pleasure centers of my emotive circuits, but I am troubled. Did I do the wrong thing?"

"What do you mean by 'wrong'?"

"I worry that Kolix may have lied about the actual necessity of the act, and that I may have—as the expression says—been taken advantage of."

Zak grinned. "That's one of the times when you can end a sentence with a preposition."

"Oh, Zak, you think I shouldn't have done it!"

"On the contrary, I'm inclined to believe that Kolix was indeed dying. I also believe that you saved his life by helping him control his lower brain functions."

I was enormously relieved. "Then I don't mind having to save his life in that particular way."

"Lucky Kolix. Now I think we can stop talking about

sex and go on to other relevant points of the mystery. What did you learn from the shape of Vush's abductor?"

"The shape?" I admit that I was still thinking about sex so it was hard to focus on what Zak was getting at. There—another sentence ending in a preposition. I can't seem to help it.

"The physical shape of the abductor. Describe."

"He, she, or it was encased in a bulky space suit so I learned little of what could be inside."

"Arda, you are not demonstrating the combination of acute observation with reasoning and judgment possible to intelligent beings of any species, but to Erthumoi in particular."

I thought again. "The abductor's suit was too big to fit a Crotonite and had no bulge at the back for wings. The suit would fit only an Erthumoi or a slightly undersized Locrian, unless there are other two-armed creatures that size who speak fluent Galactic Basic."

"None that I've heard of." He picked up another ear of corn.

"You're eating too much, and with butter."

"Arda!"

I quickly said, "I think the abductor doesn't know Kolix is deeply in love with Vush and has turned aside from criminal activities. Therefore he, she, or it thinks it will be easier to trade Vush's life for treasure if Kolix is not around to object to giving up said treasure."

"Good reasoning," Zak said. He examined the ear of corn he'd picked up. It seemed flawless to me, but I wondered if the food replicator or the local grocery store had sent something inferior. Zak seemed to be meditating over the corn.

To my surprise, he then got up and put the ear of

corn—uneaten—into the refrigerator, sighing heavily. Zak, not the refrigerator.

I bestowed a congratulatory smile upon him and said, "It's so romantic—Kolix saved by the sacrifice of my maidenhood in time to go rescue his wife from the abductor who may or may not be a former confederate in crime."

"Sounds like one of the seven basic fictional plots."

"Are you saying my deductions are fiction?"

"Not at all. I'm educating you as a writer, unless you want to concentrate on nutritional guidance of senior writers."

"Sorry, sir."

"You weren't clear about it, but I gather that as of this moment the four of you stalwart agents are hot on the trail of Vush's abductor and her pursuing spouse."

"Yes, we—four of us? Hjeg, too?"

"Hjeg, when not writing long narrative poems, works for the Galactic Alliance Archaeological Association."

"You should have told me earlier, Zak."

"I didn't know. I did some research. You could have, too."

"Sorry, sir."

"How did Dee-four get on the trail so quickly?"

"She tracked the ion trails of both ships, and they're definitely headed for Cephallonia. It can't be a coincidence that the Naxian trees told me I'm supposed to go there also, with the royal ruulogem, to help the Suffering Ones."

"Your assumption is undoubtedly correct. I wish we knew who the Suffering Ones are and how you're to help them. Did the trees put any images in your head that might clue us into the nature of the Suffering Ones?"

"No. I only saw the planet Cephallonia and that lighter patch of ocean."

"And you were given the ruulogem. Are you sure it's the royal ruulogem?"

"My positronic brain had stored the exact dimensions and spectroscopic analysis of the royal ruulogem. This one is identical."

"And remarkably beautiful," Zak said.

I turned the gem over and over in my hand. It seemed to have taken on a new power to scintillate, catching the light of Dee-four's cabin in a million brilliant rainbows that were almost too bright to watch.

"Arda, do you grasp the implications of the fact that the ruulogem was not destroyed?"

I thought I did. "It means that Elson did not take it after all, doesn't it?"

"Yes. What else? Describe the last you saw of the ruulogem before the tree gave it to you."

"Before Elson stunned me, I saw it in his hand after he'd taken it from Vush, but he must have given it back, slipping it into Kolix's pocket."

"Why would he do that?"

"I don't know, unless he changed his mind about the theft, perhaps because Kolix had been so severely injured. You'd think he could have reasoned that the ruulogem would serve as payment for his surgical services."

"I don't think so," Zak said.

"No. I guess he just changed his mind. He couldn't fit the gem back on Vush's crest, so he had to put it into Kolix's pants pocket where it would be safe. Then he stole the Crotonite bibs containing the small gems. I don't know why he dropped them on your balcony, where Hjeg found them."

"Don't worry about it, Arda. The bibs and the small

gems are not important. What about the ruulogem ending up in your pocket?"

"Oh, blast."

"Your favorite new epithet?"

"Naxo uses it. I think it's striking."

"When used by an android, it sounds as if your inner works are achieving critical mass . . ."

I drummed my fingers on the computer console and shut him up. "I'm angry, Zak."

"At me?"

"No. At Kolix. Because of the royal ruulogem being in his possession all along. That's what he meant when he referred to the Naxian tree as 'thieving vegetation.' The tree had taken the ruulogem from him when it stripped him naked."

"No doubt."

"But since Kolix had not told anyone that he had the ruulogem, then he must be lying about loving Vush."

"I don't follow that."

"You, Zak? Not follow something?"

"That will do, Arda. Why does it mean he doesn't love the princess?"

"Because if he loved her, he wouldn't have let her think Elson had taken her ruulogem. It means Kolix wanted the ruulogem for himself." I indulged in the epithet. "Blast."

"These are the only implications?"

"I must be right. It means—oh, Zak, it nullifies my good deed! I should not have saved Kolix's life! He is a villain!"

Zak settled back in his chair, a sleepy expression on his face, his eyes half-closed. "Explain."

"Elson wasn't much of a villain. He may have intended to steal, but he changed his mind. Kolix is a bad villain because when Elson's change of heart gave him the opportunity to possess the ruulogem, he . . . he . . ."

"Go on. Don't be afraid of your deductions, Arda." Zak opened his eyes wide. "Even if they may be wrong."

"Don't you see, Zak? Kolix not only kept silent about the ruulogem he'd hidden, but he then decided to kill Elson in such a way that it would look as if the ruulogem were destroyed."

Zak yawned. "Then what's all that business about Kolix's need for atonement?"

"Kolix may have regrets about Elson's death. He probably does genuinely have some regrets. Maybe it's his first murder. Vush said she'd heard him mutter about death and atonement, and so did I. Yet it seems clear to me that Kolix did deliberately murder Elson, one of the handsomest, most charming . . . and a skillful, compassionate doctor, too."

"Arda, I'm afraid that there was indeed a murder. But we can't prove it. Not until you accumulate more evidence."

If I'd been organic, I would have been trembling with rage and regret. "I did not think through the implications . . ."

"May I remind you that at the time you had sex with Kolix you did not know he had possessed the ruulogem?"

I paused. He was right. My emotive circuits calmed down. "But the fact remains that I have had sex with a thoroughly evil being. I shouldn't have saved Kolix's life."

"You had to. You're an android. Stop worrying, Arda."

"Is my reasoning logical? Is it true?"

"I'm glad you recognize that logic and truth are not necessarily synonymous in the real world. As it happens, genuine truth is hard to come by when one is dealing with intelligent beings. Especially if said intelligent beings are having a hard time staying sane."

"Kolix?"

Zak stared gravely at me through the hycom screen. "Arda, I'm not sure my theories are correct in this case, but I think more is at stake than a ruulogem or a couple of lives."

"What are your theories?"

"Right now I'll keep my theories to myself, because I find it useful to get your reactions to things just as they happen. The fact that you can remember every detail, when pushed . . ."

"I don't need to be pushed. Thank you for finding me useful, but I'd like to know . . ."

"Not yet, Arda. Approach every event and every being with your capacity for observation, your refreshingly naive emotional reactions . . ."

"I'm not as naive as I was!"

"No." He sounded almost sad. "Well, it's probable that when you find the lock fitting that key you're holding, you'll find many other answers as well."

"But according to the nuances of Galactic Basic, the word 'key' can have symbolic meaning. The ruulogem must be only a metaphorical key," I said.

Zak shrugged. "Perhaps it is, but please keep your possession of the ruulogem a secret for now. Don't concentrate on the Crotonites anymore until after you find the Suffering Ones."

Chapter 22

When Dee-four brought her ship out of hyperspace, Cephallonia was directly ahead of us, an oblate spheroid the size of Earth but colored deep turquoise and surrounded by an Earth-type atmosphere, which at the moment was full of fluffy clouds.

I had told my comrades about the lighter patch of ocean, so Dee-four looked for it. On space-normal drive, we circled the planet without seeing a lighter area, although we did see ships that seemed to be chasing each other in and out of the clouds.

"Go lower, Dee," Naxo said. "Those clouds in the atmosphere are hard to see around."

"Going low enough to get under the clouds will mean taking days to examine the entire planet."

"Go very fast, Dee-four," Hjeg said.

Naxo said, "But at high speed we won't see anything but a blue blur."

Hjeg was pressed to the viewport. "I can see at any speed."

"So can the computer," I said. "In fact, Dee-four, if you ask the computer to scan through the clouds for the lighter part of the ocean, it might be able to find it from this height."

"My Locrian brain isn't working. I should have thought of that." She touched the computer panel.

One more quick pass around the planet and then the ship descended to half a kilometer above the surface of the water. The other ships were not in sight.

"There's the lighter patch," Naxo said. "It's the top of an underwater building!"

It was now easy to see that the silvery patch on the ocean was an immense metallic dome close to the water's surface.

Hjeg said, "I've been to Cephallonia once, for a poet's conference, but it was held in one of the air-filled spaceships the natives keep for visitors. I didn't see much of the planet, I suppose, because it looked as if there wasn't much to see from the air. I certainly never noticed this structure."

"I've never been here," Dee-four said, "but from all I've read, I know that the Cephs don't live inside any buildings. It doesn't seem possible that the thing below us could be part of Cephallonian civilization."

"It probably isn't," Hjeg said. "The Seventh Species gave the Cephallonians an automated factory, but it's inside an underwater cliff. There's no need for the Cephallonians to go inside the factory since it's run by a computer programmed to supply them with a new spaceship if one gets destroyed."

"Seventh Species," Naxo said with a slight sneer. "Having to help out nontechnological races."

"Like us Samians and these Cephallonians," Hjeg said matter-of-factly. "Each of us was given the means to leave our planet. Our spaceships are the only technological devices we and the Cephallonians use. I only wish Samians and Cephallonians could remember the Seventh Species, but the gifts were given so long ago, and in such a way that our ancestral memories contain no evidence of what the Seventh Species was like."

"Well, they were kind and generous," Dee-four said. "That we know."

Naxo ran his tongue over his fangs. "We Naxians did not need to have any gifts from anybody. We were able to achieve civilization by ourselves."

Suddenly I remembered that the Naxian trees, although related in some distant evolutionary way to the serpentoid Naxians, had telepathic ability that extended through hyperspace to this planet, in another solar system. Not only that, but the trees took the ruulogem from Kolix because they knew it was some sort of key to be used on Cephallonia.

"Naxo," I said, "it's possible that the Naxian trees have a faint memory of the Seventh Species. Perhaps they don't remember what the Seventh looked like, but they have talents that go beyond the confines of your planet. The Naxian trees know that another telepathic creature is here, hidden on Cephallonia and in danger. How could the trees have such a talent unless the Seventh Species had helped them, perhaps for a purpose we do not understand except that it must have something to do with Cephallonia itself?"

"I suppose you could be right, Arda. My people will be glad to know that the Seventh touched our planet so lightly, giving telepathy to the trees."

Dee-four said, "But, Naxo, the Seventh must have done quite a lot on your planet. Arda reported that the Naxian trees told her of danger to beings far away but related to them, and that the trees and the others came from the same place. Locrian scientists studying Naxia have suspected that since the Naxian trees were once free-living creatures, related to you, it's probable that you both came from a common ancestor who was free-living. Now doesn't it stand to reason that the Seventh

Species must have removed some of those ancestors and hidden them somewhere on Cephallonia?"

"That makes sense," Hjeg said. "It would explain the telepathic link between the two planets, and the urgent need of the Naxian trees to send us here to help the Suffering Ones."

"What do you think, Arda?" Naxo asked. "The tree told you, not us."

"It was not very clear, but I think Hjeg is probably right about the common ancestor."

I did not tell Naxo that the communication from the Naxian tree had been worked on by my positronic brain. The tree had indeed tried to tell me that the intelligent beings of Naxia were related to the Suffering Ones on Cephallonia. The tree had also told me that both came from the same place—and now it seemed clearer to me that the "place" was not either planet.

I did not know what or where the place was, and neither did the trees, but I had the impression of vast distances.

Naxo was so proud of the Naxian "history" of evolving from or with the trees, on their own planet. Until I was more certain, I didn't want to tell him that the Seventh Species could very well have brought his remote ancestors from a planet so far away that it was probably in another galaxy.

Hjeg said, "Look at what's coming into view."

My positronic brain was sufficiently rattled by the necessity of concealing information from Naxo that my penchant for banality took a turn for the worse.

I said, "It's a scene I've always wanted to write—wicked predators encircling hapless victims."

"Not at all," said Hjeg. "I know Cephallonian ships, so I can tell you that the big ones are Cephallonian police patrol ships sending out holding beams. One of the two small ships caught in the holding beams is the Crotonite royal yacht that Arda and I traveled on with Kolix and Vush. The other must be the Erthumoi ship that took the princess."

"We'd better find out what's going on," said Dee-four.

I said, "Dee-four, wait! I think we should call Zak for advice about this development. After all, we've arrived smack in *medias res.*"

The Latin expression had jumped out of my memory banks, which seemed to be working peculiarly. I wondered if my recent sexual encounter had affected more than my emotive circuits.

Naxo sniffed. "What's *medias res*—cosmic excrement?"

"It means we've barged into the midst of things," I said.

Dee-four nodded. "Ah, yes. Even in nonfiction writing, starting a section in *medias res* is exciting, but it does result in the necessity to account for the events leading up to the present moment, using tricky exposition of plot that doesn't slow down the narrative momentum."

"Great Galaxy!" Naxo yelled. "You writers are crazy, maundering on about writing instead of coping with reality!"

"Oh, we try to cope," Dee-four said grimly. "I'm just not sure what to do in this situation. Perhaps Zak . . ."

"He *is* a genius," Hjeg said.

Naxo's upper body gyrated. "Don't be ridiculous. Even if he were, it's stupid to rely on the judgment of a human whose brain is glued to his word processor while his body is glued to Earth. We are far away, supposedly helping the mysterious Suffering Ones, and we can't do that until we rescue Vush—from the Cephs as well as from her abductor."

I was about to say that Zak had told me to find the Suffering Ones before attending to the Crotonites, but Dee-four was moving her head up and down in agreement with Naxo.

"I see what you mean, Naxy. We must rescue Vush at once. The police ships' holding beams are vibrating the other two ships, maybe not enough to damage brains, but enough to nauseate everyone. I don't much care if Kolix gets nauseated, but I am getting to like the little princess."

"So do something!" yelled Naxo. "We must act now! Damn the story momentum!"

From Erthumoi history in my data banks, I couldn't resist adding, "Full speed ahead," but no one paid attention to me.

Dee-four touched her comm panel. "Cephallonian patrol, this is the Locrian Dee-four speaking. I am one of the alien agents employed by the Terran Federal Bureau of Investigation. My Naxian partner and I, with the help of Erthumoi agent Arda and the Samian writer, Hjeg, left Naxia to chase that Erthumoi ship you've got in a holding beam. It contains the Crotonite princess, abducted by someone whose identity we do not know . . ."

"I know his identity!" Kolix's head appeared in one corner of the visiscreen. "Dee-four, tell those soggy nitwits to release my ship! I'm here to get back my beloved wife from a rogue. It's Granston!"

Naxo said, "You mean the writer of hard-boiled . . ."

"Yes, yes. At the time the Cephallonians put a hold on our argument, Granston was trying to sell me Vush in return for opening up that underwater dome. And I was trying to tell him that scans of the dome show there's no door in it."

"So much for plot exposition," Hjeg muttered.

Granston's face appeared at another corner of the visiscreen. Behind him we could see Vush, trapped in a closed net hung from the ceiling of his control room. He said, "Kolix is lying."

"You lie!"

"Shut up, Kolix. You think you're a romantic hero, but you'd never make the best-seller list . . ."

"I have! Frequently!"

An expression of disgust passed over Granston's reasonably handsome face, and I wondered why I was not drawn to him as I had been to Elson's good looks. Possibly it was because Elson had been charmingly friendly, until he had to stun me. As I thought about it, I realized that I had forgiven Elson for doing so. He must have been confused and frightened over stealing the ruulogem from Vush. So frightened, perhaps, that after rendering me unconscious, he decided to give back the jewel. I hoped that the act of stunning me had also bothered him and influenced his decision to stop being a thief.

"My books," Granston was saying, "also hit the best-seller lists, and not just because they have great sex scenes, although if I do say so, the way I describe sex would send any species into terminal orga . . ."

I was not listening with the conscious aspect of my mind. I was thinking about Elson, who had oozed sex appeal, an expression I have always liked although it is probably not used in great literature. Dear Elson. What would it have been like to open my body to him?

Now Kolix was yelling, louder than Granston. "Deefour, tell these police that the Crotonite government will sue them if they don't rescue the crown princess!"

"Bah," Granston said. "My business here is legit. Dee-four, get that across to the Cephs and tell them to let up on the holding beams before I puke."

"Abducting the princess is legitimate business?" asked Naxo.

Granston shrugged. "I was assigned to prove that Crotonites have stolen Seventh Species artifacts from that dome, because if it's true, they'll be hauled before the Galactic Alliance as criminals. I was supposed to take the Crotonite princess, to force Kolix into opening the dome, but when it looked as if Kolix had been eaten by a tree, I figured Vush would know the secret. But she won't give it out."

Vush thrust her fist through the webbing and shook it at him. "I've told you I know only that we think Crotonite explorers may have found our lost royal ruu-logem somewhere in this sector of space centuries ago."

Dee-four said, "Granston, who assigned you to this job?"

"The Terran Federal Bureau of Investigation, of course."

Naxo laughed. "I've never seen so many idiot writers moonlighting as agents. But I don't believe you, Granston. Dee-four and I were never informed by the TFBI that you are one of their employees."

Granston said, "I've been recently hired, by a particular organization uniquely qualified to deal with Crotonites . . ."

Kolix gasped. "You could *not* be working for Smith's!"

"Oh, but I am, Kolix."

"Shut up, both of you," Dee-four said. "I'm calling the Cephallonian police. Please reply, space patrol."

We were granted a view into the immense water-filled control room of a police ship, where two large Cephallonians manipulated the equipment with their stubby four-fingered hands. An even larger Cephallonian faced the visiscreen, and at his side was a much smaller one I recognized as Pleltun.

The largest Cephallonian said, "I am Xuln, Captain of the Cephallonian space police. The writer Pleltun here says he knows you, Locrian."

Pleltun smiled, his face suddenly taking on the good-humored expression of a Terran dolphin. "I am acquainted with the poet Hjeg as well. She has the reputation of being trustworthy. The same cannot be said for the writer Granston. As to the Erthumoi named Arda, I know only that at the Galactic Writers' Society banquet, she was supposed to be Fortizak's new housekeeper."

Xuln opened his pale blue eyes wider. "The famous Erthumoi writer—the real Fortizak?"

"Yes, sir," I said proudly.

"I have always enjoyed his work. Does he really write all the time? Tell him to do a sequel to . . ."

Kolix flapped his wings. "While Fortizak fans are indulging themselves in adulation, we in this ship are vibrating. I wish I had some of Fortizak's books here to throw up on. We're all sick here. Turn down the beams!"

"Very well," Xuln said, gesturing. The images of Granston, Vush, and Kolix seemed to relax.

Xuln turned to us again. "The holding beams will still keep the intruders safely in orbit above our ocean, which is so sacred to us that we do not permit alien vessels to enter the water."

"Then how can we search for the Suffering Ones?" Naxo asked.

"Who?"

When Dee-four explained, the Cephallonians looked startled. So did Granston and Vush.

"We, the dominant species of Cephallonia, eat only plants," Xuln said. "A few small and very stupid herbivorous animals are eaten by slightly larger predatory animals, but that is the way of carnivores, who kill so quickly that the prey does not seem to suffer much. In addition to us, there are no other intelligent creatures in our waters, certainly not any who have been suffering for a long time. The Naxian trees must have made a mistake."

"I don't think so," I said. "Maybe the Suffering Ones are inside that dome."

Xuln said, "The dome has been on Cephallonia since before my species became civilized, and as far as we know, it has never opened. We have explored the outside of the dome many times, finding no visible entrance. A large antennalike device protrudes from the top of the dome and emerges into the air, but we have never discovered its function."

"If it's hollow, that must be the way in," Granston said.

"The device is much too small in diameter to accommodate the body of any member of the Six Species."

Hjeg said, "My small components could enter it."

"Not possible. The top of the device has no opening and looks as if it never did."

"We have only your word for that," Granston said.

"If you wish to confirm Cephallonian findings, you must leave your ship and enter one of our tourist airseabuses. One is coming to pick up those who wish to view the dome."

Granston frowned. "Wait a sec while I speak to my boss, Director Smith."

We could see her face appear in a small screen at

his side. She listened impassively as Granston finished summarizing his exploits in trying to establish Kolix's part in an artifact racket run by Crotonites.

Smith said, "Captain of the Cephallonians—I am sorry we of the TFBI have troubled you, due to Granston's stupid means of trying to persuade Kolix to relinquish the site of his secret hiding place."

"But why did the TFBI believe that the artifacts are in our underwater dome?"

"We did computer analysis of all the possible hiding places for a great number of artifacts, on all the planets and asteroids of the Six Species. This was the only suitable place not already explored."

"I assure you, Director Smith, that the dome is sealed and always has been. This is the truth."

"Yes, Captain, I believe that this is what you believe. However, I respectfully request that my agents be allowed to inspect the outside of the dome thoroughly."

"We Cephallonians wish to aid the Galactic Alliance in the recovery of stolen artifacts," Xuln said, glancing at Pleltun, who nodded. "Our tourist boats will take the outsiders on a careful inspection."

Throughout this dialogue, Kolix had said not a word. He seemed to be watching Smith and Xuln warily. Now he spoke.

"And if there's no way into the dome, will you Cephs remove my princess from the clutches of that brutal Erthumoi and give her back to me?"

"It shall be done."

"Granston," Smith said sharply, "it was stupid of you to assume that the princess would know anything about the stolen artifacts. She is an archaeologist. Kolix would not tell her."

Kolix looked at Smith and said, "Director, I would never do anything to endanger my wife."

A muscle twitched in Smith's jaw. "I am glad to hear that. Perhaps the TFBI has been presumptuous in assuming that you are still a criminal, Kolix."

"I am not."

"I realize, Kolix, that Crotonite looting of artifacts began before you were born. I am even willing to believe that perhaps it was only an accident that you killed Doctor Elson, with the resulting loss of the royal ruulogem."

"Shall we call it a truce, Director?" Kolix asked.

"I am willing. Granston, your job has ended. Smith out."

Her image vanished before I could disagree with her new assumptions, yet I could not say I was certain that Kolix murdered Elson without revealing that the royal ruulogem still existed, and Zak had ordered me not to tell. I felt the ruulogem stowed in the inner pocket of my tunic, and visualized Elson's face as he held it. He'd been so solemn. Was it because he was wondering whether or not he should give it back?

The tourist boat arrived, attaching itself first to the air lock of our ship. Dee-four and Naxo hurried to the air lock, but Hjeg moves slower, so I took a minute to step into Dee-four's cabin to get some privacy. I called Zak and gave him a verbatim account of the new developments.

"It's all over, isn't it, Zak? I doubt if I could now convince Smith that Kolix deliberately killed Elson. We'll all view the dome, Granston will give Vush back to Kolix, and . . ."

Zak interrupted me. "Remember to help the Suffering Ones."

"Of course. I guess I'd better hurry—Hjeg will be at the air lock by now."

"Wait, Arda. If you ever meet Kolix alone again, tell him I said he's got to choose."

"Choose what?"

"He'll know."

I was still thinking about our conversation when I rejoined Hjeg and entered the tourist boat, which was filled with air and manned by Cephallonians in water-filled suits. Then we picked up Granston and Vush.

In spite of the fact that Smith had more or less fired him, Granston looked as arrogant as ever, coming over to sit beside me and place his hand on my thigh.

The princess was subdued and sad until the tourist boat joined air locks with the Crotonite vessel.

"Dearwing!" she cried, embracing Kolix as he emerged from the air lock. "I have missed you so much. I was so worried, and I'm so glad the tree didn't devour you."

"I'm fine, Vush. I missed you, too, and I was terribly worried about you."

"My prince!"

"My princess! I love you. I will always love *you*."

"This is more nauseating than the holding beams," Granston said as the boat headed down to the planet and plunged into the living ocean of Cephallonia.

Chapter 23

In the oceans of Earth and several other Erthumoi planets, humans and robots have built small undersea cities. On Cephallonia, nothing like those cities exists.

Pleltun had joined us and, like the tour guide, was in a water-filled suit, but Captain Xuln had gone off in the Cephallonian patrol ship. Pleltun was trying to help the rather young tour guide who seemed intimidated by the fact that this was the Crotonite royal tour to Cephallonia.

"We have only two buildings," Pleltun said, "the factory under a cliff, and the huge dome no one has ever entered. There are, nevertheless, substitutes for buildings. All our spaceships can go underwater, too, and at any one time, a few are in the ocean for use as schools for our young to learn about the rest of the civilized Galaxy."

I saw several such schools, but I was most impressed by the Cephallonian underwater gardens, which covered the high sea cliffs and plateaus reached by sunlight. Seen close up, the gardens were like a softly waving carpet of muted colors.

"Some of the gardens are for food, some for beauty," said the tour guide timidly.

"It all looks beautiful to me," Vush said politely.

Since the Crotonites seemed to color their possessions as gray as their skin, I wondered if she could actually see the colors of the Cephallonian plants— so different from the prevailing dark green of Earth's seaweed. On Earth's ocean reef, it is the animals who sport myriad colors; in a Cephallonian ocean, it is the plants.

"Crotonis has no oceans," Kolix said, "but we don't need them. There is plenty of colorful beauty for us on land."

I thought he was being tactless, if not deliberately insulting. Vush must have thought so, too, for she took his hand and squeezed it gently. Kolix sat back and closed his eyes as if terribly bored.

If I hadn't been such a noble, virtuous—in the general sense of the term—and hardworking android on a mission of mercy, I'd have kicked him. I thought that I should have pulled aside those fibers for myself and left him in the Naxian tree.

The ruulogem felt heavy in my pocket, and sometimes it seemed as if it were hot and vibrating, but when I imagined this was happening, I'd touch it, and then it was cool and still.

Was it so valuable that Kolix killed in order to keep it? As Vush's husband, he would have had access to it, but if it remained the royal ruulogem, it couldn't be sold for the fabulous price it was worth. Yet who would buy it?

If the ruulogem was a key to something, did Elson know that? Was that why he tried so hard to steal it? Yet he didn't keep it, and Kolix did. Perhaps Kolix knew the secret of the ruulogem, yet he didn't stay on Naxia to try to get it back from the tree. He left to rescue Vush.

My mind was not getting very far on unwinding the problem of all those "yets," so I decided to let it rest.

I leaned back, too, looking out through the plastiglass sides of the tourist boat as it headed for the dome.

"Is that all you Cephs do—eat and swim and sing?" Granston asked the tour guide.

The Cephallonians looked so contented in their clear blue ocean. The young ones played like frolicking dolphins; the older ones conversed, sang together, and browsed in the vegetable gardens. I hated to agree with Granston, but the Cephallonian life seemed almost too placid to me.

The tour guide answered Granston as if he'd been asked the question many times before by tourists. "We Cephallonians live simple lives. We always have, and always will. The Seventh Species gave us space travel, and we enjoy visiting other worlds, but this is our home. As the Erthumoi would say, we have always lived in Eden."

"No serpents in Eden?" Granston asked, causing Naxo's lip to curl up and reveal the Naxian fangs.

"None. There is abundant animal life, most of it small. We have no large predators."

"What's that?" Dee-four pointed to a bulky shape that swam by accompanied by a similar, much smaller one that suckled the other from time to time. They looked familiar to me.

"Those are air-breathing Terran creatures bioengineered to tolerate our ocean water and to eat the weeds that tend to entwine and choke our food plants."

"Manatees," I said. "Harmless and friendly."

"We Cephallonians love and take care of the manatees. Here they will never be in danger of extinction as they are on Earth, where boats hurt them and people eat them."

"None of you Cephs are tempted to have manatee steak?" Granston asked.

The tour guide shuddered. "Never. Although we have discovered the pleasures of cooked food, even cooked animal matter, we do not kill our animals for food. We import Terran cooked delicacies in degradable packets suitable for emptying into our mouths underwater. We use this food only for special treats on special occasions."

Ahead, the dome loomed up, shiny white, many kilometers wide, and higher than it looked because its base was embedded in the floor of a deep canyon. The space between it and the dark blue canyon walls was big enough for the tourist boat to zigzag up and down to show us the entire dome surface.

"If you become hungry while we circumnavigate the dome, we have Erthumoi refreshments for your pleasure. We also imported a supply of Crotonite nutrient capsules for the royal tour which, unfortunately, started off on a hostile note because we had no idea it *was* the royal tour."

"You could not help that," Vush said. "You were expecting ships to follow normal diplomatic procedures when entering your space, as the royal tour should have done. Instead you got a criminal in a strange ship followed by a Crotonite ship, both threatening to violate your ocean. Prince Kolix and I are grateful for your forbearance, and hold no grudge against the honored world of Cephallonia."

It was a gracious speech, coming from an obviously scared little princess huddling next to her husband in a corner of the tourist boat. Yet it was Vush who had her arm around Kolix, as if consoling and protecting him. He was withdrawn, opening his eyes only when Vush gave him a food capsule to replenish his strength.

"The walls are impenetrable!" Dee-four exclaimed

when she briefly pulled back her eyecover to see into the dome.

"Seventh Species mischief," Naxo said. "Let's eat."

Hjeg was plastered against the boat's transparent side, perhaps absorbing energy or enjoying the view. I wanted to tell Hjeg that we were still friends although I could not yet permit her to read the contents of my mind, but Granston occupied my attention, offering me half of his cheese-filled pita bread, which I refused.

"Just as well, Arda. You should preserve that gorgeous and stimulating figure of yours."

At that, Kolix laughed, but no one mentioned why I do not eat. It amused me to let Granston believe I was human.

Pleltun pointed to the dome. "You'll notice that the dome tapers upward, each hundred meters marked off by a narrow band of shinier material, embossed with what is believed to be an example of the unknown language of the Seventh Species. Scholars come from all over the Galaxy to study the marks, but they have never been deciphered."

Hjeg said, "Didn't you have a plausible theory about those marks in your last novel, Pleltun?"

He blinked—Cephs have exotically long eyelashes—and said, "I did. I imagined that the writing on the bands describes the complete history of the Seventh Species, beginning with their origin in another galaxy, and ending with their plans to return to that galaxy."

"I liked that novel," Dee-four said sleepily. "It made sense and was not as watery as the others, Pleltun."

The rest of the tour was repetitious, for no matter how many times the tourist boat zigzagged around the dome, it looked the same.

Granston and Naxo were obviously bored, and occupied themselves in finishing the food and seeing who could muster the strength to lift the biggest case of bottled drinks. Naxo won.

The Crotonites went on eating food capsules, with no ill effects. They talked only to each other, in whispers.

Pleltun, Hjeg, and Dee-four argued about writing. As a would-be writer, I tried to listen in, but gave up when they switched from the idiosyncrasies of editors and publishers to the poetical nuances of their respective native languages.

By the time the boat had circled to the top of the dome, I believed the Cephallonians. The walls of the dome gave no evidence of any doors anywhere.

The antenna at the top was of the same silvery metal as the decorative bands on the dome. It was no bigger around than my wrist, much too small for anything but a Samian mobile component to squeeze inside, and that was impossible because there wasn't even a crack to permit entry. The seamless metal of the antenna extended around its tip, which protruded only twenty centimeters above the surface of the water.

"Maybe it's a broadcasting antenna," I said to the tour guide. "If a living creature is inside the dome, then perhaps it broadcasts a distress message through the antenna."

"I suppose that is possible, but our ships have never picked up any such message, or any electrical transmission of any sort from the antenna."

The ships would not, if the message were telepathic. I decided the antenna did somehow transmit a telepathic distress call from the Suffering Ones to the Naxian trees, and I wanted to tell Zak about it.

"Is there a private space aboard this vessel?" I asked.

"Only the control room, where visitors are not allowed. Oh, and the toilet facilities for aliens like yourself."

The tour guide also did not know that I am an android, in no need of toilets. But perhaps my hair needed combing. I rose and found the toilet room, which was only large enough to accommodate with comfort an average Erthumoi or a small Locrian.

My hair was hanging in disarray. I had not even combed it since my Naxian escapade. I was ashamed, thinking that perhaps everyone believed me to be an Erthumoi of the messy type. In Dee-four's ship I had wiped off some of the fluid from Kolix and the lubrication that my genitals apparently secrete when sufficiently stimulated. I had not examined myself in a mirror because there was none. Locrians do not use them.

I combed my hair and straightened my tunic, thinking of how Vush always kept her foot claws polished and her Crotonite clothes neat. It shouldn't have mattered to me. I didn't care what her husband thought of the messy Erthumoi he'd used to straighten out his blasted lower brain—did I? Her blasted husband was a selfish, thieving murderer and I didn't like him. . . .

Zak had said you didn't have to like someone to pity them. But what was there to pity about Kolix? He had what he wanted—the position of crown prince and being married to a female who adored him. He'd escaped imprisonment and death, thanks to me, and soon the difficult royal tour would be over and he could go home—never facing judgment for his murder of Elson or his theft of the ruulogem, the only thing he'd wanted that he did not now possess. I had no pity for him.

I studied my face in the tourist boat's mirror. Even Zak, on first seeing me, had said I was good looking. I was not sure what that meant. Did it mean beautiful, or pretty, or that I looked like a good Erthumoi?

If my particular face had been put on a different android, activated not in Manhattan but in a farm colony on some distant Erthumoi planet, what would that android have been like? How would the face have correlated with the android's experiences, the ongoing activity of her cognitive and emotive circuits?

There was no answer except that any other android would have been different, even with my face. This made me decide that what I looked like was not as important as what happened to me, what I thought and felt and, above all, what I did.

"Arda!"

I opened the door. Dee-four stood outside.

"What do you need this place for?"

"My hair."

"Well, it looks fine now, and I've got to use the facilities, worse luck. Barely enough room to squeeze my tush onto that device."

"Your *what*?"

"I learned the word from Fortizak. When speaking in Galactic Basic, that word is a lot shorter than the Locrian word for my other end."

I had not called Zak, but I left the toilet room and sat down near the tour guide, who seemed tired. Perhaps wearing those water-filled suits was exhausting after a while, especially when one had no legs.

"Pardon me," I said to the tour guide, "but I've just noticed that your suit has short legs. How do you manage . . . ?"

"To grow legs?" The young Cephallonian looked amused. "We don't. We are able to manipulate micromotors that work the suit's artificial legs. It was once thought that wheeled suits would be easier, but wheels don't go as many places as legs."

"That's right, Arda," Pleltun called over. "We Cephallonians have the best of both worlds, air and water."

Kolix lifted his upper lip, showing his pointed teeth in a decided sneer. He was very good at sneers.

"None of you Cephallonians, in fact no one from any of the other Six Species, knows what the best is. You have no wings."

"You Crots can't swim," Granston said. "With an aqualung I can go anywhere the Cephs can go, and with a power pack I can fly just like you Crots."

"Erthumoi flight by individual power pack is a travesty of real flight," Kolix said. "You will never know the joy of genuine flight, the air currents lifting your wings, the soaring and turning and . . ."

"Mating on the wing," Vush said happily. Kolix kissed her.

"Are there any packets of chocolate cake left?" Naxo asked plaintively, but I thought that for once Naxo was tuning into the prevailing emotional currents and was deliberately changing the subject to keep Granston from further argument.

It was useless. Granston said, "Terran mammalian sex is the only sex worth mentioning."

"Granston, you have no idea . . ." Kolix began.

I went over to the Crotonites and said softly, "Don't argue with Granston. He's not worth it." I still don't know why I said that, unless it was because I was feeling sorry for Vush.

She stroked Kolix's hand and said, "I'll be so glad when this tour is over and we can go home."

"I feel the same way, dearwing."

I chose that moment to do as ordered. "Kolix—my boss, Fortizak, wanted me to tell you something."

"Go ahead."

"He says to tell you that you must choose."

Kolix's gray face went almost white. "Did he explain what he meant by that?"

"He said you would know."

Vush frowned. "Is something wrong, dearwing? What has the writer Fortizak's remark done?"

Kolix relaxed, his color returning to normal. "Writer. Of course. I do know what he means. I must choose between my former writing career and being an archaeologist. I am going to study archaeology and help you, Vush. No more fiction writing for me. I was tired of it, anyway."

I thought Kolix's words applied equally well to his career as a criminal, but as yet I had no proof that he had been involved in the theft of artifacts. I was determined to get that proof and show it to Zak.

But Zak had told me to ignore the Crotonites and concentrate on finding the Suffering Ones. I had to help them. I had to get the ruulogem to them. But how?

Once more it felt like a fire in my pocket. I left the Crotonites and sat on a bench at the other side of the tourist boat. Surely the sensation that seemed to come from the ruulogem was purely my own emotive reaction to thinking about it. The gem was again cool when I touched it to make sure.

"Got an itch inside that tunic, Arda?" Granston said, coming over to sit beside me. "Want me to help scratch?"

"No, thank you." His hand plunked down on my thigh and I removed it and tried to edge away from Granston.

"That antenna is so intriguing," I said to Pleltun.

"Are you sure there are no other intelligent creatures on the planet?"

Pleltun answered angrily. "Can't you believe that we are the only intelligent natives of our planet? All this talk about Suffering Ones living on Cephallonia is insulting to our species. We would never allow any other intelligent creature to suffer, wherever they were."

"If you've never been inside the dome you couldn't know if there were intelligent, suffering creatures inside it."

Pleltun and the tour guide looked at each other. Pleltun said, "You can ask any of us. We know nothing of what is inside the dome. It is impossible for scanners to penetrate it."

"You're just scared to break into the dome," Granston said.

"Even if such an act were possible—and according to Erthumoi engineers who have tested the surface, the dome cannot be cut by known methods—we Cephallonians would never desecrate the largest artifact left by the Seventh Species."

Kolix stirred uneasily. "The tour's over. We've been round the dome, and there's no way in. Are you convinced, Granston?"

"I suppose so."

"Then inform your Director Smith that the rumors the TFBI heard are untrue. Crotonite ships have not come to Cephallonia to take away illegally obtained Seventh Species artifacts." Kolix said this loudly and precisely, as if that would help persuade Granston, or perhaps convince me.

"Just because the sealed dome confirms the Cephallonians' statements doesn't mean you Crots haven't been stealing artifacts from other planets."

Vush rose, rustling her wings. "I am tired of being

insulted by that Erthumoi who thinks he's a secret agent."

"He even thinks he can write novels," Kolix said. "We will go home to our own planet now, dearwing. I have called for our ship to meet us. We thank the Cephallonians for this tour, but please take this boat out of the ocean so we can transfer to our ship and leave." He then whispered into his communicator.

The boat lifted into orbit, the Crotonite ship joined air locks, and the Crotonite captain came board the Cephallonian boat to deliver my suitcase to me.

Kolix said, "Arda, it is not necessary for you to journey with us anymore. We are going home to Crotonis, where we will be safe and do not need a bodyguard. We will transfer funds to Smith's Agency for your services."

He propelled Vush through the air lock and the Crotonites disappeared into their own ship, which immediately lifted above the atmosphere and vanished, along with my job.

Chapter 24

The Crotonites no longer needed me, but I still had the task of finding the Suffering Ones. I was not accomplishing it, and said so.

Dee-four tilted her head to one side. "There's something wrong. There's no communication coming from that antenna and no way into the dome. Perhaps there is Seventh Species equipment inside the dome, but it doesn't seem likely that any living creatures could have existed there for the millennia that the dome has been on Cephallonia."

"I agree with you, Dee-four," Hjeg said. "Arda, is it possible that you could have misinterpreted the mental picture given you by the Naxian trees?"

"I don't know—for certain, that is," I said.

Naxo yawned and uncoiled. "We had to come to Cephallonia anyway, for the royal tour, but if Arda's not certain about the Suffering Ones, let's not stick around here. Dee and I should be working on our tour story for *Spacelog*."

"Which will be rather skimpy on Cephallonia," Dee-four said severely. "Naxo, you concentrated on food as usual. Did you use your camera at all?"

"A couple of times, but you can show only so much of underwater life here without sending readers into terminal boredom, unless they want to study the Seventh Species language on the dome bands."

"Possible," Dee-four said. "Since no one's ever deciphered the language, we could feature photographs of the bands and turn the whole article into a sort of mystery story."

"Good. Let's ask *Spacelog* for more money," Naxo said. "I now suggest that we return to my planet and find out if the trees can explain the whole thing better to Arda."

"No," I said, "the mystery is here, on Cephallonia. We must continue the search."

"Would someone explain the mystery to me?" Granston asked. "I don't understand what you're talking about. Let me in on the plot. After all, it's so hard to make a living as a writer that I just took on that moonlighting job because the TFBI pays well. I don't much like Smith's, or Smith. I think she disapproves of me, the old prude."

When Dee-four told Granston about the message of the Naxian trees, he said, "Quite a mystery. Where are the Suffering Ones? Have you considered the possibility that there are no Suffering Ones, that the whole thing is a figment of Arda's imagination brought on by being held prisoner inside a tree? In the company of a villainous Crotonite?"

"Arda, do you have an imagination?" Naxo asked. "I mean, does any an . . ."

Hjeg interrupted him in time. She must have surmised that I had not told Granston I was an android. "Arda has plenty of imagination. She is creative, and hopes to become a writer."

"Good God, another competitor," Granston said. Then he leaned toward me and added, "But I'll be happy to instruct you in the finer points of creating great literature."

"Like yours?" Dee-four said. "The style of slam-bang-shoot-'em-up until the body count is high? Don't listen to a word Granston has to say about writing, Arda."

"I won't. Listen, everybody, I still think the Suffering Ones may be here on Cephallonia, and Zak ordered me to find them."

"You must be wrong, Arda," Naxo said. "Let's go ask the Naxian trees for clarification."

"Makes sense to me," Granston said. "If Arda wasn't hallucinating when she thought the trees talked to her, then she must have got it wrong. The trees must have meant some other planet, and I can help find it. My ship is on loan from the TFBI, and has complete records of every known planet in the Galaxy. Let's split up—Arda will come with me, and the rest of you follow me as we investigate likely planets."

Before I could object, Hjeg said, "I don't think that's a good idea, Granston. The best plan is Naxo's—to return to the Naxian trees for more information."

"Let's go back to Locria first," Dee-four said. "We have better records of where Seventh Species artifacts are found. If the Suffering Ones are the Seventh Species themselves, it will be easier to trace them through the artifacts. We could even take some of the artifacts to Naxia to show to the trees."

"That's crazy," Granston said. "The TFBI computer . . ."

"But the blasted trees are on *my* planet!" yelled Naxo.

They went on arguing about it while the tourist boat waited for them to make up their minds.

I remained silent, although I was still convinced that the Suffering Ones were on Cephallonia, and the only place they could be was inside the dome. We'd already seen the antenna through the plastiglass sides of the tourist boat, but I wanted to touch it. I thought that if I were in the open air, perhaps the ruulogem in my pocket would vibrate. It was supposed to be a key— to what?

Yet I could not reveal that I had the ruulogem. True, the Crotonites had left, so Kolix would not know that the tree gave it to me, but Zak had said to keep it a secret. I said nothing.

The others finally agreed to return to Naxia and ask the trees where the Suffering Ones could be.

"Since we've decided to return to my planet," Naxo said. "Let's go before we waste any more time."

"Please come with me, Arda," Granston said. "It's time you and I got to know each other better."

"Make up your minds," said Pleltun, after conferring with the tour guide. "This boat must return to the ocean for an evening class in which our children practice donning space suits and walking."

"Okay, we'll go," Cranston said, rummaging around in the basket which had held packets of cheese wafers. He found one left, took his time opening it, popped it in his mouth, and chewed methodically.

The tour guide, obviously exasperated, signaled the control room of the tourist boat, which lifted from the ocean of Cephallonia and started toward the orbiting ships.

"Come on with me, Arda," Granston said.

"I prefer the company of my friends."

"I'll be a good friend. One might almost say a great and good friend, my beauty."

The tourist boat joined air locks with Dee-four's ship. Naxo slithered over to me, extruded a hand and took my arm. "Coming, Arda? We are much better company than Granston."

"What are you after, Naxo?" Granston asked. "The Erthumoi government is trying to get the Galactic Alliance to ban cross-species sex."

"Arda and I are friends. Aren't we, Arda?"

"Yes, Naxo, but I want to examine the dome again."

"We've got to talk to the trees on my planet."

Suddenly the tourist boat's hycom screen lit up and Captain Xuln's face appeared.

"Don't leave the boat yet," he said. "An urgent message is coming through from Crotonis."

His face was replaced by that of Princess Vush. She had been crying.

"Kolix is missing! Abducted!"

"Wait a minute, Princess," Dee-four said, "tell us exactly what happened."

Vush sniffed and dabbed at her cheeks with a gray handkerchief. "We just got home, only a few minutes ago. Kolix insisted on racing through the gravity well of Crotonis and then said he had to be alone for a while. He told me to wait for him in the palace, and before I could stop him he flew out the air lock, heading for the cave where he lived as a bachelor."

"Cave? You Crots live in caves?"

"All of them but the royal family, Granston," Dee-four said. "The elegant cliff caves of Crotonis are famous."

"Hey, Princess, are you upset because you think Kolix has another female, stashed away in his old home?" Naxo asked.

"Certainly not. That is—I may have wondered why he left so quickly, as if the matter he had to attend to was urgent. I can't believe it was another female. I know it wasn't—for I followed him."

"Then you must know where he is," Hjeg said.

"No, I don't. Kolix's cave is large, with an outside

terrace where his private hyperdrive yacht is kept. Although the cave has many rooms and halls, there's only one entrance. I was far behind him, but I saw him enter the cave. I waited a few minutes and then I went inside, too. But he wasn't there!"

Dee-four's voice was as soothing as possible. "You must have been so anxious that you could not have found every room in the cave. I've read that the caves of wealthy Crotonites have many halls and rooms."

"I know," Vush said tearfully. "They do. But I am quite sure that I searched each room. I went back out, thinking that while I was in the back rooms Kolix had gone past in the hall and gone out the front door. But when I went out to the terrace, his private ship was still there. I called the palace and he had not gone to it."

"Simple," Naxo said. "He's gone for a good slug of whatever you Crotonites drink when you've had a rough day. After all, he'd been captured and stripped by a tree and his wife abducted. Maybe he's just drinking himself into oblivion somewhere."

"Kolix does not drink. Besides, the Crotonite main computer system says he is not on the planet."

Dee-four's angular head jutted out. "That's impossible."

Vush sobbed. "It is possible—if Kolix were dead. The computer system keeps track only of living forms. I am now certain that one of Kolix's former business partners—I do not know who they are—has waylaid him here on Crotonis, killed him, and hidden the body."

We were all silent, for her reasoning seemed plausible, especially to me, since I was convinced of Kolix's criminality.

"Why would anyone want to kill Kolix?" Naxo asked naively.

Vush sobbed again. "Kolix doesn't know that before they were willing to agree to my marriage, my parents investigated his family. Kolix's parents and grandparents became wealthy, but no one knows exactly how they did this. My parents believe that some of the wealth may have come from illegal activities, all too prominent in Crotonite life. But I persuaded them to let me marry Kolix because he is so handsome, and so interested in my own field of archaeology."

"Yeah, selling archaeological riches," Granston said.

"No, no. Kolix promised me that he would honor the ethics of a true archaeologist."

"If Kolix is dead somewhere on Crotonis," Dee-four said, "shouldn't the Crotonite police handle this?"

Vush said, "If I ask anyone at the palace to help me find Kolix, my parents will know and be upset. You must help me."

"What can we do, Princess?" asked Naxo, flexing his coils.

"Your ships have scanners—you'll pick up traces of his presence, and find his body. If you can't, that means he's left Crotonis in a ship I know nothing about. If so, your ships will be able to track him."

"Well, I guess we could do that," Dee-four said.

"I'm sure my dearwing is either dead or in mortal danger, as he has been ever since that awful banquet at the Galactic Writers' Society. Please help."

"Certainly," said Dee-four. "Come on, Hjeg, Naxo. You coming with us, Arda?"

"No. I'll go with Granston." Zak had said to find the Suffering Ones before becoming more involved with the Crotonites, and that was what I intended to persuade Granston to help me do. Besides, I'd already rescued Kolix once, and he'd fired me.

"Good. Best that you travel with me," Granston said. "I don't trust that Kolix, and I can protect you."

Naxo, Dee-four, and Hjeg went into the air lock, and I waved good-bye to them.

Once in his ship, Granston ushered me to his cabin. "You just freshen up, honey, and I'll be right back."

I put my suitcases in a corner, and on one of those impulses that roboticists call burgeoning robotic intuition, I opened it and put on a clean, prettier tunic.

I also found Zak's gift, and read again what he'd written on the package—"For Arda, when she is thoroughly discouraged."

Had I hit that point yet?

Granston would be back soon, presumably after he freshened up. He seemed terribly intrusive, so I didn't want to share anything personal with him. I did not open the gift or call Zak.

On another odd impulse, I put Zak's gift into a plastipak and stuffed it into the inner pocket of my tunic, along with my communicator and the ruulogem.

I could hear Granston's footsteps coming to the door, so I quickly opened it, walked past him, and said, "I want to try again to get into the dome. I've been assigned to help the Suffering Ones, and that's where they must be."

"Nonsense, honey. They're on Crotonis, trapping Kolix, who's probably been stealing their artifacts."

"Granston, are you saying that the Suffering Ones are members of the Seventh Species, hidden on Crotonis?"

"Why not? I've set my ship's control on automatic, headed for Crotonis. While my colleagues Dee-four, Hjeg, and that hulk of a Naxian are trying to rescue that bastard Kolix, you and I will find the artifacts. In the meantime, we have enough time for a little fun."

He grabbed my waist, drew me close, and kissed me hard.

I tried to squirm away without revealing that I was much stronger than he. "Please, Granston. We can't have sex. We have a task to perform."

"This is the only task I feel like performing at the moment." He swarmed over me, whispering, "Lovely Arda—just what I need after such a nonrewarding day."

I resisted; he persisted.

"Come on, Arda!" he yelled, his sweat smearing against me as he grappled and groped, "Take off that damn tunic. I want to wine and dine on your body, not be almost castrated by whatever the hell you've got in your pockets."

We were in the ship's control room, but the visiscreen wasn't on, so I didn't know where we were. "Have we left Cephallonia?"

"We will as soon as you and I have made fantastic love."

"Granston, I will consider your proposal immediately after I've looked at the dome again. Please take your ship down."

He stared at me. "You're crazy, but what the hell, anything to satisfy a lady, and believe me, I know how to satisfy."

He turned on the visiscreen and I watched the ship move lower until it stopped when the antenna was still many meters below. "Don't want you to decide to go for a swim instead of playing with me, Arda."

The air lock was at the side of the control room. I went into it, opened the outer door and leaned out, touching the ruulogem in the hope that I might hear sounds from the antenna below me. I could only hear

Granston's breathing and the soft stirring of the ocean's waves.

"There's nothing of interest down there, girl. You've been on a wild-goose chase."

I was about to tell him I had no interest in wild geese when I remembered that this was another human metaphor. "I suppose you are right, Granston. We should move on to Crotonis."

As I said this, the ruulogem suddenly seemed hot again. "Sorry, Granston. I was wrong. We can't leave Cephallonia. The Suffering Ones are here."

He grunted. "Now I know you're crazy. I'm the one that's suffering. I need to put out my fire in your body."

He pulled me into the control room and kissed me hard enough to bruise an organic Erthumoi as he also fondled lower portions of my anatomy with ungentle hands.

I wanted to render him unconscious with a tap on his skull but had no excuse because he was not endangering my life, just making it unpleasant and keeping me from doing my job. Not knowing how to handle the situation, I did not struggle when he insisted on taking my possessions out of my tunic pocket.

First he found my communicator and asked if I had it tuned to Zak's frequency.

"He is my employer. I am to report to him daily."

"Lovers?"

"Certainly not."

"You can use the communicator later to report on how great sex is with me, but now it's in my way." He tossed the communicator in back of him and took out Zak's gift.

He guffawed at Zak's message. "Thoroughly discouraged? You can't be, when you're with me."

He dropped Zak's package on the floor, thrust his

hand into my tunic pocket once more, and found the ruulogem.

"Now what's this pretty thing? It's as big as the ruulogem the Crots lost. It must be an imitation. Is it?"

"I don't . . ."

"You couldn't afford to buy it if it were real." He turned it over and over, the gem scintillating as no imitation could do.

"Please return it, Granston. It's a present, given to me."

"Oh? Which lover bestowed an imitation ruulogem on you?"

"No lover. The stone is a key of some sort. The Naxian trees gave it to me so I could use it to help find the Suffering Ones. Let me find them, Granston."

"Key? That's a laugh. Now I know you're either inventing the whole story to conceal the fact that you've stolen this from somewhere, or you were definitely hallucinating on Naxia."

"Please, Granston—I need it!"

He put the ruulogem into his pants pocket, where it added to the bulge already in his pants. "My beauty, you'll get your bauble back only after you lend me your lovely body." He opened his fly to show his erection.

I could not cope politely any longer. "Granston, have you discerned any beating of my heart?"

"Arda, my hard-to-get sweet, the hearts of all girls beat faster around me."

I pulled his head down to my bosom and said, "Listen, Granston. You won't hear a heartbeat because I have no heart. I'm not human. I am an android."

Granston lifted his head so quickly that he hit my chin, which hurt him, not me. His square jaw had dropped like a lift that's lost its antigrav.

"But you must be human. You look so very human, and Fortizak always has human housekeepers."

"He had no choice but to hire an android to help him with the Galactic Writers' Society banquet. You can check with Smith's Employment Agency."

"By God, you're one of those humanoid robots taking jobs from real people, pretending to be what you aren't, and all the while you are an abomination!" Veins stood out on his red forehead, getting so much redder that I worried about his circulatory system.

"I'm sorry, Granston. I can't help being an android. Let me find the Suffering Ones. Please return the ruulogem."

"No. I'm keeping it."

"I'm very sorry, but I must have it." I seized both his arms in one hand and held him until I could remove the ruulogem from his pocket. During this procedure he was swearing unusually biological oaths.

I released Granston, picked up Zak's present, and added it to the ruulogem, now back in my tunic pocket. I was about to retrieve my communicator but Granston stood in the way, and now he had a gun in his hand.

"The last time I shot you, Arda, I had the setting only high enough to knock out a human, but I've reset it to fry an android's brain. Give me the ruulogem or I'll shoot."

I stepped into the air lock again. "Granston, be reasonable. It would be murder . . ."

"I don't care what the law says about filthy androids. Nobody will prosecute me for killing you when I say that you went berserk and tried to kill me, so I had to defend myself."

"Naxo will sense your emotions and know you are lying."

"Naxians aren't allowed in Terran courts."

"I need the ruulogem, Granston. The Naxian trees say it's the key to saving the Suffering Ones."

He waved the gun at me. "I don't care about alien creatures. Give me that gem and you can stay locked in my cabin until we get to Crotonis, where I'm going to get the artifacts Kolix has been hiding. When I'm finished, I'll return you to Smith's without insisting that you're a defective robot, which you probably are. Give it to me or I shoot."

I moved to the outer rim of the air lock. "If you shoot, I'll fall into the ocean with the gem."

He touched a panel in the control room and the ship abruptly tilted, tossing me to the floor of the airlock.

"Arda, stay right there. I'm going to close the inner door of the air lock and take the ship out of normal space. I've read that hyperspatial fields are lethal to positronic brains, so it will seem as if you've had an unfortunate accident. I'll retrieve the ruulogem after you've deactivated."

"I'm a living, sentient being, Granston. Don't kill me."

"You're not alive. I want you dead. No one must ever know that I tried to fuck an unholy machine."

What happened next is difficult to write. Difficult, that is, for an android imbued with the laws of robotics. Yet I had to protect my own existence, according to the third law. The problem was in avoiding conflict with laws one and two.

I threw the ruulogem at him, not as hard as an android can throw because then he would have died. I aimed precisely. The ruulogem landed exactly where I aimed it, on his right testicle, which hung down slightly lower than the left.

I may have violated the first law somewhat, but I had tried to avoid permanent harm to Granston, who was by now doubled up and groaning in pain. I retrieved the ruulogem and my communicator, and put them in my pocket along with Zak's present.

I did not take the gun. I was having enough trouble with the laws of robotics.

"You manufactured bitch," Granston muttered, trying to stand upright and move toward me. "I'll have you sent to the factory and taken apart."

I went back into the air lock and jumped out.

Chapter 25

Before the blue ocean of Cephallonia closed over my head, I saw Granston's ship leave the atmosphere, so he must have recovered from my attack. I was relieved, but as I sank I felt it necessary to sort out the problems affecting both my cognitive and emotive circuits.

How could I be a combination bodyguard-detective when those I was supposed to guard tried to kill me, used me sexually, abandoned me, and then fired me?

How could I think clearly (I was clear on the fact that I was not thinking clearly) when I had to overcome all the prohibitions against hurting a human?

This was particularly problematical because while said human had attempted to kill me, to say nothing of reviling me because he despised robots, he was nevertheless a genuine human.

But my life had been in danger, had it not?

No, not if I'd agreed to give up the gem right away.

Yet giving it to Granston would have—well, might have—endangered the Suffering Ones.

I didn't even know who the Suffering Ones were. They probably were not human. Perhaps it was too vague a reason for hurting a bona fide human.

As these thoughts assailed me, I discovered another problem: androids are waterproof, but we do not float.

Perhaps Zak would say that this list of grievances

does not add to the narrative momentum, but I want to show the state of mind I was in by the time I hit the bottom of the canyon and began thinking with greater clarity.

While cursing myself for not escaping with a power pack, my memory banks disgorged the fact that all robots, including androids, can swim, which helps if you've been designed without flotation factors.

I swam up the side of the dome in solitude, for no Cephallonians came by—free-swimming or in boats. The water was clear and cool, the dome as enigmatic as ever.

As I neared the top of the dome, my back was poked.

I turned around to see two manatees nuzzling me. They explored me from top to bottom and seemed disappointed when I had no food to offer them, so I stroked their heads. This was a mistake, for they were delighted and would not go away.

The huge dome tapered sharply near the surface. When I swam over to the highest point to hold onto the antenna, I discovered that when I stood up on the slippery top, my upper half was out of the water, the small waves lapping at my waist.

From above the surface, I looked through the water at the dome top, which curved markedly down to the first embossed band of metal. Starting at this first band, the dome's curvature was much less, so that it sloped gradually all the way out to the widest perimeter of the building. From there the walls went straight down to the canyon bottom.

With manatees begging for attention, I examined the antenna but saw nothing of use. After a while the manatees grew bored and swam off to a floating web of vegetation, presumably their lunch.

I very much wanted to confer with Zak, but when I

tried the communicator it was waterlogged and would not work. Not every Erthumoi device is as well made as an android.

Next I brought out Zak's gift, wondering if water had seeped into the package. When I unwrapped it, I saw that it didn't matter, because the gift was a small plaque bearing a note from Zak, completely sealed in transparent plastic. I read the words on the note.

"Dear Arda,

Here's my advice on how to stay sane in spite of being intelligent, self-aware, and ultimately mortal:

Cope with the uncertainty of the universe with courage and by remembering that you are not alone, but are part of the universe, connected to all the other parts, some of which may need your help. Don't forget to accept yourself and to be mindful of what is.

Good luck—Zak"

I did not feel alone, not with manatees near and with Cephallonians and tourist boats that would eventually pass by.

What I did feel, in spite of Zak's words, was unconnected. I was the only android on the entire planet. Being part of the universe was no comfort when I now knew for certain that I was mortal, that prejudice against androids could be lethal, and that whoever needed help was not getting any from me.

Ruulogems were supposed to promote higher thought, so I took it out and held it close to my eyes. It was even shinier because it was wet. I stared at it for five minutes with no discernible increase in cogni-

tion, yet I did experience a strange calming effect and
the words "what is" came back from Zak's note.

What is? Did that mean the reality of the moment?

I looked around me. Present reality seemed to con-
sist of the ocean, the dome, the antenna, myself, the
ruulogem in my hand . . . the ruulogem. It had dimensions that would fit inside the cuplike top of the antenna. I placed it there.

Under my feet the dome top suddenly vibrated. As I
held onto the antenna to keep my balance, it seemed
as if the first of the embossed shiny bands of the dome
were sinking, until I realized that it was the sharply
curved section of the top moving up, gaining in height
and flattening out as it went.

Soon I was out of the water, standing on a flat surface. I was still holding onto the antenna where the
royal ruulogem of Crotonis sparkled in the sunlight.

Motion stopped. I waited, but the dome and its antenna were as mysterious as ever.

"Erthumoi! You are under arrest for desecrating
our dome!"

Over my head hovered a water-filled Cephallonian
patrol boat. The police could not come out to get me,
but the boat was equipped with formidable guns.

"I haven't desecrated your dome," I shouted. "It rose
all by itself." That was not strictly true, for the ruulogem had set it into motion, but I had not known that
would happen.

A grappling hook reached toward me from the patrol boat.

"You will be placed in an air-filled detention cell and
questioned about your activities, Erthumoi. Do not
resist."

I gave up. I had no means of leaving the planet
anyway. There was even a chance that I could explain

my actions satisfactorily to whatever government the Cephs had.

I yelled to them. "Don't worry about finding me an air-filled cell because I'm an android. Just take me aboard your boat and I'll answer all your questions. I willingly surrender to Cephallonian authority."

As I reached this defeatist peroration, I remembered the ruulogem I'd put in the antenna cup. I plucked it out and instantly the floor beneath me vanished. As I fell through the dome top, I looked up in time to see it closing up again over my head. I was sealed off from pursuit by the Cephallonian police.

I fell only a short distance, landing undamaged on something soft. Looking around, I saw that I was lying in a shallow round depression lined with soft, billowy cushionlike material.

I sat up so I could look over the rim of the depression. Surrounding my cushioned cup of a seat was a wide metal platform embedded with crisscrossed shiny wires. On the left-hand curve of the metal platform was a gigantic stasis box. It was one of the transparent kinds sold throughout the Galactic Alliance for storage of large perishable items, and it was over half full of what looked like large semicircular green mats.

Beyond the metal platform was a linked series of curved metal boats that resembled odd canoes fitting together because the intended bow of one fit around the pointed stern of the canoe in front. They formed a chain of small boats resting in cradles jutting from the metal platform.

I got into one of the canoes and peered over the edge. If I'd been Fortizak, I'd have had an acute attack of acrophobia, for there was nothing between my head and the ground far below except air. The only connection to the distant bottom of the dome was a thick metal pole upon which the central cushioned seat rested.

Studying the situation, with automatic analysis of the exact distances involved, made it clear to me that I would be unable to reach the pole unless I climbed over the side of the boat, swung on its bottom to the underside of the metal platform, and made my way thence to the pole.

Unfortunately there were no handholds beneath the canoes or the platform, and the pole itself looked exceptionally smooth and slick. The logical conclusion was that getting off my perch by sliding down the pole was not only inadvisable but extremely unlikely to be possible.

With a power pack I might have reached the bottom intact, but I did not have one, and anyway my expertise in flying with one was admittedly poor. I seemed to be stuck on this strange high perch inside the Cephallonian dome.

I sat back in the canoe and contemplated the rest of the dome. From top to bottom, except for the open space around and under my perch, the inside of the dome was a terraced garden. I say garden because it had obviously been planted, although there seemed to be only one type of vegetation.

I thought of the plants as trees although they did not resemble any Terran or Naxian tree I'd seen. They had thick, short, dark blue trunks sprouting long fern-shaped bright blue foliage spattered with gold along each frond. Trees in the far distance looked like blue fog ornamented with gold sparkles.

Where the terraces ended at the central open space, they joined a ramp that connected each layer. The ramp spiraled all the way down to the bottom of the dome. I wanted to inspect the trees, but I had no way of getting across the space to the top ramp unless I found out how to work the canoes, which I assumed were small antigrav boats.

While examining the control panel of the boat I was in, I heard a noise from over in the terraces. It was the sound of wings, like an immense bird in flight.

Huddling down inside the boat, I waited as the sound came closer. Then, from the broad space between the lines of trees, Kolix flew out into the open and crossed to land on the metal platform next to the stasis box.

Fortunately my canoe was not close to the stasis box, and Kolix had landed facing the box, not me. He walked up to the box, opened it, and took out an armful of green mats. They must have been heavy because he staggered a little under their weight. He put them down on the metal platform so he could close the box.

I almost called out to him, but I was afraid. I'm not sure why. Detectives—and is not an investigator just that?—are supposed to be cautious and observant. I waited and watched.

Kolix picked up the mats again and opened his wings. I saw that he was wearing two power packs, but he still seemed to be having trouble getting airborne. Finally he took off and flew the mats back to the trees. He was soon out of sight among the trees at the distant perimeter of the dome.

I realized that for a Crotonite, the atmosphere inside the Cephallonian dome would be too thin. He was not wearing a breather, and it must have been difficult for him to breathe easily, much less fly.

There were still many mats in the stasis box. He would be back. I had time to study the situation some more. It was then that I noticed how the foliage of many tree-ferns was faded, limp, and disorganized. The fronds of healthy trees were not only firm but curved into a neat upward semicircle. The only difference between the two kinds was that the base of each healthy tree was encircled by green mats.

I could not be certain unless I went over to examine them, but the arclike arrangement of branches in the healthy trees appeared to be enclosing objects suspended in air.

I waited until Kolix returned. I was about to speak to him when the ruulogem in my pocket began to throb. As I reached in to hold it, the fronds of the healthy trees started quivering in time with the ruulogem.

Kolix paled and faced the vibrating trees. Soon their vibration turned into singing, soft and full of words. I could not understand the words any more than I'd understood those of the Naxian trees, but the meaning of the song filled my brain. The trees were singing of hope.

The singing was not a telepathic message given only to me, and it was not my hallucination, for Kolix heard it, too.

"Be patient!" he shouted into the vast inner space of the dome. "I am doing my best, as fast as possible."

The singing grew louder, more joyous. It seemed to me that Kolix did not know it was about hope. I held the ruulogem, and that somehow made the meaning of the song clear to me, but to Kolix, it must have been frightening.

"Trees of Cephallonia!" Kolix cried, "I cannot help what has happened in the past, but I promise you it is over. I am atoning, even if I will probably be killed for it."

The music rose to a climax and ended, although a faint, happy noise continued as if the trees were vibrating with pleasure. Kolix wiped his high, peaked fore-head and returned to his work.

I stood up. "Why will you be killed, Kolix?"

The load of mats he had picked up dropped from his arms and he turned to face me. For a moment I was afraid, too, wondering if he had a gun with him.

He just stood there staring at me, his wings limp.

"Kolix, why will you be killed for what you're doing?"

He blinked and swallowed. "Hello, Arda."

"Hello yourself."

"I suppose you and the others—but I don't see them. Where are Dee-four, Naxo, Hjeg, and that idiot, Granston? Who worked the control panel?"

"I'm the only one here, Kolix. The others must be helping Vush look for you."

Kolix abruptly sat down, his head in his hands.

"Kolix? Are you all right? We got a message from Vush that you'd gone to your cave. She followed you, but when she couldn't find you, she was afraid you'd been killed. Everyone went to Crotonis."

"Then you did find the control panel. Why didn't the others come with you? Why didn't Vush come?"

"What control panel are you talking about? I haven't yet been able to figure out how to use the one in this canoe."

"Not the boat! Didn't you come from Crotonis. . . ?" He stopped. "No, you didn't. I thought it was an earth-quake, but it must have been the dome opening. How did you do that without letting water in?"

I was reluctant to show him the now quiescent ruu-logem concealed in my fist. I said, "I never left for Crotonis with the others, and . . ."

"Why not?"

"The others thought the Suffering Ones had to be on another planet, not here. They were going to return to Naxia to ask the trees for better information, but then Vush called and asked for help. Naxo and Hjeg went with Dee-four, but I got in Granston's ship to persuade him that the dome should be investigated once more before we decided the Suffering Ones were not here."

"Are you in league with that scoundrel?"

"Everyone says you're the scoundrel, Kolix."

He stamped his clawed foot. "Arda, what happened!"

"It's rather embarrassing . . ."

"You and Granston decided to have sex. I saw him leering at you. He has a terrible reputation at the Galactic Writers' Society, you know."

"I didn't. And we didn't. The fact is that Granston was going to kill me, so I jumped out of his ship into the ocean. I swam up to the top of the dome and when I touched the antenna in a certain way, the dome's top section rose, and then a trapdoor at the surface opened. I fell in."

"So that's what the cushioned area is for. I've always wondered. Why did Granston want to kill you?"

"It's a long story, but the gist is that he hates androids."

Kolix laughed. "Poor Arda."

"It's not funny, Kolix."

"No, it definitely is not. Sorry. I suppose you want to know what I'm doing here."

"I think the Suffering Ones are these trees that you're helping back to health by placing those mats around their trunks. The trees are grateful."

"They never said so before, but it's reassuring to know that's the case. Yes, I'm replacing the mats."

"Replacing?"

"My story is longer than yours, Arda. It begins on

Crotonis, with cruelty and greed. I'd rather not tell you."

He was so pale, his wings trembling, that I thought I'd better help him out. "You can tell me if I'm wrong, Kolix, but I think I've deduced what's been going on. The Seventh Species built this dome as a museum housing their artifacts. I don't know why or how each object is held by the tree fronds . . ."

"When healthy they generate a field that suspends and protects the artifacts."

"Okay. The trees get sick and can't generate the field when the green mats are removed. You Crotonites took mats so you could get the artifacts. Since you didn't enter the dome the way I did, you must have come another way, but none of the Six Species has invented matter transporters. Is this metal platform a transporter invented by the Seventh Species?"

"Yes. The only other one I know of was discovered on Crotonis a long time ago by my grandfather, who told my father, who told me. That's why my family has been so wealthy. We've never discovered how the transporters were made or even how they work. They just do. You step on the platform, touch certain patterns in it with your feet, think of your goal, and you go."

"How convenient for you Crotonites to be able to plunder the Galaxy's most fabulous museum, reached by the Galaxy's most important invention, all of which you Crotonites kept secret."

Kolix took a deep breath and pressed his hand to his forehead as if he had a headache. "Don't, Arda. I'm trying to make amends."

"Why?"

"When I met Vush, I asked her what she would do if she found a Seventh Species invention of great value.

Like the good being she is, she said she'd give it to the Galactic Alliance so that scientists of all the Six Species could work on developing the invention for the use of all species. I may do this yet."

The trees were beginning to sing again, and this time it was in a sonic register too high for most organic beings to hear. Crotonites, however, are a lot like Terran bats, with extraordinary hearing. Kolix listened to the trees, puzzled.

"What are they singing, Arda?"

"I don't know the words, only the general sense of happiness. I think it's a message they are sending to the antenna, which must transmit it again through hyperspace to the Naxian trees. When you learned about my contact with the Naxian trees, why didn't you tell us that you knew where the Suffering Ones were located?"

"Don't be stupid, Arda. My family were the ones that turned the dome trees into the Suffering Ones."

"And you only decided to help them after the night of the Galactic Writers' Society banquet. When you realized you were evil and you had to reform."

"Evil? Yes, I was—I am evil. But I had decided before the events of the banquet to take the mats back to the dome trees."

"Do you expect me to believe that, Kolix?"

"Please try. You see, Arda, when I met Vush, I fell in love—at first sight and for the first time. I hardly knew her—we hadn't had our mating flight—but I wanted to change for her sake. I stopped stealing artifacts, brought back all those that hadn't been sold, and began to replace the mats. My decision to change resulted in deaths. . . ."

He shuddered. "I will never atone enough. If I'm killed, it will serve me right."

"Kolix! Don't fall apart. I'll help you. I can carry a lot of mats if you carry me across to the trees."

"These Crotonite power packs are too small, and even with two I cannot fly carrying both you and the mats."

"Can I take a boat?"

"I think the Seventh Species intended that visitors to the museum would view the artifacts from the boats, but I don't know how to make them work. I had medical training; I'm not equipped to deal with alien machinery that doesn't respond to thoughts."

I was studying the control panel again when part of my brain reviewed what Kolix had just said. "Medical training?"

He did not answer, for at that moment the metal platform began to hum.

"Kolix! What's happening?"

He took off into the open space, circling around to land beside me in my boat.

"Get down, Arda. Someone's transporting!"

He put his wing around my body as if to shield me, just as five columns of shimmering mist appeared in midair.

The columns stabbed down to touch the platform, the humming stopped and the mist resolved into five organic figures.

The wrists of one of the figures were neatly handcuffed in front of him. I was pleased to see that it was Granston, glowering.

"Hello," said Dee-four. "What have we here?"

Chapter 26

We all worked with Kolix to take the mats back to the Suffering Ones. Once removed from stasis, the mats came alive, rippling as we held them. Although their green color resembled dark moss, the mats were not moss but composed of springy, interwoven strands of a semifirm substance like a cross between overcooked noodles and soft mushrooms. When two mats were molded into a circle around the base of a tree, they immediately grew fine tendrils that pushed into the ground. As they did so, the fernlike fronds of the trees rippled, too.

By the time every mat was back in place, Hjeg and I were the only ones not exhausted. Everyone plunked themselves down on the soft padded central area to rest, but I stayed in one of the boats, from which I could easily see and hear the others.

"Could someone lend me a communicator, so I can call Zak?" I asked. "Mine is still wet and I fear it will never recover."

Naxo tossed me his. "I have another in the ship, so you can keep that one, Arda."

I reported, so quietly no one else could hear, and when I finished, I was glad to see a smile on the tiny image of Zak.

"Good work, Arda."

"I endeavor to give satisfaction."

"Yes, Jeeves. You do. Now I want you to leave the communicator on."

"But . . ."

"No 'buts.' Rejoin your comrades, but before you do, attach the communicator to your tunic, face outward."

"I thought you were working."

"I am. I always am, but I can still listen in. The dubious virtue of modern hycom is that through hyperspace I can communicate instantaneously with anyone anywhere, as long as my housekeeper doesn't soak the technology in ocean water. Right now I have a curious desire to listen to what the others say."

"But you hired me as your eyes and ears so that you could go on writing and wouldn't be bothered except when I call once a day."

"This time I may want to make a comment to the others."

Feeling unaccountably miffed at having to share Zak, I attached the communicator with the screen facing outward, and then I joined the group, explaining that Zak wanted to be part of the conversation.

Naxo stretched his body out. "Hyah, Zak. We organics are plumb tuckered out as you Erthumoi would say."

"Not this Erthumoi."

Naxo yawned. "Anyway, I'm glad I didn't have to do that chore wearing a breather the way I did back in the putrid air of Crotonis, if you'll forgive the expression, Princess."

"We Crotonites know the effect our air has on aliens."

"I'm also glad the air here is suitable for me," said Dee-four, systematically cracking each joint of her arms as she tested them. "Vush—Kolix—are you okay after that work in what to you is thin air?"

"Somewhat winded," said Kolix, "but we're managing."

"Well, I'm not okay," Granston complained. "My back is stiff and my muscles ache from lifting mats out of the stasis box with my hands manacled together. Can't you release me now?"

Granston had actually refused to help until Dee-four ordered Naxo to coil around his body and give him a Big Hug, which wasn't necessary because just the threat made Granston leap to the stasis box and start taking out the mats.

"You're still under arrest, Granston," Dee-four said. "Endangering the existence of an android is a crime in the Galactic Alliance."

"You have only Arda's word against mine."

"I sensed your emotions, Granston," Naxo said, "and you were lying when you said Arda had tried to kill you. Just relax and Dee and I will take you back to Earth when we report to the TFBI in person."

"Director Smith will forgive me for getting mad at Arda," Granston said. "She probably doesn't like androids."

"She hired Arda," Kolix said.

"And Arda is a good agent." The words came from the middle of my chest, where Zak's image reposed. I was pleased.

"I'm hungry," Naxo grumbled. "Where can we get some food?"

Nobody knew. The thought of going back to Crotonis didn't appeal to anyone, but the ships were there. Since there did not seem to be any way of leaving the dome to beg food from the Cephallonians, the organics would have to stay hungry.

In the meantime, the organics rested, Hjeg absorbed energy, and I thought of how proud I was of my non-Erthumoi comrades. On Crotonis, Dee-four had used her deeplook to hunt for Kolix's body, and instead had found peculiar machinery behind a hidden, locked doorway in Kolix's cave. Hjeg had managed to get inside and unlock the secret room, which had a floor that Dee-four scanned and said was a matter transporter.

When Vush insisted that they use the transporter to follow Kolix, Dee-four deciphered its secrets. They were about to leave when Granston showed up, so—as the old Erthumoi stories used to say—he was clapped into irons and brought along.

Once Kolix had explained about the mats and the Suffering Ones, no one but Granston objected to helping. Dee-four probed the mechanism of the antigrav boats so we were able to use them to transport the mats across to the terraces, from which the two Crotonites flew with mats to each needy tree.

Kolix seemed to be resting quietly now, but during the actual work of helping the Suffering Ones, he had constantly hurried us, as if time were running out.

Yawning, Dee-four now turned to him and asked, "What was your big rush, Kolix? We'd called your royal in-laws to tell them you and the princess are safe. Naxo and I told the TFBI where we are and what we're doing. Hjeg let her people in on the secret of Cephallonia. Granston called his lawyer who threatens to sue everyone. Now Arda has reported to Zak who's with us by hycom."

"You don't understand and I can't explain." Kolix sat with one wing draped around Vush, but it was he who leaned on her, not vice versa. "My life is . . . forfeit."

"What does that mean?" asked Vush.

Zak, who really was listening, said, "It's an Erthumoi

expression, meaning that when someone has committed a crime, a penalty must be paid."

"Perhaps with my life," Kolix said softly.

"No, no, dearwing. You should not keep brooding about the accident at the Galactic Writers' Society banquet. You wanted to stop Elson, not kill him. It's not your fault that the ship exploded. For involuntary manslaughter, the penalty is surely not death."

"Not for any of the *other* Six Species," Naxo said. "Not even for murder."

"It was not murder," Vush said.

Zak did not comment, so neither did I.

Dee-four reached out to touch Kolix briefly. "Perhaps you are worrying about your family's crime of stealing the mats and endangering the life of these trees. I do not think you will have to pay a penalty for that because we've restored them. Look, the trees are coming back to life now, the branches springing up and curving just like those of the healthy trees."

"Symbionts," Hjeg said. "The trees and mats."

A voice said—*Yes. We are symbionts.*

"Who said that?" I asked. When everyone turned to look at me, I realized that the voice had been inside my mind. I'd been fingering the ruulogem in my pocket while listening to the others talk. Now I grasped it tightly and tried to think clearly.

I asked in my mind—*Who are you?*

—*You call us trees, but we are plants from another galaxy who were made Guardians.*

—*Guardians?*

—*Of this museum. It is the Museum of History.*

—*The history of the Seventh Species?*

—*That is what you aliens call those who built the museum.*

—*They brought you and the mats. . . .*

—Without the mats, we cannot remain conscious and we lose our power to hold and guard. Tell our rescuers we thank them, even the one who took our symbionts from us, as did his father and grandfather.

"Arda," Naxo said, "I can't read the emotions of androids, but from the rapt expression on your face I suspect that you're having a peculiarly mystical experience."

I said, "It's not mystical. I'm being talked to telepathically by the plants in this dome. It's very much like listening to the Naxian trees, but I can understand these plants better. They speak Galactic Basic." I repeat what the Guardians had told me.

There was a tone of amusement in the Guardians when they said—*We learned Galactic Basic from listening to the Cephallonian tourist boats. They could not hear us, but we could hear them, through the antenna.*

I told my comrades this, and everyone laughed.

—We Guardians are pleased that so many of the display objects are now back in place. We hope that the rest will be returned, but if this is not entirely possible, the museum will still be worth viewing.

When I repeated this message of the Guardians, Zak said, "Ask them how the museum can function as a museum when nobody can get in without first going to Crotonis or by falling in from the dome top the way you did."

Vush said, "Yes, ask them, Arda. As an archaeologist hoping to interest the public of all Six Species in such a wonderful museum, I would very much like to know if the museum is accessible in some easier way."

I began to try to think out these questions, but the Guardians interrupted my thoughts.

—No need to tell us. We hear what the others say,

*but at the moment we can talk only to you because you
hold the key.*

—*Could you talk to the others telepathically if I let
them each hold the key?*

—*No. Only you and perhaps*—*we are not sure*—*one
other. The museum was to have been made accessible to
all intelligent species a long time ago, but the key was
lost. It is you who can restore it.*

I said this out loud, noticing the surprise it engen-
dered in my audience—well, not in everyone. I looked
down at the communicator on my tunic and saw that
Zak seemed maddeningly complacent, if not positively
smug about something.

—*Now, nonorganic Erthumoi called Arda, please
place the key upon the marked center of the seating area.*

I explained what I was supposed to do, and the others got out of the central depression. I stepped onto
the resilient cushion and stopped, puzzled. I could see
no marks.

"What's the key you are supposed to use?" asked
Naxo.

Suddenly I felt as if the others should not see it, so
I did not bring out the ruulogem, and I did not answer
Naxo. "I can't see any place to put the key."

Dee-four retracted her eyecover. "Arda, deeplook
shows that there's a metal device under the exact center. Feel for it."

"I've found it. I see now that the silver color of the
cushion is faintly lighter there."

"Hurry, Arda. Put the key on the center," Kolix said
in an oddly tight, harsh voice.

"But what *is* the key?" asked Vush.

I kept my hand in my tunic pocket, the ruulogem
clutched in my fist. I wondered desperately if the ruulogem had a strange hold over me, but I said nothing.

"Arda," Zak said, "it's time."

I took out the ruulogem. "It's your royal ruulogem, Vush. Elson didn't take it after all, and it wasn't destroyed."

Kolix did not even blink.

"But how did you get it?" Vush asked.

"Don't explain, Arda," Zak said. "Just use the key."

I bent down and placed the ruulogem on the exact center. At once, the building vibrated again, this time longer and more powerfully. Vush shrieked and Kolix held her.

"'What's happening?" Granston yelled. "An earthquake?"

"No," I said. "Watch."

The flattened top section of the dome, the only one without a terrace attached to it, moved up once more. It also widened and became transparent.

Dee-four peered up at the dome above us. "I think the top has turned into a landing platform for tourist boats. Yes—hangar doors have appeared in it."

"Great Galaxy!" yelled Naxo, pointing downward. "The whole blasted dome is becoming transparent!"

Zak said, "I advise you to watch out, my friends. With all the reporting you agents did, you forgot to tell the Cephallonians. They have surrounded the dome with guns."

We all stared at the Cephallonian police, who were in armed antigrav boats above the top and swimming— well-armed—in the water around the dome. As I wondered how I could inform them before they shot at us, water locks pouched out from the now transparent walls. The police could enter—after putting on water-filled suits.

The Guardians spoke again, this time aloud. "You may remove the key, Arda. We have used it to accomplish our task and it is no longer needed now that it has restored the museum and our vocal abilities. Give the key to the Crotonites as our gesture of good will, in the hope that from now on Crotonites will help take care of our museum instead of stealing from it."

Kolix bowed his head. "Thank you, Guardians. I have not failed after all. Soon I must return to Crotonis, and then to Earth, to face judgment for another crime."

"Not just yet." Pleltun, dressed in a water-filled space suit, had entered the dome. Using a power pack, he jetted up to join the group.

"Kolix, you and I have been members of the Galactic Writers' Society for a long time. I know you and have always believed the rumors that you are a crook. If you've reformed, you must explain what has happened to our dome. What you say to me will be broadcast to the rest of Cephallonia."

Kolix pointed to me. "She's responsible. She held the key." He was not going to admit that he'd stolen the ruulogem and that the Naxian tree had stolen it from him.

"Arda, explain only what's necessary," Zak said.

I told the Cephallonians almost everything, omitting Kolix's possession of the ruulogem and his sex with me. Granston writhed as I told what he had done, but I wasn't sorry about making *him* uncomfortable. I also omitted various new ideas agitating my mind. When I was finished, I handed the ruulogem to Vush.

The princess kissed her husband and then flew to the nearest Guardian that had no object to hold in its energy field. Hovering with her wings and power pack, she held the ruulogem in the space between the curved fronds. When she opened her hand and let go, the ruulogem remained suspended there.

Vush saluted the Guardians. "I give back the ruulogem, for it is an important artifact of the Seventh Species. Let tourists and archaeologists enjoy its beauty, and perhaps benefit from its positive effects."

She smiled at Kolix and added, "My dearwing has reformed. The museum will be safe, for Crotonite guards will make sure that only genuine tourists use the matter transporter on Crotonis."

Naxo reared up. "As the Erthumoi say, three cheers for the Crotonites."

All of us cheered, including the Cephallonians.

"I will take you on a tour of the museum," Kolix said. "I know it well and have restored many of the artifacts."

With Kolix and Vush flying slightly ahead, we each took one of the antigrav canoes. On automatic, the canoes followed a set course beginning at the top, spiraling into and down the layers of terraces until we'd seen all the artifacts.

A few were like those in the Locrian museum, but most were different. The top terraces held what seemed to be the earliest artifacts, because we could imagine the uses to which they might have been put. Vush thought that many of the early pieces were jewelry, often featuring ruulogems, but there were also variations on the one type of woven artifact—circular cloths made of metallic thread that had not tarnished. Up in the early section there were also decorated containers ranging from deep bowls to shallow trays, and implements that might have functioned as eating utensils, but with handles none of us could use.

As we traveled down the series of terraces, the artifacts became more complex and harder to understand, until the final levels, when they looked simple again, but much more mysterious.

"Remarkable," said Zak, who had not worked at all

but had watched eagerly from the communicator. "Plel-tun, your Cephallonian talent intuited the function of this museum before you ever saw it. As in your novel, the display is a complete history of the Seventh Species, or will be, once the archaeologists get through figuring it out—eh, Princess?"

"Yes," Vush said. "It is a priceless treasure of beauty and information. So interesting that what we think are the latest artifacts seem to be simplified sculpture in odd forms."

"Probably not sculpture," Dee-four said. "I deeplooked them, and they are objects like tools for creatures who didn't have hands resembling any of ours. Perhaps they are devices to be worked by telepathy. Do you know, Guardians?"

"We do not know the function of any of the objects. Our purpose was to hold and guard them, not to explain them. We came to consciousness only after those who made the museum, those you call the Seventh Species, left Cephallonia. We never saw them."

Zak's voice issued from the region of my chest. "'Perhaps the Seventh Species did not wish to explain too much for reasons of their own. Perhaps they also hoped that eventually the different intelligent species of this Galaxy would—when sophisticated enough—solve the meaning of each object."

"Even if we did that," Hjeg said, "we still might not know what the Seventh looked like, or in which galaxy they originated, or what happened to them."

Zak nodded. "I think the Seventh Species would want to give few clues about what happened to them, although they may have expected that eventually we would guess, whether they left definitive clues or not."

Dee-four said, "I'd like to find out what other galaxy evolved a species as remarkable as the Seventh."

Zak said, "Somehow I doubt if that's terribly important. What's more important is their whole history in *this* Galaxy, and why they had to make it hard for archaeologists to decipher."

"So why did they?" asked Naxo.

"I'm not sure," Zak said.

"But we must find out," Hjeg said. "Archaeologists from all of the Six Species will want to know why the Seventh Species did not wish their history to be easily understood."

"And understood too soon," Zak said.

Dee-four said, "I don't understand that. We of the Six Species, who now dominate this Galaxy, could learn so much from their history. Why hide it from us?"

"You forget how many millennia it took for all of us to become civilized," Zak said. "Especially us Erthumoi, who run the Crotonites a close second in self-defeating bouts of prejudice."

The word dropped into the conversation like an exploding asteroid.

"Prejudice?" asked Hjeg. "I have never understood that."

"You're lucky," Zak said. "There's still a lot of it."

"I don't understand it either," Pleltun said, "but since we don't yet know the history of the Seventh Species, I suggest that we forget about it for a while and enjoy refreshments."

"Yeah, yeah!" Naxo shouted.

Pleltun added, "It's time for us Cephallonians to make amends. We are bringing in food and drink from our Erthumoi stores for a party down on the floor of the dome."

"I must leave," Kolix said.

"Not yet." Vush pulled at him. "This is the last stop of the royal tour. Let's make the most of it."

"I thought we already had," Kolix said grumpily.

With the ranks of terraces and their vegetation looming up on all sides, higher and higher, the setting of the party was almost overwhelming. I took off the communicator to hold it close to my mouth so I could speak more privately to Zak, but I saw that he had turned his back on us and was writing furiously. I put the communicator back on my tunic and hoped no one would think Zak was being impolite. As it was, I was ignored, because I didn't eat or drink but sat off to one side.

Finally Hjeg, having had champagne poured onto her block, slowly made her way over to me. "Arda, are we still friends?"

"Yes, Hjeg."

"But you don't want me to touch you yet."

"No. Sorry."

"Then there was more to the story than you told."

"Only a little. Personal."

"I don't mind. It's a good party. I see that Zak is busy."

I looked down at my tunic and saw, upside down, that Zak had heard and turned around.

"Hi, Hjeg. Take care of my housekeeper, will you?"

"Isn't all the danger over?" she asked.

"No."

"I will try to take care of Arda although she doesn't want to be touched. I'm sorry that it tunes me into her thoughts, but I can't help it, Fortizak."

"Arda, are you listening?"

I said, somewhat acerbically, "Of course I'm listening. You're typing on my chest."

"Hardly. I want Hjeg to go with you from now on, as your bodyguard."

"But I don't need one! I'm the bodyguard for the Crotonites, or I was until they fired me."

"You're just afraid Hjeg will think badly of certain of your activities," Zak said. "They don't matter, Arda."

"Because I'm an android?"

"Because you're a good person. Now I'm going back to work, and leave the damn communicator on and yell if you need help."

"From you, Zak? You're on Earth. If I'd had my communicator with me in the Naxian tree, I probably would not have bothered calling you. How could you have been of any use?"

"Brains are always useful, my stubborn housekeeper. If you'd called me, I could have notified the Naxians to let you out. Fortunately Kolix did that. Hey—go after him!"

Kolix was flying up through the open center space of the dome. His princess, left behind, was not screaming because she'd been stunned and was unconscious.

I flung myself into a canoe and sped after him. It all happened so fast that I forgot I was supposed to take Hjeg along.

"Arda, he's going to the matter transporter. Stop him."

"I'm trying to, Zak."

By the time I made it to the transporter, Dee-four, Naxo, Granston, and Hjeg—carrying Vush on her back—were following in another canoe, and Pleltun was coming up with his power pack, but they were too late.

Kolix's form was winking out, and I went with him.

Chapter 27

The air was full of molecules that would make it poisonous to any organic nonCrotonites except a Samian. Kolix and I were standing on a transporter platform exactly like the one in the Cephallonian dome. On the floor around the transporter were empty boxes, nothing else. The room's one door was open and its other side was camouflaged to make it seem part of the natural cave walls of the next room.

I had expected to find that the inhospitable planet Crotonis was as gray as its dominant life-forms, but the room in which we arrived had walls of iridescent stone, shimmering with color. I began to understand why Crotonites kept their clothing and furnishings simple in shape and hue.

"Go back, Arda. I'm closing the transporter setting for Cephallonia."

"All the more reason for me to stay, Kolix."

He touched a panel beside the Crotonis transporter and the pattern in the metal floor changed color. "No one can follow from Cephallonia now. Damn you for being here, Arda."

"I'm here, too, Kolix," Zak said. "So to speak. And you need Arda."

Kolix sighed. "Fortizak, you don't understand my situation, what I have to do, and why."

"Oh, yes, I do."

Kolix seemed to sag. "Arda told me what you said."

"About choosing? Have you?"

"I made the choice long ago."

Zak said, "The night of the Galactic Writers' Society banquet, wasn't it, Kolix?"

"Yes, but I must face the consequences of my choice. I do not know what will happen."

"The confrontation is not necessary."

"It is, Fortizak. I once made certain . . . commitments. They must be undone."

"You undid the commitments when you made your choice."

Kolix clenched his fists. "Not completely. It's not easy, for such as I. You don't understand. You can't possibly know what my situation is like."

"That's true, but I think you're making a mistake. Open up the transporter so Vush can join you here. Then go to the palace. Stay on Crotonis for good. No need to return to Earth."

"I must."

"If you must, take Arda with you."

"No, she'll be in danger, Fortizak."

"I'd have preferred that Hjeg be along to help, but since she isn't, Arda is strong and capable. Hire her again as your bodyguard, Kolix."

A wan smile lit Kolix's pointed gray face. "Okay, Arda, you're hired."

"Are we going to Earth now?" I asked.

"In my private spaceyacht. I'm setting a timer on this transporter so that Vush can come home after I've left. On the way out I'll show you the family manse. No one lives in it now, so we won't be seen."

As he and I started for the door he said, "I hope Hjeg didn't ruin this door lock. Grandfather went to a

lot of trouble to disguise this door from other Crotonites, including his own family. He pretended the next
room was extra storage space but too damp for much
use, so only he came here."

The next room led to a broad corridor, big enough
for a Crotonite to fly through it, but Kolix took my
hand and we walked. He opened doors on each side,
pointing out the lush furnishings in each. The bed-
rooms had web-beds and seating cushions much more
elegant than those in the Crotonite royal yacht. The
dining room was huge, presumably so family and guests
could fly easily to capture their live food.

Some shelves and tables had faint circles or squares
of various sizes on them. I pointed to them and asked,
"Were Seventh Species artifacts once there? Did you
take them to Cephallonia, along with the mats?"

"The mats were always in stasis in the dome. And
yes, I took back the artifacts we pretended we bought
throughout the Galaxy. There are none left here."

The hall ended at the cave opening, which gave upon
a broad terrace jutting out from the mountain. To one
side was a parking cradle containing the smallest
hyperdrive ship I'd ever seen. I looked out over a canyon with low purple and yellow vegetation, humming
with small winged creatures, growing at the bottom
and along the rim. The canyon walls themselves were
bare and sparkling with brilliant color. It almost
seemed as if fireworks were going off inside the stone.

Except for the canyon, the landscape consisted of
mountainous cliffs honeycombed with caves. I mar-
veled as I watched the citizens of Crotonis flying from
cave to cave, or up to a large building perched on the
highest cliff across the canyon. This structure was re-
plete with landing terraces.

"That's the royal palace of Crotonis," Kolix said.

"Are we going there first?"

"No. We're going right to Earth." He turned and got into his ship. "Coming? You'll have to ride in the cargo bay. There's only room for two Crotonites up front."

I opened the cargo bay and had started to get in when Kolix suddenly pulled me back.

"Wait, Arda! I'm not sure the cargo bay is shielded enough from hyperspatial fields. I tried to kill you once, but I will never do that again. Androids are people, and as alive as any organic. I know that now."

"Bravo, Kolix," Zak said.

I said, "I can fold up to fit next to you in the pilot's section. Folding up would be uncomfortable for a human, but not for me. I'm an android."

Laughter shook Kolix, and continued until I thought that he could not stop. I shook him.

"Control your lower brain," I said.

"It's not out of control at the moment, Arda. I'm just releasing emotions. Organics do that, you know."

I said, "Sometimes I also feel like laughing hysterically or crying or both, except that I can't cry. Perhaps androids need to release emotion, too. Do you agree, Zak?"

"I think I do. Kolix, where are you going after you arrive on Earth?"

"That depends, Fortizak. Is it day or night?"

"I don't vouch for the rest of Earth, but here in Manhattan the sun has not yet set in the golden west."

"Then there's still time. Please call the TFBI, specifically Smith's Agency, and tell Director Smith I will surrender myself to her in her role as a representative of the TFBI. If, after hearing my story, she believes it's necessary to turn me over to the Terran police for unintentional murder, I will comply."

"You'd better come to my apartment, Kolix. I'll tell

Smith to meet you here. Arda and I will be your witnesses."

"An excellent idea. Much safer. Make Smith start out for the meeting now. My ship is small but has powerful hyperdrive, so we'll be on Earth soon. Keep Smith waiting in your apartment because I must do some errands first, and I don't want to have any official interference."

"What kind of errands? Where are you going?"

"I know three places on Earth where illegal artifacts are stored. First I'll go to the freight garage under our embassy."

"Under?" I asked.

"Arda," Zak said in his scolding tone, "remember that the Crotonite embassy is on a man-made island in the East River. It makes sense to have the freight entrance underwater and—hey, Kolix! Did the embassy builders use the old midtown tunnel that's under the river bottom?"

"Yes, Fortizak. To make a secret storehouse, my grandfather broke into another part of the tunnel which I enter through my private dock in the embassy garage."

"So you're going to retrieve the rest of the artifacts stored there—and then?"

"I'll go to the family apartment, where we had appointments with confederates involved in our business dealings. It's in Rivway, that luxury building on the East Side near the GASworks. The third place is on the West Side, and after all the artifacts are in the ship, we'll go on to your apartment."

"I'm calling Smith now," Zak said, turning off the hycom. In a moment it was back on. "All fixed. She'll be here in about an hour. Arda, you stick with Kolix, and Kolix—be careful."

"You can trust me to show up, Fortizak."

"I do, but you may be in danger. Just in case, what's the code for the door lock of your apartment?"

"NonCrotonites have been inside, but none has ever been told the lock code of the family hideaway."

"Interesting old Terran word. Interesting that you should know it. Now be logical, Crown Prince. Communicators can break. If something goes wrong, I want to be able to get to Arda. And, Kolix, may I congratulate you on your command of your Crotonite flight muscles as well as Erthumoi colloquialisms."

"You do understand."

"Yes. For some time."

"How did you guess?"

"There were lots of other clues. My hired robot Y50 scanning Arda, responding only to her, and programmed to embarrass the Crotonites at the GWS banquet. Elson both doctor and thief. The red herring of the ruulogem, which turned out to be an important key that no one—including the villains—knew about. Arda wondering if the laws of robotics applies to nonhumans. Naxo's talent nullified when he was tempted with drugged capsules. The drugged Locrian fizz fortunately able to paralyze Dee-four's eyecover, or she might have been killed."

Kolix winced.

"I was also impressed by the anatomy of Crotonites, by Elson continuing to wear his surgical mask so his mouth stayed covered, and by your reactions to death, beginning with the finding of DNA in Elson's ship. And, of course, you always knew too much. Now I think you'd better tell me the door lock code for your apartment."

"We don't use the front door, which is sealed, but the fortified terrace door. Small ships like this one can land on the terrace, as well as airtaxis and flying Crotonites. The code lock is 7-32-97-2."

"Got it," Zak said. "I'll keep your secret unless you don't bring my housekeeper back to me. Wait a moment while I call Cephallonia."

"What for?"

"In view of what you've done in the past and the conciliatory royal tour you've just completed, I think it would be wise if I told Pleltun to take Vush and the rest of Arda's colleagues to Earth in the fastest Ceph ship. We'll *all* meet in my apartment for the final showdown."

While my memory banks were accessing the word "showdown," Kolix grinned and said, "Go ahead, Fortizak."

"You can call me Zak, Kolix. We never used to be friends, but I think we can manage now." The communicator went blank while Zak presumably called Pleltun.

"I don't understand," I told Kolix. "What does Zak know that I don't?"

"Nothing, Arda," Kolix said wearily. "He's more intelligent than most people, organic or nonorganic." He looked tired enough to collapse, or perhaps he was mostly worried about whether or not he'd have to be arrested.

"Kolix, I have believed you to be a deliberate murderer, but I don't think so anymore. It has something to do with medical training, doesn't it?"

Before he could answer, my communicator came back on and Zak said, "It's all fixed. Pleltun and the others are on their way to Earth at top warp drive."

"Top what?" I asked.

"Sorry. Been watching too many old shows. Top

hyperdrive speed. Vush is greatly relieved that she will soon see her beloved."

"I hope she forgives me for rendering her unconscious on Cephallonia. I have to leave, and she would have stopped me."

"Your princess is in love with you, I fear," said Zak.

"Fear?" Kolix's eyes watered. "My criminal past is a danger to her, but from the first moment I saw her, I loved her and wanted to be part of her noble life."

I said, "Is that the truth, or did you badly want to be a crown price?"

"Arda, when I took over the smuggling business from my father, I was more interested in the artifacts than in the money made from selling them." He paused, his wings drooping. "I admit that my family was rich by then, or I might not have been so fascinated by Vush's archaeology. The Crotonite royal family has never been wealthy."

Zak cleared his throat. "There'll be time later to grovel in guilt."

Sharing the pilot compartment with Kolix was somewhat humiliating but manageable. By folding myself upside down, my too-long legs occupied the space meant for Crotonite wings.

Kolix started up the engines. The ship left the cave and was soon out of the Crotonite atmosphere and into far orbit, where hyperdrive could be engaged.

"Arda," Kolix said, gazing down at me. "I have come to believe that Crotonite females are the loveliest creatures in the Galaxy, but I admit that you do look beautiful even upside down."

"You leave my housekeeper alone, Kolix."

"I keep forgetting we have a chaperone this time."

Kolix didn't talk during the voyage, and I was busy

thinking—trying to undo previous appraisals and arrive at what Zak might have deduced long ago.

By holding the communicator up, I could see Zak typing, his back to me and the hycom screen he used for our communications.

"Zak, I'm thinking about how novels are written."

He didn't look around. "I'm not thinking about it. I'm writing one that's due in a week."

"Please, Zak. I want to learn. For instance, if the leading character is trying to decipher the plot by putting together clues, is it best if she—I mean, the leading character—doesn't reveal the thought processes until certain?"

He grunted and said, "By 'certain,' do you mean that point when the plot unravels enough so that the reader ought to be able to figure it out, too?"

"Yes."

"The author should make sure that he, she, or it shuts up until then."

"Even if the book is in first person?"

Zak looked at me over his shoulder. "Wallowing in the inner thoughts of the narrator is vastly overrated, to say nothing of being egocentric."

"Okay."

"You disturbed me for that?"

"Sorry. I'm not sure there's anybody else to ask."

As Zak raised his eyebrows, the ship came out of hyperspace just above Earth's atmosphere, and went zooming down.

"Kolix," Zak said, "what about your, um, confederates? Will they be penalized?"

"Not if I obtain the artifacts for restoring to the museum on Cephallonia. I want the confederates to have a chance to start over. To be honest."

Zak said. "That would be an admirable reformation,

Kolix, but you can't count on it, especially since there's murder involved. Did these confederates help you steal from the dome on Cephallonia?"

"No. Only my family knew about the Cephallonian museum and the transporter on our planet. In ships from Crotonis, we took the stolen artifacts to be sold through intermediaries in Manhattan, where it's easy to find willing confederates."

"Willing crooks. Of all species?"

"Not exactly."

Zak laughed. "Uh-huh. You can think of Arda and me as your new confederates. Arda, continue to leave the communicator on, although it is lousing up my work day. I want to see what's happening."

Kolix nodded. "Zak, I never thought I'd say this, but that is a great relief to me. Arda is strong, intelligent, and helpful, but I hesitate about telling her the truth."

"I understand," Zak said. "Are you stiffening up in outrage, Arda?"

"Well . . ."

"Don't. Truth is hard to take sometimes, but it will all come out in the wash."

I was marveling at the oddities of Erthumoi colloquialisms as Kolix piloted the ship through traffic to the East River, into which the ship plunged to enter a water lock giving into the Crotonite freight garage.

Kolix touched a switch and his parking space was enveloped in steel. When he opened the air lock, a section of wall slid back so that we faced a dark section of tunnel filled with boxes.

"Wait here, Arda. Only one box is still full." He ran out, brought it back, put it in the cargo bay, and returned to the pilot's seat. "Poor Grandfather. He would not have approved."

"Did you know him, Kolix?"

"No. When he was dying, he told my father about Cephallonia and the transporters. Father didn't particularly want to continue the stealing and smuggling, but Mother proved to be a marvelous crook, running everything until she and Father both died in a ship accident. They'd already put me to work in the business, so I knew all the secrets."

"You're not proud of your parents."

"Not of my grandfather, or my mother, but my father might have been proud of me for loving Vush and wanting to become an archaeologist. For a Crotonite he was such a gentle being, kind and . . ." He leaned toward the control panel as if in pain.

"Is your lower brain giving you problems?"

"More than you can imagine."

"I'm sorry your father is dead."

"Arda, my father would never forgive the other things I've done. Never, never forgive the death . . . death . . ."

"Kolix! You must finish what you've started!"

One sob escaped him and then he went to work. The steel barrier slid back, the ship left the garage and the East River.

Soon we landed on the terrace of Kolix's "hideaway." I was surprised to find that the apartment was one big room, so large that the original rooms must have been combined to make a space in which Crotonites could fly.

The only items of luxury were the couch, chairs, and table of a size to be used in business dealings with two-legged, tall beings like Erthumoi and Locrians. A Crotonite web-bed hung unobtrusively in the darkest corner, shelves—bare except for a few books—lined the walls, and on the floor were two large Erthumoi rugs of the type called Oriental, their vivid gold and russet colors brightening the prevailing Crotonite gray.

"I've been robbed," Kolix said at once. "On the shelves there were two Seventh Species bowls and a piece of sculpture. I came here before my wedding, but decided to return the artifacts to the dome after the royal tour. I didn't want Vush to find them in our ship and know her husband was a thief. Now someone's been in since then. Zak, did you tell anyone the door code?"

"No. Are you going to inform the police?"

"Don't be ridiculous. I'd have to explain how I got the artifacts, and I'd humiliate the Crotonite embassy. I must go to the last place. The artifacts may be there. Have the others arrived at your apartment?"

"They've all said they're on their way."

"I'll have to risk it. Come, Arda."

We got back in the ship and traveled across town to an ultramodern penthouse facing the Hudson River. The building was so high that no others looked down on it, so whoever lived there had remarkable privacy. The low-walled terrace was full of exotic human statuary and a variety of potted trees, but there was still plenty of room for Kolix's ship to land.

I gave Zak the address.

"Anyone in the apartment?" he asked me.

"I can't see. Trees are between the ship and the terrace windows of the apartment."

"No one can be there," Kolix said. "I'm getting out."

"So am I," I said. "I want to see the view."

I unwound myself from the front seat of the ship and got out of the air lock before Kolix, who seemed angry.

"Just look at the view, Arda," Kolix said. "There's no need for you to go into the apartment."

I walked to the west end of the terrace and looked over the wall. "Zak, there's a gorgeous view across to the Jersey Palisades, and on the riverbank below us there are swimming pools and gardens. You should move here, Zak."

"I'd never leave Central Park or consort with wealthy thieves. Kolix, why don't you want Arda to go into the apartment?"

"If I expect my confederate to reform, I must ensure that privacy is maintained. I'll only be a moment. When you've seen the view, Arda, wait in the ship."

He walked around the pots of trees. Through the leaves I saw him tap a code into the lock of the terrace door, which looked as fortified as a Manhattan apartment door can be. The door opened and he went into a dark apartment.

While I waited, I enjoyed the western view. "Zak, look at all the boats on the Hudson. I've heard that there are boats that take tourists to the underwater canyon in New York Bay. I should like to see that some time."

"Okay." He was busy typing again.

"So many of those private pleasure boats look like old-fashioned sailing or motor vessels that just travel on top of the water. Why would anyone want to do that when antigrav boats go above it, with no waves to cause human seasickness?"

"'Some humans prefer old-fashioned things."

"Like human housekeepers."

"Now, Arda . . ."

"Zak, Kolix is still inside. There must be a great many artifacts in here. I think I should help him." I walked over to the terrace door.

"Zak, these terrace windows are polarized. I can't see in. What should I do? Kolix seems to feel that this confederate will be more likely to reform if no one has invaded the privacy of this apartment."

"Wait, Arda."

I did, another minute. "Kolix said he'd be only a moment. How long is a moment?"

"It depends on one's emotional state," Zak said. "I think you should wait for him as he said, back in the ship."

I returned to the ship, while Zak went on typing and I went on worrying. After five minutes, I opened the air lock and got out again. Then I ran to the terrace door.

Zak said, "What are you doing, Arda? Go back!"

But I was already trying the terrace door.

"Arda!"

The door was electrified, and the shock I received the moment I touched the handle threw my nervous system into spasm. I collapsed.

"What are you doing on the terrace floor? Are you all right?" Zak shouted. I was prone so he was getting a few of the terrace tiles.

It took a full minute (with Zak yelling all the time) before I could respond. "I was temporarily paralyzed by a barrier field. Fortunately, I had not taken a firm hold of the door handle or the paralysis might have been severe. I have just performed a systems check, which shows no permanent impairment of android function."

"Go back to the ship and lock yourself inside and . . ."

"But, Zak . . ."

"Arda, do as I say!"

"Yes, sir." I walked back to the ship.

"Dammit, if you could only run that ship and take it to my apartment terrace."

"Accessing."

"Accessing what?"

"Everything I learned about Crotonite machinery from the computer in the Crotonite ship."

"You mean you can now run a Crotonite ship?"

"Yes, sir."

"Then leave at once."

"But what about Kolix?"

"I don't think you should wait to find out what he's doing. The apartment is clearly dangerous for androids. Leave!"

Chapter 28

Getting into the pilot section was a tight squeeze, and I had some difficulty arranging my body across both seats so I could use the control panel and still see where I was going.

"Hurry, Arda."

"I can't fly this thing blind." With another bend of my body I made it. I could now work the panel and see out as well.

The sun had set and Manhattan's lights were coming on, but with the apartment windows polarized it was fairly dark on the terrace of Kolix's confederate.

"Zak, I think you're wrong. I should stay here until I find out what Kolix is doing in there. Perhaps something happened to him or surely he'd come out and tell me what's going on. If he can't get the door open, he could fly out a window because he's wearing one of his power packs. I think I should try to get into the apartment again and find out if he's all right."

"He may have decided to team up again with his confederates, so it's too dangerous for you to stay, Arda."

"But Kolix . . ."

"If he's made another choice, then that's his decision. You don't want to join them in crime, do you?"

"No, Zak."

"Then I order you to come home."

" 'Order' as in the advice given by a boss or a friend, Zak? Is it possible for humans and androids to truly be friends? I fear that you are talking to me the way a human orders a robot like Y50 to perform its duties, and I want you to believe that androids are people."

I did not look down at the communicator to see his face, so I don't know what he did during the moment of silence that ensued after my outrageous remarks that I expected would get me fired, and would lead to a bad report on me for Smith's Employment Agency. I was worried, so I quickly turned on the ship's engines.

"Arda, I don't need a robot housekeeper . . ."

"It's all right, Zak. I will return to Smith's and you can hire a human . . ."

"Dammit, listen to me. You're a *person*, and a friend, and if you don't come home to safety at once, I will turn off my word processor and come over there!"

I was about to access the computer drive sequences when I heard a sound and felt the cool evening air on my face.

"What's happening?" The communicator was below the control panel and Zak could not see out. "Is something wrong, Arda . . ."

Zak's voice broke off just as I experienced a sharp burning sensation in the center of my chest.

I looked down. The communicator had melted into a useless lump of plasti-metal. Underneath it my synthoskin felt slightly charred, but my internal machinery was not damaged.

I turned to see that the ship's air lock was open and Director Smith was pointing a gun at me.

To use a human expression not strictly applicable to androids, I was getting fed up with having guns aimed in my direction, but I did not attempt to fight. She was not only my boss, but a human being.

Smith said, "Arda, you are under arrest. The TFBI will be lenient because you probably did not realize the extent of Kolix's criminality, but your stupidity includes you in some of the guilt. Turn off the motor and get out of the ship."

I hesitated. Zak had told me to go to his apartment, and I felt considerably more loyal to him than to the Director of the Agency, however tied to the TFBI it was.

"Arda, may I remind you that I am a human authority, that you are a robot, and that you work for my agency?"

I got out and submitted while Smith put handcuffs on my wrists. "Director Smith, how did you know we'd be here?"

"I can monitor all the communicators given out by my agency. Fortizak had changed the code on yours, but when you began using Naxo's, I learned about the stolen artifacts and where you and Kolix were going. Walk ahead of me, into the apartment."

We entered an expensive living room. Gold and white drapes and upholstery set off the gold-veined white marble floor. Clear plasti-glass cabinets held an array of what were surely Seventh Species artifacts. There was everything from small plates to sculptured tools of unknown use.

It was, however, not the artifacts that drew my attention, for along one side of the room was a veritable forest of the usual exotic alien houseplants favored by Erthumoi. The plants were set in a semicircular basin full of multicolored rocks and silver jets that provided continual misting for the leaves.

Along the opposite wall was a huge piece of furni-

ture, old and dark in contrast to the rest of the room,
with a Crotonite-sized power pack lying on its top. This
sideboard, as I believe it is called, looked so heavy that
it was no wonder Director Smith had handcuffed Kolix
to one of its front legs.

Kolix was moaning through a tight gag, his eyelids
moving up and down. He was evidently waking up from
a dose of stun.

Smith used a third pair of handcuffs to fasten the
ones on my wrists to the other front leg of the
sideboard.

"Arda, you are strong enough to move this furniture,
but doing so will activate an electric field that will
prove lethal to an android brain."

"Is this the way TFBI agents make their prisoners
wait for the police to come?"

"There will be no police. I'm handling this myself."

"Director Smith, Fortizak Human will worry about
me."

"You are only an android housekeeper. He will hire
another. I doubt if he will bother to trace you tonight."

I said, "I think he'll come, and he'll bring the Crotonite princess and maybe also his writing colleagues
Pleltun, Granston, and Hjeg, with . . ." Fortunately,
she interrupted me before I could say that Dee-four
and Naxo would be sure to come along.

"I doubt it, and if he or anyone else shows up, the
building monitors down in the lobby will inform them
that I have left. If Fortizak comes in an aircar, he'll
think we've gone because the apartment will look dark
from outside."

"He'll try the terrace door and get an electric shock."

She rubbed her hands. "Serve him right if it proves
lethal. No one can enter this apartment except when
I choose. I've turned on an electrical field that will

render unconscious anyone attempting to get through the sealed doors and windows, even a disassembled Samian. If any of them so much as walks on the terrace, they'll be hurt. And no one can shut off the field because the electrical power comes from a generator inside the apartment."

"Don't you want Granston to enter—isn't he working for you?"

"You heard me fire him. He's an idiot. Lie still, Arda."

She vanished into another room and I hoped against hope that Zak would come with Dee-four. More fervently, I hoped that Dee-four would deeplook at the apartment before anyone got out of the aircar. She'd see the electronic circuits operating to create the deadly intruder-proof field. She might even see the generator inside the apartment. That wouldn't get me out of the apartment, but it would protect my friends from being hurt.

They were all my friends. Well, maybe not Granston, but the others. I wondered if I would ever see Zak again, or be able to let Hjeg touch my mind and share my knowledge.

Smith returned, carrying a box and followed by a man who looked very much like a taller, dark-haired Elson. He walked stiffly and stared straight ahead, with no expression on his handsome face.

"Meet Elson's . . . *brother*." It was said with a curious little giggle. "He and I are going to perform a little surgery on Kolix. First we'll remove something from Kolix's chest . . ."

"Something metal, and it isn't a pacemaker," I said, hoping my guess would stimulate her to reveal more.

"That's right," she muttered as she opened the box. "Nothing wrong with that Crotonite heart."

"Smith, what did I help Elson insert into Kolix's chest?"

Rummaging through the box, she paid no attention.

"Director, please answer me. If I helped install something lethal into an organic being, then my positronic brain will be badly affected. I must know . . ."

"You stupid robot! It makes no difference to me what happens to your positronic brain. It's coming out anyway. I have a new one for you, already programmed."

"But android brains are too complex to be programmed."

"But I succeeded in programming an android brain!" Smith's vanity was touched, and now she was talking.

"I was a roboticist before I started my agency, and I know all about robot brains. I managed to install a set program into an android brain. He was perfect, so perfect . . ."

"Elson?"

"Oh, my darling, my darling Elson!" It was a cry of anguish.

"Elson was an android," I said slowly. "He was programmed to operate on Kolix, giving Kolix a third, robotic brain you could control. Then you could make Kolix continue the artifact racket that he wanted to stop because he was marrying an archaeologist."

Kolix was making sounds, trying to talk through the gag.

"Shut up, Crotonite. Arda, you are intelligent after all. One of our better models." As Smith momentarily closed her eyes and smiled, her face smoothed out and I could see that she had once been fairly pretty.

She opened her eyes and frowned. "But a robot like you can't fathom my triumph in creating an android who could insert his *own* brain into an organic being."

I felt as if I were trembling inside as I thought about

that night of the Galactic Writers' Society banquet. I'd been so smitten with Elson, so upset when he turned from doctor to thief and was "killed," that later Zak didn't want to tell me the truth.

Perhaps my emotionality made Zak fear that androids are as psychologically vulnerable as humans. Perhaps we are.

"His own brain?" I repeated, hoping she'd talk.

Now she seemed eager to brag. "Try to understand the fantastic marvel of my achievement, Arda. I planned it all. When Elson removed his own android brain, his skull still contained a small robot brain like Y50's, just intelligent enough to continue the operation and escape into the aircar."

"That is remarkable," I said carefully, for my emotive circuits were almost out of control. "Did you program any other android? Did you insert programming into—me?"

She was taking instruments from the box and putting them together. In eerily matter-of-fact tones she said, "The android positronic brain is designed to be activated in an unprogrammed state, except for the installation of the laws of robotics. All androids must learn like children. Fortunately, they do it quicker. I tried various modifications of positronic brains, but they deactivated when programmed. I ended up using an advanced positronic brain like yours . . ."

"*Like* mine?"

"That's what I said."

"Then android brains can be programmed. You did do it."

"Not on you. I wanted a male android. You are an ordinary, unprogrammed female android."

The laws of robotics do not take into account the strong wish for suicide that can occur in an intelligent robot that has emotive circuits. If she'd told me I was another Elson, I think I would have wanted to be deactivated.

In great relief, I said, "Smith, if android brains deactivated when you tried to modify them to accept programming, how did you succeed with Elson?"

She caressed her left breast as if she needed stimulation. "I nurtured him. From the moment of activation, he was mine, taught by me to love and obey me."

"That's not programming. That's training. You did not actually insert programming . . ."

"He's a robot! I programmed it!"

Her eyes looked so wild that I was more frightened. "Smith, perhaps you meant to help androids . . ."

"Help you robots? I wanted one to take the place of Kolix, my *business* confederate, who had betrayed me by insisting that he would never steal for me again. Can't you understand that?"

"Yes. I understand. Elson was so very handsome."

She stopped putting instruments together and pointed to Kolix with obvious repulsion. "Compare that with Elson's beautiful body. Elson was, and will be again, wholly mine."

"Director Smith, did you really love him?"

"I still do. He is my husband. We were married by a human city official who had no idea Elson was anything but human. As Elson's legal wife, it was incredibly painful to have to destroy his perfect body in the aircar explosion."

I was surreptitiously testing the weight of the sideboard, wondering if an electronic field would actually be set off if I lifted it, and if so, whether or not it would kill all three of us.

"Lie still, Arda. You will die if you disturb the sideboard. I will not. I am wearing a device that will ground the shock."

"Smith, I feel sorry for you. What pain you must have suffered when you began to suspect that Elson's transplanted android brain was beginning to malfunction . . ."

"Not malfunction. On Cephallonia, Kolix got back control from my Elson. At first I thought it was happening soon after Elson's brain was linked to the organic brain of this Crotonite monster, but later I knew that Elson had been in control then."

"Now I understand something that puzzled me," I said, trying to speak slowly to give any would-be rescuers time. "I thought it strange that after Elson finished the surgery on Kolix, he kept his surgical mask on and seemed to be talking through it. But he wasn't, was he?"

"No. Elson's implanted brain directed Kolix's vocal cords to speak the words, through an intercom to the robot. You heard the robot apparently speak, but it was Kolix, lying prone so you would not see his lips move."

"Clever," I said.

"Of course."

Kolix writhed, his lips bleeding from his attempts to bite through the gag.

Smith slapped his face and tore off his clothes. "Look, Arda, at this disgusting shape. I cannot bear to think of that night, when Elson's body was in a trillion bits, and this ugly Crotonite was about to take his supposed bride on their mating flight. I had to shake this repulsive Crotonite hand of his. Arda, you are an Erthumoi, with the proper form of an Erthumoi. Could you bear to be touched by a hand like this?"

"I . . ."

"The handshake was for the purpose of transferring

the royal ruulogem over to me. Instead he refused the handshake and was cruel to me. I decided that he merely had another plan for us, and the next day I was reassured when I visited the Crotonite embassy before you all left on the royal tour. Kolix was pleasant to me, so I knew it was Elson speaking."

"But later?"

"Later Elson could not control this ugly creature." She was holding a scalpellike knife and plunged it into Kolix's thigh.

"You've hurt him, Smith."

"I'll do more than that."

"It's not necessary . . ."

"It is! You don't understand everything that's happened. Elson did not report to me what he had learned from Kolix's brain, so I hired Granston to find out where Kolix had hidden the artifacts. I had to know the location of the hiding place in case . . . in case . . ."

"In case Kolix did dominate Elson's brain?"

"Yes." She gritted her teeth. "I was so worried, yet when everyone arrived at Cephallonia, and Granston reported to me, I heard Elson speak through Kolix's horrible mouth. He spoke the right words to me, and I was happy."

She stabbed Kolix again, harder. "But then the Crotonite took over. I did not know until I heard you speak through Naxo's communicator to Fortizak. I learned that Kolix had gone to Crotonis and returned to Cephallonia using a matter transporter, and that the artifacts were being restored."

"Didn't you know about the museum?"

"I knew Kolix was getting artifacts from a secret hiding place, but I did not know for certain what it was or where it was. Finally, Dee-four reported that the ruulogem was there."

"The ruulogem is beautiful, Smith. It's too bad you didn't have a chance to keep it in your hand for a while, because it promotes noble thoughts and purpose."

"Nonsense. It promoted Kolix's greed, which grew worse as he gained control back from Elson's brain. The ruulogem was mine."

"The ruulogem was never yours, Smith. You are the greedy one, are you not?"

She almost spit at me in her fury. "The ruulogem was to be the symbol of our love! It was a measure of my Elson's obedience and devotion to me."

The Elsonlike android continued to stand rigidly next to her, saying nothing.

Smith gripped the knife and spoke to Kolix. "Elson, Elson, why, why did you let this monster take control of your brain?"

I tried to stop her, but I could not break the handcuffs. "Smith, you haven't realized . . ."

"Elson!" Her voice rose to a quavering shriek. "I believed in you, because you looked at me through the hycom and affirmed our love. You said you would never do anything to endanger your wife. But you were not strong enough. You let Kolix betray me. You let him give back the ruulogem, and come to Earth to remove the artifacts he knew were here. Those in his apartment I took, and I waited here because Kolix said he would take the rest of the artifacts to Cephallonia."

"Smith, the artifacts belong on Cephallonia."

"Don't argue with me, Arda. It was Kolix, not Elson, who complimented you on your beauty. Elson! Listen to me! I know you're inside this repulsive Crotonite skull, helpless, but you can hear me. If only you'd had enough control over Kolix to affirm that I am your wife! That would have stopped him."

Kolix was struggling to talk. I hoped the gag would last, but I was beginning to believe that rescue would not come. Where was Zak?

I told her the truth. "Smith, you're wrong. Kolix thinks his real wife is Vush."

Her thin, withered lips stretched into a grimace. "Elson will know I'm his wife when he's back in an android body. And I intend to have a new body, too. Mine is old and ugly."

Kolix nodded "Yes." Smith kicked him and said, "Such a waste. It was all so much trouble."

"But so brilliantly conceived," I said.

"I had to make everyone believe lives were in danger so it would be necessary to have a doctor on hand during the GWS banquet. I made Elson drug Crotonite food capsules because I knew Naxo would want to try them, and I had to make sure he could not reveal that Elson's emotions were not readable and therefore not organic. Elson also drugged the fizz so Dee-four could not deeplook and see that he was an android. If Naxo and Dee-four had not been incapacitated, Elson was programmed to kill them."

"No android would do that!"

"I programmed Elson to believe that the laws of robotics did not apply to nonErthumoi organics. I was careful to order him to make certain that Naxo and Dee-four did not reveal his identity."

Zak, please show up . . . please . . . please. It kept going through my head, and I tried to think of other things to say to this madwoman.

"How did you get human DNA for Elson's robot body to take with him into the aircar?" I asked. "Did you tell Elson to kill a human for the purpose?"

She shrugged. "It was easier to do it myself. It was a derelict I made certain was not registered. It was necessary to have DNA fragments in the aircar so everyone would go on thinking that Elson was human."

Kolix moaned again, his face a paler gray.

She gripped the knife and bent over Kolix, so I said, "Wait, you haven't explained why Elson's brain, in Kolix, should have become controlled by the Crotonite."

"I'm sure it is only a temporary malfunction, due to the proximity of Elson's android brain to the primitive nervous system of this Crotonite. He'll be himself after I've put his brain back where it belongs, in this new Elson."

"There's no use taking out the android brain that's in Kolix," I said desperately, trying to make myself believe that what I was about to say was the absolute truth. "Elson's not inside it."

"You don't make sense, Arda."

"Smith, you didn't take into account that the double brains of Crotonites are completely different from the brains of any Erthumoi, human or android. You know it's impossible to have a successful mind transfer between human and android brains, so you should have guessed that it wouldn't work with Crotonites."

"You're wrong," she said, inspecting Kolix's chest as if deciding where to cut. "It was not mind transfer. Elson's brain was simply implanted on top of the Crotonite lower brain and hooked into the nerve pathways to the upper brain. This should have made it possible for the android brain to capture all the memory patterns in the Crotonite upper brain and to control it as well. Then it would be Elson who would do Kolix's thinking."

"Ingenious," I said, trying not to look over at the wall of plants. I'd caught a glimpse of small black objects erupting along with the mist from the silver columns.

"I am always ingenious." She stared up at nothing, muttering through a litany of her perfect plans that had, after all, not been so perfect.

"So ingenious . . . perfect scheme to prevent Kolix from destroying our lucrative business . . . Elson to take over Kolix's body . . . to acquire all the artifacts Kolix had intended to give to the archaeologists . . ."

She had gone back to her study of Kolix's throat and upper chest. I asked, "And what was Elson supposed to do then?"

"Very simple, Arda. He was to return to me so I could perform the operation I am about to do—remove the android brain and replace it in this new android body. He came back here but said I must surrender the artifacts so that he could take them to Cephallonia. I knew it was Kolix talking. I'm going to . . ."

"Wait, Smith. Did you tell Elson that this operation to remove the android brain would kill Kolix?"

"It does not matter. Kolix will die. He must die, for his brain may retain a residue of memory of Elson."

"Elson might not want you to kill Kolix."

"Certainly he wants it. He's trapped inside that repulsive body, yearning to get out to be with me once more. And I have programmed him. He knows the laws of robotics apply only to Erthumoi."

"But they don't."

"You're a romantic fool, Arda. Elson knows better. After Kolix is dead and my Elson restored, I will remove your silly brain, Arda, and replace it with a positronic brain to which I have transferred my mind patterns."

"It won't work! The new Arda will be psychotic!"

"I must try. I want to be an android as strong and beautiful as you, for my Elson."

Hjeg's components had disappeared. I couldn't see what had happened to them. Had they touched the protective electric field and been killed?

Smith touched the scalpel to Kolix's upper chest.

"Stop!" I yelled. "It's useless! Elson is *dead*."

"That's ridiculous!"

"Yes, he is. Listen to me, Smith. Elson was your husband . . ." I wanted to say "slave" but dared not . . . "confederate. A functioning android brain would never have allowed Kolix to control it. The only way Kolix could take back his own body was to deactivate the implant."

"You're wrong. It was a temporary weakness, allowing Kolix to take over . . ."

"No, Smith. If Elson's brain had continued to function, he'd have carried out your schemes. What you're looking at is Kolix, the Crotonite, whose upper brain took control."

"I know that. I've been telling you the same thing."

"What you don't realize is that you underestimated the power of the Crotonite upper brain. Kolix stole Elson's memories from the implanted brain. He knew everything Elson knew. Kolix could remember everything about you, Smith—but he hates you because you're not Crotonite. He loves Vush, not you, so he probably worked hard to deactivate the implant of Elson's brain."

"Elson . . . dead? Truly dead?"

"Consider the evidence. Hasn't Kolix behaved like a Crotonite all along? Kolix knew how you felt about Elson, so it was easy for him to say things that helped you believe, until it was too late, that Elson was still alive. Smith, think back over everything that's happened. If Elson's brain had been intact, there would have been better evidence for it."

She began to cry.

"Listen to me, Smith. There's no point in committing murder again. No one will be able to trace you to the unregistered human from whom you got the DNA. You'll get away with that, but you won't get away with murdering a Crotonite. You can let him go. Kolix will be too ashamed to reveal that he has a defunct android brain inside his chest, so you won't be arrested for what you and Elson did to him."

"But I must test Elson's brain, make sure there is no hope, that my Elson is really dead . . ."

"He's dead."

"I need him!" She raised the knife. "I'll take out the brain. If it's deactivated . . ."

"But Kolix will be dead, too."

"He should die for murdering my beloved!"

"No, don't remove the brain and kill Kolix! I'm an android, and I tell you that Elson . . ." I could not finish.

"Dead. You're sure he's dead."

"If you kill Kolix, you will not be able to have this wonderful new Elson for your own, Smith!" I yelled.

"My—own?"

"You're not thinking clearly at all. Don't you realize that you have a perfect android lover in this new Elson? All you have to do is insert a new positronic brain in this Elson's head, and train—I mean program it. He will be better than the old Elson because he will not have any memories of being Kolix—and of having sex with Vush."

She turned from Kolix to me. "I will do that, but I must be rejuvenated. I must have your body, Arda."

"You'll be killing my *self* if you remove my positronic brain. Killing an android is illegal."

"No one will arrest me for accidentally deactivating

a malfunctioning android when I was attempting to repair you. I will remove your brain now and . . ."

The lights went out. With a well-placed kick, I rendered Smith unconscious, and then I lifted up the sideboard so Kolix and I, our wrists still handcuffed, could free our arms.

I was removing Kolix's gag when the front door of the apartment opened and Zak came in, followed by Dee-four, Naxo, Granston, Vush, a suited Pleltun, and a posse of Manhattan police. The apartment seemed crowded.

"Okay, Hjeg," Dee-four called. "Disconnect the barrier fields and then turn the generator back on."

Zak undid Kolix's handcuffs first so the Crotonites could fall into each others' arms, and then undid mine.

"You figured it out," Zak whispered to me.

"Smith is the monster."

"'Murderers usually are. Unfortunately, some can't be prosecuted."

I hadn't kicked hard enough to kill or severely injure, so Smith was recovering consciousness. She stood up shakily.

"Officers," she said to the police, "I have been attempting to repair this malfunctioning female android, who had injured this visiting Crotonite."

"Is anyone pressing charges?" asked the police sergeant.

No one spoke until Kolix said hoarsely, "There won't be any charges, Smith. The android is not malfunctioning after all. I have a suggestion for you, however."

"What is that?"

"I recommend atonement. It helps combat the loneliness."

Smith said, "Kolix, you remember . . . him. You must know what he really thought. Didn't he love me?"

"Director Smith, you loved *him*. He did his duty."

She sighed and picked up Kolix's power pack from the sideboard. "Elson, attend me. We're not staying at this party."

"Yes, ma'am," the robot said.

"Come with me." She walked to the terrace with the robot beside her.

"Smithy, it's theater time in Manhattan," yelled Naxo. "You'll never get an aircar."

But Smith had risen into the air with the power pack. She held the robot's hand and jumped off the terrace.

Kolix and I ran out there. He was shouting.

"Smith! My power pack is meant to be supplemented by Crotonite wings. It isn't strong enough for you and the robot!"

I looked down. "It's too late, Kolix."

On the edge of the swimming pool below, Smith's body lay crumpled, and beside her was a smashed robot.

Chapter 29

Kolix and I were alone with Zak on his apartment terrace.

"I must leave," Kolix said. "Vush is waiting for me at the embassy. She and I will take the rest of the artifacts to Cephallonia. Thank you both for your help."

Zak grunted. "I'm glad you thanked Dee-four and Hjeg. I knew the barrier field was lethal, but Dee-four's deeplook found the electric generator and the misting apparatus inside Smith's apartment. After that it was simple for Hjeg to enter the water pipes. People make such complicated plans to protect themselves, but they always forget something."

"Yes, they do," Kolix said. "Like forgetting how strong the laws of robotics are."

"Good luck on the rest of your life," Zak said.

"I shall need it. Vush said she thought Elson's deactivated robot brain should be removed from my chest, but I told her I didn't want more surgery. She agreed. She loves me, and I really love her. I know who and what I am now."

"The one and only hybrid?" asked Zak.

"A murderer, for the laws of robotics do apply to nonhuman organics."

Zak nodded. "Smith lied to you about that."

"And in telling me that there would be no damage to the Crotonite upper brain when an android brain was inserted."

"Then Kolix's upper brain did die."

"And with it, his intelligence and consciousness. When I felt that brain die, I knew that I was killing the real Kolix, but I could do nothing to save him."

Zak said, "There are many kinds of murder, Elson. Smith murdered your potential and your rights as a free android when she inserted programming into your brain to turn you into her obedient lover and confederate in crime. And Kolix's lower brain almost murdered your own intelligence and consciousness."

"That is true. I nearly killed you, Arda, when Smith's programming was augmented by the primitive emotions from Kolix's intact lower brain, not yet under my control. Yet those primitive emotions eventually helped me get rid of the programming. I apologize, Arda, for taking so long to gain control, and for needing your help."

"It's all right, Elson," I said. "But I guess you're really also Kolix, aren't you?"

"I am. His knowledge and his love for Vush were transferred to my brain before his upper brain died. I vow that I will spend my life atoning for Kolix's death."

Zak said gently, "It will be a shorter life than you could have had in an android body, Elson."

"I know. My android brain will deactivate when my Crotonite body dies. That is part of the atonement, and will not be onerous because I will share my shorter life with Vush, as an archaeologist. Now farewell, Zak. I probably won't return to Earth, and you never leave it. But, Arda, perhaps you will visit the Seventh Species museum again, or come for a stay at the palace on Crotonis."

"I would be honored," I said.

He was wearing a new power pack. He spread his wings and flew into the night, a beautiful winged creature silhouetted against the moon.

The next morning, before I went to meet Hjeg for a tour of the Samian embassy, I took the time to observe Zak eating his breakfast of healthy cereal grains with fruit.

"Zak, I have come to a rather odd conclusion."

"So have I," he said, pointing to the cereal. "You seem to think I have entered second childhood."

"No, sir." On the surface of the cereal I had placed two raspberries for eyes, and a curved slice of peach to make a smiling mouth. "The arrangement of the fruit is to persuade both of us into a cheerful acceptance of what is."

He put sweet lactose-reduced skim milk into his coffee and on his cereal. "Acceptance of what is? Do you mean the reality of Kolix and Elson?"

"The reality of me. Working for you. With Smith gone and the TFBI under reorganization, I have no other employer, do I?"

"Nope," he said through the raspberries.

"I will continue as your housekeeper?"

"Nope."

"Oh."

"As my partner. Okay?"

"Oh, *yes!*"

He finished the cereal. "I don't think you told me what odd conclusion you've come to, Arda."

"I meant odd deduction . . ."

"Deductions are not the same as conclusions. You must understand that to be a writer means constant courage in battling the uncertainty of the Universe by choosing words mindfully . . ."

"Yes, sir. I deduce that the Seventh Species started as organic, probably not humanoid in shape, but that eventually they were robots."

"Perhaps they merely had robots working for them."

"None of the late artifacts were the sort of domestic utensils used by organic beings."

"It's possible that the robots of the Seventh Species destroyed the organics," he glared at his cereal, "by starving them to death."

"I'm sure the Seventh Species robots had laws of robotics, too." I noticed that something was missing from the table. "Where's the coffee cake?"

Zak grinned. "Deducing that the laws of robotics would probably encourage your regrettable urge to keep me healthy, I've already fed the cake—and in case you don't know, I'm crazy about cake—to the pigeons on the terrace. Look how fat they are. Can you make pigeon pie?"

"Sorry."

He sighed. "Perhaps the Seventh Species wanted to stop eating other life. If they also could not mind transfer to robots, they may have stepped aside to let their robots go on evolving, doing what any intelligent species must do—add beauty, meaning, and purpose to the Universe."

"And love."

"Love?"

"I'm being mindful of what is," I said.

Then I kissed him.

Kate Elliott

The Novels of the Jaran:

☐ **JARAN: Book 1**   UE2513—$5.99
Here is the poignant and powerful story of a young woman's coming of age on an alien world, where she is both player and pawn in an interstellar game of intrigue and politics.

☐ **AN EARTHLY CROWN: Book 2**   UE2546—$5.99
The jaran people, led by Ilya Bakhtiian and his Earth-born wife Tess, are sweeping across the planet Rhui on a campaign of conquest. But even more important is the battle between Ilya and Duke Charles, Tess' brother, who is ruler of this sector of space.

☐ **HIS CONQUERING SWORD: Book 3**   UE2551—$5.99
Even as Jaran warlord Ilya continues the conquest of his world, he faces a far more dangerous power struggle with his wife's brother, leader of an underground human rebellion against the alien empire.

☐ **THE LAW OF BECOMING: Book 4**   UE2580—$5.99
On Rhui, Ilya's son inadvertently becomes the catalyst for what could prove a major shift of power. And in the heart of the empire, the most surprising move of all was about to occur as the Emperor added an unexpected new player to the Game of Princes . . .

C.S. Friedman

☐ **IN CONQUEST BORN**   UE2198—$5.99

Braxi and Azea—two super-races fighting an endless war. The Braxaná—created to become the ultimate warriors. The Azeans, raised to master the powers of the mind. Now the final phase of their war is approaching, spearheaded by two opposing generals, lifetime enemies—and whole worlds will be set ablaze by the force of their hatred.

☐ **THE MADNESS SEASON**   UE2444—$5.99

For 300 years, the alien Tyr had ruled Earth, imprisoning the true individualists, the geniuses, and forcing them to work on projects which the Tyr hoped would reveal humankind's secrets. But Daetrin's secret was one no one had ever uncovered. Taken into custody by the Tyr, he would have to confront the truth about himself at last—and if he failed, all humans would pay the price. . . .

The Coldfire Trilogy

☐ **BLACK SUN RISING (Book 1)**   UE2527—$5.99
                                    Hardcover Edition: UE2485—$18.95

Centuries after being stranded on the planet Ema, humans have achieved an uneasy stalemate with the *Fae*, a terrifying natural force with the power to prey upon people's minds. Now, as the hordes of the dare *fae* multiply, four people—Priest, Adept, Apprentice, and Sorcerer—are drawn inexorably together to confront an evil beyond imagining.

☐ **WHEN TRUE NIGHT FALLS (Book 2)**   UE2615—$5.99
                                    Hardcover Edition: UE2569—$22.00

Determined to seek out and destroy the source of the *fae*'s ever-strengthening evil, Damien Vryce, the warrior priest, and Gerald Tarrant, the immortal sorcerer known as the Hunter, dare the treacherous crossing of the planet's greatest ocean to confront a power that threatens the very essence of the human spirit.

FOREIGNER
by C.J. Cherryh

It had been nearly five centuries since the starship *Phoenix*, came out of hyperdrive into a place with no recognizable reference coordinates, and no way home. Hopelessly lost, the crew did the only thing they could. They charted their way to the nearest G5 star, gambling on finding a habitable planet. And what they found was the world of the atevi—a world where law was kept by the use of registered assassination, where alliances were not defined by geographical borders, and where war became inevitable once humans and one faction of atevi established a working relationship. It was a war that humans had no chance of winning and now, nearly two centuries later, humanity lives in exile on the island of Mospheira, trading tidbits of advanced technology for continued peace and a secluded refuge that no atevi will ever visit. Only a single human, the paidhi, is allowed off the island and into the complex and dangerous society of the atevi, brought there to act as interpreter and technological liaison to the leader of the most powerful of the atevi factions. But when this sole human the treaty allows into atevi society is nearly killed by an unregistered assassin's bullet, the fragile peace is shattered, and Bren Cameron, the paidhi, realizes that he must seek a new way to build a truer understanding between these two dangerous, intelligent, and quite possibly incompatible species. For if he fails, he and all of his people will die. But can a lone human hope to overcome two centuries of hostility and mistrust?

☐ **Original Hardcover** UE2590—$20.00

☐ **Paperback Edition** UE2637—$5.99

DAW

Attention:

DAW COLLECTORS

Many readers of DAW Books have written requesting information on early titles and book numbers to assist in the collection of DAW editions since the first of our titles appeared in April 1972.

We have prepared a several-pages-long list of all DAW titles, giving their sequence numbers, original and current order numbers, and ISBN numbers. Also included, of course, are the authors and book titles, as well as reissue information.

If you think that this list will be of help, you may have a copy by writing to the address below and enclosing two dollars in stamps or currency to cover the handling and postage costs.

DAW Books, Inc.
Dept. C
375 Hudson Street
New York, NY 10014-3658